MORNINGSIDE DRIVE

CLAUDIA CHIANESE

'Who doesn't love a sweet ending with something left hanging? I do and I did! I enjoyed the story and congratulate you for having conceived and written it.

JV Whittenburg, PhD
Catonsville, MD

'The story arc moves precipitously within the first few pages. The protagonist's emotional state – a rollercoaster – is intensely written and believable.

Robin Polleta
Ormond Beach, FL

'I enjoyed this book! The short chapters were especially nice, making it easy to read. The storyline kept my interest throughout.

Misty Hinson
Gainesville, FL

Illustration by Kelsi Lee Lytle/Imbued Ink

MORNINGSIDE DRIVE

CLAUDIA CHIANESE

CCE PUBLISHING
Edgewater, Florida

Cover image: Kelsi Lee Lytle/Imbued Ink
Cover and book design: Cindy Casey/CCE Publishing

Published by
CCE PUBLISHING
Edgewater, Florida
ccepublishing.com
cindycaseyediting@gmail.com

Printed in the United States of America

ISBN: 979-8-9896281-0-0
LCCN: 2024903063

Dedication

In loving memory of our son, Tony ... may he rest in peace.

Table of Contents

Chapter 1

Autumn 2013 in New York City

ço

I married Ben Garner because he made me laugh. Although, it did not hurt that he was also tall and well-off. For fifteen years our lives were comfortable, if not predictable. He handed me a hot cup of coffee while I laced my running shoes. The steam circled above the mug I hugged with both hands. I love this man.

"Are we still going to Sunday brunch?" he asked.

"The reservation at Tavern on The Green is for noon," I said, then pulled an all-weather parka over my head. "There'll be eight of us."

"Great. Tweedle Dee and Tweedle Dumb will grace us with their presence."

I laughed at his characterization of our friends, Marigold and Mark. They stood up for us when we were married and we considered them close friends.

He tilted my chin with an index finger and studied my eyes. "You sure you'll be warm enough?"

We kissed goodbye. One of those everyday kisses you would never leave without. The wanting present, but scheduled, or set aside for an organized event, like brunch with friends. His kiss was reminiscent of the Sundays Jacqueline had his kids and we spent the day in bed. Going down in the elevator I thought – *kids or no kids, I could go back up* – but didn't. Today was the one day I would have time for a run, this week.

Shades of red, yellow, and orange decorated the trees in Central Park. Children played in the leaves already on the ground.

I ran past the skating rink and predicted the arrival of snow. Below-zero temperatures were a couple of months away. I jogged in place at the traffic light before crossing Fifth Avenue on my return. An ambulance idling outside our Park Avenue apartment distracted me as I weaved between cars stuck in traffic and blaring horns.

I knew something was wrong when the doorman held the door too long. Ben lay on an ambulance stretcher surrounded by EMTs. His sweater and oxford dress shirt had been cut open and defibrillator paddles rested on his chest.

"Mrs. Garner, I'm sorry for your loss," said a policeman.

The golden buttons on his uniform flashed like neon lights and his voice echoed from a broken PA system. Like Alice in Wonderland, I felt myself tumbling down a rabbit hole. My thoughts spun around and around. Ben was dead.

The lobby faded as though I had too much to drink. The loud voices echoed within a blur of confusion. When I came to, someone asked if I knew who was president.

"Barack Obama. And you are?"

"Officer Regan."

"What happened? He was fine an hour ago. How could this be?" I said in shock.

"Your husband had a massive heart attack. I'm sorry. Is there someone you can call?"

* * * * *

I sat in a stupor waiting for Marigold to arrive. She pushed through the yellow tape and rushed past the white sheet draped over Ben to hug me.

"Joy, I'm so sorry.

"He was fine when I left for my run." My words were interrupted by tears … "We joked about brunch …" and stuck in my throat.

Thank God, Marigold had come quickly. I was inundated with questions about hospitals and funeral homes. She made notations on scrap paper while I couldn't answer, as though I had a severe head injury.

Later, with Marigold by my side, I phoned Ben's ex, Jackie. She preferred Jacqueline and often corrected him. I took the high road. "Jacqueline, this is Joy. You better sit down. I have bad news." I choked back my tears while listening to hers. "I can contact the kids unless you prefer to."

Bryce and Scarlet were Ben's children. After his divorce, I was the live-in nanny. It was the perfect situation for me. I attended City College, while the kids were in school, and studied hard on the weekends they spent with their mother.

We didn't plan to fall in love … but did, and after a few years, we married rather than give Jackie an excuse to pursue full custody. His kids and I were close. However, with their father gone, I feared Jackie would claim they now belonged to her exclusively. The pending loss felt like a steam roller ironing out my chest.

Between deep breaths, she said, "I'll tell them. Please, let me know about funeral arrangements." She paused. "Do you know if I'm in the will?"

Thanksgiving came less than a week after the funeral. I

begged off invitations to dinner and offers to "come at halftime for a drink." Even Jackie offered, "How about I come for coffee and we watch the parade? You love the parade."

I declined all their good intentions. It pained me to watch another family's celebration.

December was a blur. Settling the estate and responding to condolences kept me busy. I was exhausted and the quiet I had welcomed soon turned to dread. Surrounded by emptiness, I wore pajamas, rather than stand in our closet deciding what not to wear, and if I went out, dressed in the same black turtle neck and heavy coat. The kids stopped calling and responded to my texts with a like or heart. I was alone and reality hit me hard.

Christmas Eve, I made excuses for Bryce and Scarlet and wrapped my grief in holiday paper to put under the tree. Now, they didn't have to choose between parents, I was a step, not their parent.

It wasn't a horrible Christmas. I went to Midnight Mass at St. Patrick's Cathedral and took my hurt to bed. Christmas day, I pretended to be Jewish, went to the movies, and ate Chinese food, alone. I didn't call anyone and no one called me.

I secluded myself in the apartment and bundled up in black, to sit on the outside porch, or walk, not run, through the park. Years ago, women wore black and mourned for a year. I wallowed. Besides, I was clueless about what to do ... a shell of a woman.

When the ground decided to thaw, I did too. I traded the black turtle neck for a white cardigan and accepted an invitation for lunch with the girls. I had not seen them since the funeral, and refusing one more time would have raised a red flag.

The Central Park Boathouse had good memories for me. After arriving, I checked my coat, ordered a Chardonnay, and waited for Elizabeth, Regina, and Marigold to arrive. Elizabeth arrived first, wearing a vintage Chanel suit jacket, expensive jeans, and pointy black flats.

"You look fabulous, darling," I said while air-kissing her cheek. Regina and Marigold waved enthusiastically from the doorway and hurried to join us. They greeted me with hugs and kisses and explained I had been missed. Dizzy with grief, I thanked them for getting me out but felt I no longer belonged in this crowd. They knew little about me and my secrets ... secrets I had put to sleep.

Marigold said, "Tell me, how are you coping?" She wore a colorful flowing caftan under a warm sweater with boots and carried a satchel suggesting she was running away.

Elizabeth interrupted. "Let's order first." She signaled for the waiter. "I have an appointment at three with Allen."

Allen was her lawyer.

"I'll have a Bloody Mary and the crab cakes," said Regina. She closed her menu and continued, "Joy, you look pale. Are you okay?"

My last kiss with Ben played in my mind over and over again like a movie scene.

"I didn't know our last goodbye would be our last," I mumbled.

Uncomfortable with the attention, I turned to Regina, "I'm fine." And to the waiter, "Crab cakes, and another chardonnay, please."

He nodded and took my menu.

Elizabeth chewed a nail and said, "Bring me a double Titos, on the rocks with a twist of lemon, and the shrimp salad." She removed her cheaters and slipped them into her red Michael Kors bag.

"You look like shit," Elizabeth exclaimed. "You need to

get away."

"I'm thinking of driving to Daytona." I was annoyed by her attitude.

"Daytona Beach in Florida? You are kidding. What could possibly be worth seeing there?"

"Besides a beautiful beach and eighty-degree weather? My father."

Everyone's eyes turned toward me. Even I was surprised by the admission.

Marigold commented. "You have family in Daytona? I think my parents went there on spring break in the sixties. You never mentioned your father before."

"We're somewhat estranged."

Although thoughts of Dad haunted me, I had kept them to myself, and could not recall being asked about my past. Consequently, I never had to lie.

"Yes, I have family in Daytona." I examined the faces of these women I had spent so much time with. Their interest in me was as an accountant's wife. Our friendship was convenient and without substance.

Regina cleared her throat. "Your dad must miss you. It might do you good to visit him."

Elizabeth looked out on the lake that was once a swamp. "The Foundation spends an obscene amount of money on this pond, and it's still an ugly shade of green ... I'm divorcing Tom."

No one looked surprised.

My cell rang. I studied the number. "I need to take this," I said and walked outside.

On the patio, planters overflowed with winter pansies. Black cast iron tables and ice cream parlor chairs decorated the space where patrons sat in the spring and summer. I listened to Jacqueline leave a message.

"Joy, can you please return my call? The kids want to know if they get the apartment."

The sun disappeared behind the clouds. The sky turned dark and dreary. I pulled my thin white sweater tight around me. I had taken Ben's love for granted, and now ... it was gone.

Without companions, Elizabeth and I would be excluded from future gatherings. Nothing made sense anymore. I felt lost and alone.

The memory of saying goodbye to my father overcame me like a tidal wave. We had fought about my returning to Stetson University in DeLand. When the bitter discussion ended, he had slapped the tuition money on the table and said, "Do whatever the hell you want, you spoiled brat," and walked away. At the time, he didn't know I was pregnant or that I suspected him of murder.

Did my dad miss me? Maybe? I had been gone for thirty years. That goodbye would be our last unless I returned and solved the mystery.

Did he kill Diane and Tammy Martin?

I shivered. It was time to go home.

Chapter 2

Groundhog Day 2014

༄

There were times, I forgot Ben was dead. It was especially true a few days later when I left Manhattan via the Holland Tunnel. Traffic was light at five in the morning. Traveling against commuter traffic, I crossed the Delaware River in no time and stopped in Harrisburg around noon.

Ben had convinced me we could travel west and get to Florida. He grew up in the Panhandle and said, "We'll go south starting in Roanoke, Virginia. You must see the Blue Ridge Parkway."

We were newlyweds, so I raised my eyebrows when he was not looking.

The view was everything he had promised. As the smoky mist retreated above the mountains, a bluish hue descended and stole my breath away. The twists and turns of the man-made curves, fifty-two years in the making, were like a roller coaster ride. Dizzy from the near-death experience of kissing the mountain's side, I screamed. We stopped in Fancy Gap, a small town with a population of two hundred and thirty-seven people.

I made a reservation at the same bed and breakfast we had honeymooned. When I arrived it was late, and exhausted from the ride, I crawled into bed.

In the morning, I reached across the covers for Ben, but he was not there. I stretched and yawned thinking he would return with coffee; of course, he didn't.

I dressed and walked alone to the Early Birds Café. A lively group of men occupied a white metal table (the kind my grandmother had in her kitchen) near the front window. The establishment's name was scrolled in cursive. A waitress greeted regulars with, "Good Morning," and saved the "I'm Lorie, your server," for strangers like myself. Duct tape, used as a bandage, stretched around her hand securing a gauze pad in place.

Time was frozen; it might have been 1965 or 1996, the year we were married. I studied the menu halfheartedly and listened to the men's banter.

Jake, a robust man with a white beard and railroad cap made manly man noises. I imagined him scratching his head and passing gas. It was not pretty. Luther wore suspenders. His thin curly hair was pulled back in a ponytail. Several other men's stomachs lay beneath the tabletop, threatening to tear their pants. They discussed Obama Care and then moved on to love.

Luther cleared his throat and said, "What negative feelings do you bring to the relationship?"

A bell chimed when a patron opened the restaurant door and prevented me from hearing his response.

"Are you talking about me throwing the remote at the television or Jane catching it?" Jake chuckled.

"You could've cracked the flat screen," Lorie commented, refilling glasses with a water pitcher.

"Jane catching it," Luther scratched his stomach, "that would have pissed me off."

It was a familiar scenario from the past. Ben and I had enjoyed the back-and-forth repartee and laughed at the locals together.

Rather than cry in public, I asked for my coffee to go. And drank it rocking on the B&B front porch, wondering why I had come this way; then gathered my belongings and checked out.

Daytona Beach was eight hours away.

* * * * *

The view of wild sea oats and shrubs relaxed my frayed nerves. As I gazed at the view and soaked up the sun, I wondered if anyone would recognize me after all these years.

Whitecaps danced among the turquoise waters, then tangoed to the water's edge. Several people sat on beach chairs under an umbrella. A cooler served as a table for their beer. The Florida sun warmed me as I exhaled my apprehension.

I grew up here, "The World's Most Famous Beach," known for the Daytona 500, Bike Week, and Spring Break.

Today's local newspaper's headline, "Murder and Missing," was an anniversary issue about cold cases. The featured mother and daughter I believed were not missing, but dead. The peace sign necklace Diane Martin wore in the picture was in my pocket, its velvet pouch worn.

All these years, fear had plagued me, and the eleven hundred miles between Daytona Beach and New York City did not help me forget. I was afraid of the truth when I left and have returned with the same fears. It was as though, I washed a favorite sweater with a tissue in the pocket, and some of the shriveled lint was caught in the seam forever.

Things were familiar at the Maverick Resort Hotel in Daytona Beach. I waitressed here in high school. I brushed the sand off my feet, walked through the lobby, and climbed the stairs to my room.

The one-bedroom ocean view suite was clean and near Morningside Drive, my family home. The swish-swish sound of rumbling waves soothed my mood.

I unpacked, hung my dresses in the closet, and arranged shirts and shorts in the bureau. Then stared at the empty suitcase, and remembered Elizabeth's disdain at the mention of Daytona, certain she would describe the motel as a dump. City life demanded perfection; so many people, yet no one to talk to. The loneliness was now a fading feeling because I was home.

I sent a text to Marigold saying I arrived. Wondering if we would stay in touch, the friendship was beginning to evaporate in my mind, already.

After dark, I drove to Morningside Drive. The lights were on. Through the open drapes, I caught the silhouette of my father, Frank Webb, reclining in his chair.

He was probably wearing an old Seabreeze High School t-shirt and worn-out flip-flops. More than likely, he was watching Fox News and held an empty can of beer in his hand.

Enjoying himself was what he did best, and as a child, I loved him for it. Today, I imagined him as a selfish old man.

The light in my upstairs bedroom was off, the way I had preferred it. The scent of night jasmine lingered in the air.

Spring of 1984, I studied the world from that window, blew cigarette smoke through the screen, and watched my father escort Diane Martin and her daughter, Tammy, to his car. Several days later their family reported them missing. No one saw them again.

I removed Diane Martin's peace necklace from its pouch to study the effect of its being concealed.

I watched Dad struggle to get out of his chair. He walked to the window, and pulled the drapes closed interrupting thirty years of worry. I put the car in drive and eased away, to rehash the past alone in a motel room.

In the morning, birds squawked overhead, as whispering waves kissed the shore. The air was humid. The sun not yet strong, The Maverick opened for breakfast at seven. I chose an outside table and settled in as a server walked toward me. It was Carrie, wearing a coat of indifference. We were best friends in high school. I was shocked she still worked here.

Carrie held a pot of coffee in one hand and an empty mug in the other, and said in an early morning voice, "Coffee?"

I nodded yes. Our eyes met.

"Do I know you?"

It was too late to run or hide.

"I'm from out of town," I said laughing.

At forty-eight years of age, my black hair was now salt and pepper, and no longer pulled back in a ponytail but cut short to capture its natural curl. I weighed the same, although things had shifted. A black t-shirt paired with crisp white Ralph Lauren shorts suggested money. Hopefully, my large dark sunglasses created doubt. It felt awkward, and I debated how to handle the situation.

Carrie was heavier. Her thin hair lacked color and suggested she no longer went by the nickname Red. Deep cigarette-induced creases decorated her upper lip. Her posture was slouched and her stomach was paunchy. My eyes scanned the menu pretending to decide what to eat.

Carrie asked with a forced smile, "You ready to order? I can come back."

"Two eggs over easy, bacon and rye toast."

"I'll get that right out," she said and walked away.

I sipped the cup of coffee, in silence. Damn, just my luck she still worked here. I remembered late-night discussions about boys, solving world problems while smoking, and not talking about my father's drinking. I had missed her.

Carrie returned carrying a weathered brown tray loaded with orders. Her eyes no longer struggled to remember me.

"You visiting?" she inquired while serving my eggs.

"A New Yorker. I decided to get away from the cold," and refrained from addressing the elephant in the room. "I'm not a beach person though."

"The Big Apple. I hear the weather is a bitch, the temperatures in the teens and below."

"Today's temperature feels like a heat wave to me."

"Well, most Floridians spend February indoors. If you're looking for something away from the beach Blue Spring Park is about an hour away. Manatees migrate inland this time of year. Those gentle cows are something to see. Ask the front desk how to get there."

Life returned to her eyes as she chatted, refilled my coffee, and slipped a receipt face down on the worn table. She watched me stir a packet of sugar into my coffee, and fold the emptied paper into a minuscule speck.

"Anything else?"

"No," I mumbled, relieved she did not say she recognized me. After eating, I left cash and headed to the beach.

The waves lingered around my feet in a way I had missed for thirty years. The hard-packed sand offered security. The water was clear with layers of blue, a diverse contrast to the dark troubled waters and jagged shoreline I had left behind.

Morningside Drive was not far from the beach. Deep in thought, I wandered home. Daylight exposed its shabbiness. The flowerbeds had weeds. The walk was stained, and several news-papers defaced the driveway.

My mother would have cringed to see the house in such neglect. Missing her, I choked on the regret of not attending her funeral and felt an overwhelming love for her.

Dad had denied his involvement with Diane Martin pre-viously, and given the chance, would again. Doubt consumed me, coming back felt like a mistake, and staying away for so long was an even bigger one.

I fingered the jewelry bag in my pocket and turned to leave when the screen door slammed. An old man shuffled down the driveway toward the newspapers.

It was Dad, grumbling, "You want something, girlie?"

Eyeglasses dangled on a chain around his neck and bounced off his chest. His face and clothes were dull and wrinkled. I had anticipated he would look older, but not broken.

"No sir. Just looking at the house," I shouted.

"You realtors are all the same, want me to sell cheap. Don't even think about trespassing, or else!"

His threat of "or else" was familiar, an expression he often said during my childhood and often accompanied by, "Do it again and I'll kill you." I remembered his threats.

"Sorry sir, no harm intended."

I pondered this place of no turning back as he stooped to re-trieve the daily paper. I recalled Marigold's question. "Do you love your father?" Once again, I did not have the answer.

After hearing the front door slam, I walked away and glanced back at the house that once shined in a sugary lemon-ade yellow color with a robin's egg blue front door, crying.

I returned to the Maverick, climbed into bed, and fell into a heavy sleep. I woke up disoriented, surprised by my surroundings, and calling out for Ben. The memory of Ben's death hit me like a bolt of lightning and why I had returned to Daytona became rusty in my mind. Nevertheless, I dressed and set out to Main Street.

Little had changed. The street made famous by Bike Week was lined with Harleys. Mannequins, in sequined leather chaps and skimpy halters, were displayed in store windows. I cut across to International Speedway Blvd and absorbed the view of the Halifax River and Daytona's City Island crossing the bridge.

Things looked different on the other side of the bridge. The buildings were occupied, not empty like in the eighties when Daytona was the Spring Break Capital and girls went missing. Daytona Speedway was under construction. Work vehicles crowded makeshift parking lots. Metal pilings decorated the sky. Bill France Boulevard had not changed. I turned at Mason onto Valor and parked in front of the Daytona Beach Police Department.

For thirty years, memories of Diane and Tammy Martin with my father had been etched in my mind. I finessed the necklace from the faded blue pouch, secured the peace sign around my neck, and opened the car door, determined to find the truth.

The building was new and modern. There were no shade trees. A few plants with a hint of color adorned the outside of the building. The double glass doors were heavy to open. Inside everything was shiny and sleek.

I approached a young cop manning the reception desk. An oil painting, featuring a surfer riding a huge wave to shore, filled the wall space behind him.

"I'd like to speak to a detective, please."

He smiled, a smile starting with his eyes. "May I ask who wants to speak with a detective?"

"I'd rather not say."

"In reference to what?" He probed further.

His baby face contrasted with the solid abs that tugged on his shirt buttons. His thick hair was gelled, not overly, in place.

"Do I have to tell you? Can't I just talk to a detective?"

"Lady, you're talking to a detective. I'm Detective Baumgardner. Is there an immediate danger, Ma'am?" He made deliberate eye contact and no longer smiled.

"Sorry, no. There's nothing immediate. It's hard to explain ... Complicated."

I checked over my shoulder for anyone who might be listening and whispered. "I have some evidence. I could be wrong, and being silly. It's been so long. If I could talk to someone, privately."

He mimicked my lowered voice and said, "Well. Speculate, hypothetically, of course. Pretend you're not being silly. What type of crime would we be talking about?"

He made a good point by whispering. Feeling foolish, I resumed speaking normally but still checked around for who might be listening.

"My concern is ... well, hypothetically speaking, it could be murder or they might be missing. People can be missing for thirty years and still alive. Well, I don't know for sure, but imagine."

"Let me get this straight. You might have information about a cold case involving two victims, who are missing ... but maybe dead, hypothetically speaking."

"Yes."

"I can phone over to our Cold Case Unit and see who's available. Take a seat."

"Thank you."

The wooden bench was hard. My bones pressed against its unforgiving surface. Doubt returned and crept into my mind. Perspiration formed on my forehead. I had rehearsed in a mirror, hundreds of times, what to say. When I found the necklace, I was frightened and fled. Uncertainty dominated my thoughts. There was no proof this necklace belonged to Diane Martin or that Diane and Tammy Martin were dead. Maybe, they did not want to be found, either. End of story. Feeling ridiculous, I told myself to put my fears aside and let the police decide the connection between my dad and Diane Martin. Perhaps they were looking for their dog ... really.

Baumgardner studied me and picked up the phone. "You busy? I got a walk-in you're going to want to see. She's talking about a thirty-year-old case."

I pressed my shoulder bag to my chest and worked hard to remain composed.

Baumgardner looked up. "Ma'am you're in luck, Ray Atwood is in the building. You'll like Ray. He's retired from Daytona PD. Works Cold Cases. He'll be out in a few minutes."

My thoughts spun. The mention of Ray Atwood made me weak in the knees and nauseous. Ray was another reason I left. In 1984, we were lovers.

As I regained composure and looked up, Ray was standing behind a glass partition in view. He held reading glasses in one hand, a pencil was tucked behind his ear and had gotten better looking. My heart raced as he moved out of sight.

Blood drained from my face. My arms tingled. A flood of emotions devoured my body, heart, and mind, like the first time we met. I was wearing baby dolls and watching Laugh-In on television, pretending to study for a geometry test. Mom was in bed. Dad was out at a board meeting, or so he said. I heard someone fussing at the front door, and then the doorbell rang. I grabbed my housecoat. Dad stumbled in, supported by a police officer, and I fell in love.

In flight mode, I approached Officer Baumgardner. "Excuse me, I'm suddenly not feeling well ... maybe I ate something. I'm sorry. You know. I am going to go."

I hurried out the door and got in my car. I had fallen in love with Ray Atwood all over again.

Chapter 3

Best Friend

९०

As I entered the driveway of the Maverick Hotel, Carrie exited. I circled back and followed her truck. The green Ford stuck out in the sea of white cars. Sun glare obstructed a clear view. However, when her truck turned right onto River Beach, and then took a couple of lefts, I was right behind her. She was not getting away.

It had been naïve not to consider Ray would be at police headquarters. Seeing him had unnerved me. The unresolved feelings I buried had resurfaced. I was 17 years old again and needed to talk to my best friend ... Carrie.

I slammed the brakes when she turned abruptly into a driveway and parked behind her.

Carrie stared red-faced at me. Her t-shirt was stained.

"Why are you following me? What do you want?" she yelled.

"To talk ... It's me Joy, Joy Webb."

"I know who you are. Joy Webb. Back from the dead wearing designer sunglasses, no longer help but a guest. Why didn't you say so at breakfast?"

"I didn't have a clue you'd still be waitressing there. I'm sorry." I removed my sunglasses and made a puppy dog face.

"You're sorry?" She shifted a tote bag on her shoulder. "Thirty years and this is the best you came up with? Stay at the Maverick and pretend you don't know me? How did you even get a room? Normally we are booked this time of year!" Her voice cracked. "Where the hell have you been?" She paused. "We worried ourselves sick, and you have the nerve to just show up looking this freaking good."

"There was a cancellation."

"Right!" She took a deep breath and composed herself, "Lucky You! The Leahys had a death in the family."

Her anger returned, "You know what? You were dead to me and you're staying dead."

She walked toward the house and unlocked the front door. A dog ran out, jumped up, and licked her face. She scratched the animal behind the ears saying, "Lucky, have you missed me?" Then squinted in my direction. "Listen to yourself." She shook her head. "You weren't snatched, you ran away! All this time, you were alive and safe. Not locked in some pervert's basement."

She pointed to my Lexus with New York license plates. "Obviously you've been living a good life in the Big Apple and never bothered to phone. Why?"

When I didn't answer, she said, "Whatever ... excuses don't matter."

Lucky jumped on me. Carrie grabbed his collar. "Get in your Lexus and go."

Dizzy with regret, I spit out, "Give me a chance to explain. Please, I can explain."

She gathered Lucky up in her arms. Smothered the animal with kisses, and went inside.

The memory of Diane and Tammy Martin with my father gnawed at me. He never informed the police. Dad, teacher of the year, concealed he had been with them. I recalled hearing the knock on the door, and the muffled conversation. Carrie never kept a secret. A flashback of Ray and me in Cedar Key for the weekend came back to me.

I told my parents the girls were going to Disney. It was a lie – Ray had picked me up Friday afternoon. We drove through Gainesville and took Rte. 27 to 24 into Cedar Key and stayed at Aunt May's Cottage. We made love every chance we had, fished in the morning, and watched the sunset at night.

Sunday, Dad bumped into Carrie in Publix and asked. "You girls back early? Where's Joy?"

Carrie blurted out, "Joy's in Cedar Key with Ray Atwood."

She spilled her guts – never thought to cover for me. Say she had to work and couldn't go to Disney. Make up any lame excuse. Carrie couldn't keep quiet about my getaway. How would she keep her lips sealed about murder and other things? When I got home, Dad inquired about Disney, and let me dig a big hole for myself. While Mom peeled potatoes in the kitchen. Her eyes focused on the door.

"How were the lines?"

"Not bad. It never rained as predicted. But the threat kept the crowds down." I lied.

"Did you ride Dumbo? I know it's your favorite."

"Yes. Dumbo and the Teacups, I love them, too!"

"What about Ray, or do you call him Officer Atwood? Is he a Dumbo Teacup fan?"

"Officer Atwood?"

Terrified of my father, I panicked. I flew up the stairs and slammed the bedroom door. Then secured it using a desk chair wedged under the handle, a technique I had read about in Glamour magazine, just in time. Dad pounded on the door, called me a liar, a tramp, and not his daughter. His rant sounded like an electric razor running up and down my spine. I had covered my ears to block the hurt.

After dark, while he snored, I tiptoed out the front door to Carrie's. Several days later I went home and pretended nothing had happened.

I sat in my car reeling from the day's events. Thirty years ago, I was afraid and fled. Today, I was not going to run.

Carrie's accusation of me living a good life now was understandable and based on appearance. She could not see inside – the scar tissue, loneliness, regret, and sorrow. The necklace was the only evidence. Perhaps Carrie remembered something else. I was determined to get her to talk.

Chapter 4

The Woman Outside

℘

Water droplets added a squeak to Frank's footsteps as he went inside to talk to his wife. "Another damn realtor, Mary Elizabeth."

He reheated a cup of coffee in the microwave, removed the protective wrapping around the paper, and sunk into a recliner opposite Mary Elizabeth's empty rocking chair. He continued talking to his dead wife as though she were alive.

"Greedy. The whole damn bunch. Realtors! They show up thinking charm will get you to list. You know the Hicks house over on River Road. Some creep bought it and tore it down. No shit, Mary Elizabeth. Tore it down. Carrie says they're building a mansion with five baths. Remember when we bought here in 1965 for ten thousand dollars?"

His eyes wandered to a wedding picture on a nearby shelf. The smiling couple, descending St. Raymond's church steps, had met at a church dance.

Her laugh had drawn Frank's attention. They would meet in Van Cortlandt Park for lunch, and he fell in love with her blue eyes and dark hair. People said they looked like Liz Taylor and Eddie Fisher. Frank insisted he was taller than Eddie.

They honeymooned in Daytona Beach. Housing was so affordable there that Frank sent applications to teach at several schools. One year later he had a job as the music teacher at Seabreeze High School and Joy was born.

"Our lives would have been different if Joy hadn't gone missing, Mary Elizabeth. I promised you I'd never sell or move away. But it isn't easy being here alone, surrounded by memories. Remember Paul? Paul loves assisted living. Hot meals in the dining room and his love life, well ... It's something I think about. I could tell the new owners where I'm living in case Joy shows up."

Frank wiped the tears from his eyes.

"I was so angry with her about not going back to school that I threw the tuition money at her. We didn't know she was missing until the tuition due letter came ... in the mail."

Something about the woman outside gnawed at Frank. He gathered yesterday's newspapers scattered on the floor. Thumbed through various sections and found the anniversary article on cold cases. He closed his eyes to recapture the realtor's voice. Then studied the newspaper photo of Joy and said, "I'm calling Ray Atwood."

Frank pressed the Daytona Beach PD number on speed dial and listened while the phone rang.

"Daytona Beach Police Department," Baumgardner answered.

"It's Frank Webb. I'm calling about Doug Dillon's article on cold cases and want to talk to Ray."

Baumgardner recognized the voice and rolled his eyes as he tapped a pencil on a notepad. "Mr. Webb, how are you? Let me get you, Ray. Hold please."

Baumgardner put the call on hold and buzzed Atwood.

"It's chronically cranky Frank on line one. He's looking to

bite off someone's head and asking for you. I told the walk-in you'd be out in a few."

Ray Atwood pressed line one. "Frank, how are you?"

"I could complain. But it won't change shit. Anyway, I won't waste your time. I'm calling about yesterday's article. Nice story, but hardly a coincidence, it being the thirtieth anniversary and all. Did the story get any play?"

"Frank, you're not wasting my time. This is difficult for everyone. We're hoping to get closure for the families. I wish I could tell you differently. There are no new leads."

"So, let me get this straight. The reporter, Lazy Ass Dillon, is trying to make a name for himself and couldn't find any real news, keeps revisiting the past. Does anyone give a crap about ripping off our scabs? I'm too old for this bullshit."

"Calm down Frank, these articles rip off my scabs, too. Call the newspaper with your rants about reporters. I'll let you know if something develops. Have a nice day."

Frank slammed the phone and studied the newspaper photo. His chest hurt and it was difficult to stand.

"Ray's working on closure for us. We can thank that Dillon guy, Mary Elizabeth." He mumbled and walked to the kitchen, tossed the paper in the sink, struck a match, and watched it burn.

* * * * *

After talking to Frank, Ray went out front and said to Baumgardner, "Frank Webb thinks Doug Dillon is a lazy ass who wants to make a name for himself. He is not a happy camper."

Baumgardner shook his head and answered. "No surprise. Was he ever not cranky?"

"He may have been less cranky before his daughter went missing and his wife died. But no. He was never not cranky. Where's the walk-in?"

"She left. Said she wasn't feeling well. Something didn't agree with her. Could have been food or Dillon giving her the once-over. Watch the security tape."

"Scott. What did she say?"

"Hypothetically speaking, something about a crime which happened years ago. Her concern was ... it could be murder or they might be missing." Baumgardner looked up. "She said, 'People can be missing for thirty years and still be alive.' She imagined. She wanted to be anonymous. Watch the tape."

Ray closed his office door and watched the footage. A woman got out of a Lexus with New York plates and entered the building.

He thought to himself, *That's Joy. How can that be Joy?* His heart raced. His hands shook and the urge to run after her produced a familiar adrenalin rush. He talked himself down remembering an incident in Tampa.

Years ago, he had pulled over a vehicle convinced the driver was Joy. He put on his glasses for a better view of the footage. The woman looked like Joy. Although her hair was short, salt and pepper, and curly. Ray zoomed in on the car's plate number. Took the pencil behind his ear and copied it down.

He stood and grabbed the edge of the desk to steady himself. It was as though an earthquake had passed through the room. He bit on the pencil to relieve the chattering of his teeth, as though he was having a seizure.

The dream of finding her is finally true. But, where had she been? Why had she never contacted him? And more important, why was she in town now?

Chapter 5

Black Coffee, One Sugar

In high school, Rockefeller Garden had been our meeting place. Ray and I would meet for coffee, sometimes lunch. Share a sub from a local deli, or peanut butter and jelly sandwiches wrapped in wax paper from home. Occasionally I fixed bologna and cheese. Ray preferred mustard and me, mayo.

After the blow-up with Carrie, I drove along the Halifax River admiring the waterfront homes, then parked at Rockefeller Garden to think.

In 1984, the former winter home of John D. Rockefeller was in disrepair and occupied by the homeless. Today things were different, even the gardens had been restored.

The sun supplied a respite from the cold I'd escaped, only days before. White clouds streaked across the sky announcing the day's end as I wrestled with the past.

My cell rang.

"You're alive," he said.

"Ray?" I whispered. My skin tingled and I was stunned. "How did you get my number?"

"I'm a police detective, Joy. Retired, but ... a police detective."

"You know I'm in Daytona?"

"The security camera has you on film. You are alive and still more than attractive at what, forty-eight? You wanted to remain anonymous, became ill, and left."

"You recognized me?"

"Yup, and ran the plate. The car is registered to Benjamin and Elizabeth Frances Garner. I guess Elizabeth Frances Webb, aka Joy Webb, married."

"Yes... Well no." I did not know how to explain that Ben had died. "How did you get my cell number?"

"The old-fashioned way, the Manhattan directory." He laughed. "Your Park Ave address and phone were listed ... your housekeeper answered, and gave me your cell."

"Ray, I can explain."

"You want to do this on the phone?"

I did not and a heavy silence lingered in the air.

"Let's meet, tomorrow morning at Rockefeller Gardens, un-official, of course. I'll bring coffee, black ... one sugar. Right? Like old times."

His voice ricocheted with sarcasm and he hung up leaving me with thick memories. Did he have a crystal ball and know I was at our meeting spot? Where we had coffee and licked our fingers clean after eating sticky buns. We had been in love. It was ironic I had come here.

Once in bed, I tossed and turned feeling like tomorrow was the first day of high school. I strategized in my sleep but had no game plan, just regret. My feelings for Ray had never dis-appeared. They had simply faded into the background of a happy marriage to Ben.

In the morning, Ray arrived ahead of me. I recognized him from behind – his one shoulder permanently lower than the other and the way he cracked his neck, head to shoulder as he watched the river's current.

I walked a path to reach him and stood beside him. He handed me a cup of coffee and our hands touched with the exchange, rekindling a feeling I hadn't felt in years.

"I can't believe you're here," Ray said and smiled the way he'd smiled at me thirty years ago.

Our embrace was familiar yet awkward. Ray wiped the tears from my face.

"I'm happy you're not dead. I never should have stopped looking for you. Damn, I knew you were alive."

We sat on a bench near the water's edge. I removed the cover from the brown paper cup and stirred the contents of a sugar pack into the hot coffee. Then I listened to the splash of the water along the shore wondering what to do or say next.

"I've missed you."

"I've missed you, too, and have regrets."

"Regrets? That's what you call this? Watching the security tape, I couldn't believe my eyes until I heard your voice. I knew it was you. But why? Why did you leave?"

Yesterday's anger and aloofness were surfacing. His tight arm muscles were obvious in a white t-shirt and his torso trim in stonewashed jeans. At fifty-one years of age, his hair was jet black and thick, with a hint of grey at the temples, and his eyes – the dark brown color of youth. A physical attraction bounced between us, or so I felt.

"So, what's the big secret? What's kept you away for thirty years?"

He waited for an answer with his arms folded across his chest. I studied his eyes. Enjoyed his crooked smile. Debated how much to share. I fidgeted with the small jewelry bag in my pocket.

"Thirty years ago, I was vacuuming, and found this necklace under my father's chair." I separated the drawstrings and emptied the contents into my hand. "Diane Martin wore this peace sign necklace in the photo of her missing."

Ray stared at the necklace. His jawbone tightened. He wandered closer to the river. I lingered and then joined him. The water was choppy and slapped the beach wall creating a splash. We both jumped back to avoid getting wet as the sun disappeared behind a cloud and the air turned cooler.

"You think your dad had something to do with the Martins' disappearance?"

"Yes."

"I have a duty and moral obligation to inform the department, first. Then all concerned parties will be notified. You'll have some explaining to do."

Ray turned to walk away, over his shoulder he said, "You may want to let your dad know you're alive."

I watched him and wondered if it was too late to hope for something. I shopped for groceries preoccupied by Ray's words. Then returned to the Maverick, and fixed a sandwich, sat on the deck, and stared at the ocean, unable to eat.

Thirty years had passed. Ray was right. I had to visit my dad. The whole truth would not be easy to tell. My insides gnawed … was I doing the right thing?

Ben was dead. My stepkids were more attached to their mother. And my son didn't have a clue who I was. I did not want to be alone.

I drove to Morningside and sat outside my "old house" wondering what to call the run-down cottage. It looked tired. Perhaps, "former residence." Better yet, "Dad's house." He lived here. Maybe "childhood home" was best.

Chapter 6

Dad, it's Me

I hadn't been inside for thirty years. Memories of growing up here, playing badminton in the backyard with Carrie, neighborhood block parties, barbecues, fireworks on the Fourth of July, and Christmas cookie swaps came to mind.

Things were good and then not. Dad guzzled beer. Mom suffered from depression. Always afraid of saying or doing the wrong thing, I lived in fear my words would trigger more drinking and more despair.

My hands gripped the steering wheel and doubt invaded me. Perhaps it would be better to stay missing. Dad may have been helping the Martins look for their dog. If my suspicions proved true, my father could be behind bars for the rest of his life.

I walked toward the house, each step heavy with guilt and filled with fear. The doorbell hung loose against the doorjamb. A missing screw suggested it may not work and a signal to leave. I closed my eyes, raised a fist, and pounded on the door.

After what felt like an eternity, Dad bellowed. "Give it a rest. I'm coming."

And he was, slowly. He opened the door and I heard myself say, "Dad. It's me, Joy."

"Joy? My Joy? Are you joking? Don't mess with me."

"Yes. I'm home, Daddy."

His hands shook as he fumbled for his glasses and moved into the sunlight for a better view to study my face then burst out in laughter as tears streamed down his cheeks. It was a genuine father and daughter reunion. But my chest hurt – the joy of being home, yet heavy with fear – was he a murderer?

"Holy Mother of God. Mary Elizabeth, your prayers have been answered. Sweet Jesus. Where the hell have you been?" Glancing toward heaven, he said, "Thank God. You're alive. If only your mother were here."

He grasped my shoulders and lamented. "To the day she died, she never gave up hope. Thank God, you're safe!"

He pulled me in for a hug. "And all grown up ... with short curly hair. Come in! Come in! No wonder I didn't recognize you!"

His laughter floated like bubbles in champagne.

Inside, the foyer was dark and dated, filled with the memory of me kissing my mother for the last time. His laughter turned to sobbing. Fraught with emotion, he stumbled to his chair and sunk into it. Out of breath and sweating, he pointed to Mom's rocking chair.

"Have a seat, Joy. Your mother died from cancer four years ago. She worried every day about you, and the worry became cancer."

He opened a tattered linen handkerchief and mopped his neck.

I knew Mom had died. The heartbreaking online obituary made me think about coming home. I decided not to. It would be cruel to confront him about the past while we both grieved.

"Now you're back, Joy. What happened? Where the hell have you been for thirty years?"

This was the maelstrom I feared. How to tell him where I had been and why? Instead, I sidetracked. "Dad, you want coffee? I'll make coffee."

"That will be great. Make it Irish. You know where the bottle is. We have some celebrating to do. Thank God you're here. Maybe I'm dreaming. Joy, am I dreaming?"

"You're not dreaming," I said on the way to the kitchen.

An old Black and Decker drip coffee maker was on the counter. The art deco coffee canister, its capital letter C missing when I left, sat on the counter. I removed the lid. Scooped coffee into a filter, put water in its pot, then listened to it drip, drip, drip, while I chewed my lips and peered out the window.

The tree we planted long ago was now a majestic weeping willow. But there was no garden, just weeds. My mother always planted a beautiful flower garden. The memories and emotions caught me off guard.

Dad nodded off, while I was in the kitchen and was startled when I returned to the living room.

"Was I dreaming?" he said and reached for the cup with two hands. "If I am, don't wake me."

"Dad, you're not dreaming."

"A parent is hardwired to their children. They never forget them." He sipped his coffee. "At first, your mother and I saw you everywhere. At the mall, we'd follow people positive it was you until we caught up. Memories triggered by simple things, a drinking glass or the jacket you hated and refused to wear."

He put the cup down and blew his nose.

"Memories everywhere. If we drove past the library, the park, or the bank, every building held a reminder of you."

Tilting his head toward the ceiling, he retrieved one.

"Silly things, like a stranger in the grocery store wearing a green shirt. Your mother said, 'Green was Joy's favorite color. Remember buying those Mickey Mouse ears at Disney? She insisted on a green pair.' A snapshot image of you, excited and laughing came to mind. Instead, I'd answer, the salad dressing is in aisle nine."

He pursed his lips in an effort not to cry, and paused lost in thought.

"And now you are here, and it's time to celebrate. Hand me the phone. I'm calling Carrie. Damn, I knew you weren't a realtor. Shit! Thank God, you weren't abducted by some deviant. Or were you? It would explain things."

Next to Mom's chair sat a dial phone with a twenty-foot extension cord. I weaved the long cord around the sofa, across an end table, and handed it to him. He punched the keypad and cradled the receiver between his head and shoulder.

"Carrie, it's Dad. Get your fanny over here. I have good news, great news."

He sounded happy and hung up. I was caught off guard by his reference to himself as her dad, and saw red, like a lightning bolt. Angry and jealous of their easy relationship, I snapped. "You're Dad to Carrie?"

I regretted my outburst. The happiness slid off his face, replaced by a look – the look. It always preceded an eruption of anger and fear bubbled in my chest. His controlled anger, not yelling, was intense. I started to sweat and fought an urge to flee. I pictured my mother sick with thinning hair sitting in the now empty chair. My emotions swung from glad to sad. Then regret. I was angry, mad, and surprised by the words coming out of my mouth.

"Carrie always called you Mr. Webb. You were very strict about it."

"Now don't get your britches in a twist. Yes, she calls me

Dad. Joy, you were gone. We were a tag team driving your mother to chemo. Carrie brought her. I picked her up. When your mother died, I was lost."

His voice was no longer soft or forgiving.

"Carrie stayed by me."

His voice went on an emotional roller coaster ride, fluctuating from bitter and loud to sweet and low.

"You got a problem with that? Where were you anyway, Joy? Locked in someone's basement? If so, you are forgiven ... But ... Why would you stay away, otherwise? Perhaps you had amnesia. Years have gone by and now you show up, Miss I'm-All-right-and-have-money. I see the big diamond ring you're wearing."

"I went to New York," I said as I fingered the wedding band on my ring finger. Ben had added anniversary stones every year. Suddenly, I was embarrassed by the size and tucked my hand under my thigh.

"You went to New York? Like to sightsee or work? I remember the fight we had and you left. Then a month later, getting a letter in the mail from Stetson University. I phoned the dorm. Your roommate, what was her name? Cheryl ... said you went home because your father had a heart attack. I had no heart attack. You were not at home. All hell broke loose."

His voice faded and my brain took flight. Cheryl was a bubbly type, you thought was dumb – she giggled so much. We hit it off immediately as roommates and explored the campus together. We were best buddies and members of the choir. Bells rang in my head and I envisioned the Christmas Candle Light Ceremony. The memory of the illuminated candles and the sound of the huge pipe organ, was like an out-of-body spiritual experience that almost brought me to my knees.

But I heard Dad saying, "You were in New York City for thirty years and didn't have a dime for a phone call? Shit, Joy!"

"I didn't know what to do after I saw you with Diane and Tammy Martin!"

"You've got to be kidding! What the hell do Diane and Tammy Martin have to do with you running away? God Damn it! Make this coffee more Irish!"

His eyes bulged and he held out his empty mug toward me red-faced.

In the kitchen, the light was no longer bright and sunny. I couldn't get the memory of Stetson out of my mind. I'd felt free and hopeful about the future until I found myself pregnant. I shut down. Cheryl couldn't figure out what was wrong and I wasn't about to tell her. I walked the campus alone, made friends with the trees, and sat in the Elizabeth Hall Chapel praying for a miracle.

The freshly brewed coffee smelled burnt. I turned the lights on. Mom would have had clean dish towels hanging, and a fresh cloth covering the table.

The whiskey bottle on the counter was an ugly reminder of why I left and hadn't come back for so long. I poured a hefty shot into Dad's mug, added hot coffee, and returned to the living room, determined to keep my composure.

"What did the Martins have to do with me leaving, Dad? … You tell me, and be truthful."

"Truthful!" Dad slammed the mug on the end table. Hot coffee flew on the rug. He struggled to stand.

"The truth? Tell me the truth." His voice rose to a crescendo. "Why or what have you been hiding for thirty years? This Martin thing is bullshit!"

A knock on the door interrupted us. I sought refuge in the kitchen and heard Ray Atwood say, "Can we come in? We have good news, Frank."

"Ray, come in, your timing is perfect. More good news, shit! I'm too old for this."

"You and Officer Baumgardner have met, I believe," said Ray.

"Let's cut the crap. I talked to you bubbleheads yesterday. There were no new leads. And today? I bet you dollars to donuts there's a new development."

"We wanted to tell you in person. After you phoned, we have good news about Joy."

I stepped into the room and completed his sentence. "Is alive and no longer missing. I took your advice, Ray."

Ray cleared his throat as Carrie opened the front door.

"I'm glad you called, Dad. Let's get a welcome home party started. Hi, Joy."

Dad hugged Carrie. "Joy's alive."

"I know. She's staying at the Maverick. She wanted to surprise you herself. Didn't you Joy?" Carrie winked at me but her eyes reflected a hurt.

Dad slipped his hand into Carrie's and they both stared at me.

"It's hard to believe after all these years. Hard to imagine a sane person would deliberately hide from loved ones, unless ... they had amnesia or were in a locked basement. However, that wasn't the case. Was it Joy? Matter of fact, Joy is ready, to tell the truth, aren't you? Let's hear it."

Ray studied the room, his eyes glancing face to face, and then stopped at mine. My heart pounded and my hands trembled as I removed the velvet pouch from my pocket and pulled out the necklace.

"Diane Martin wore this silver cross in the newspaper picture. Two weeks later I found the necklace in the cushions of that chair." I pointed at the old recliner.

"You ran away because of a newspaper picture?" Carrie said, "Why didn't you tell me?" She appeared flushed.

Ray interrupted. "Joy never told me either, Carrie. I was on that case. This information would have changed the search had I known. When you went missing months later, we considered it might be a serial killer.

My face went pale, as I glared at my father. "I never intended to be missing. I went away from you, Dad."

I felt like a snowball rolling downhill gathering momentum.

"You had to be the last person to see them. But didn't come forward ... because ... you'd be a person of interest. When I asked, you lied and said it was a mother looking for her kid's dog – a stranger. It wasn't A MOTHER! It was Diane Martin."

"What difference does it make why they came to the house? You believe I'm a killer because you found a necklace? Don't be stupid."

"Stupid? Diane Martin wore this necklace!" The pendant dangled in my hands.

Dad grabbed my hand to remove my hold on the necklace.

"Give me that. You know nothing."

"I watched Diane and Tammy get in your car from my window." Ray appeared surprised. "The three of you drove away, and they haven't been seen since!"

We struggled over the necklace and Officer Baumgardner stepped between us, "I'll take that. Mr. Webb, we'll need you to come down to the department and answer a few questions."

"Am I under arrest? A necklace doesn't prove anything. I want it back."

Dad grabbed Baumgardner's hand and pried his fingers open. Ray stepped in to restrain him as Dad kneed Baumgardner in the groin. The detective doubled over moaning in pain.

Ray locked handcuffs on Dad.

"You're under arrest now Frank, for assaulting an officer."

I stared in stunned silence as Dad was led out the door. For years, I had dreaded seeing my father in handcuffs. Now my worst fears had come true ... this was why I never came back; especially when my mother was alive. If he was interrogated, a lot could go wrong.

What had I done?

Chapter 7

The Dog Story and Mr. C

☙

The scuffle left spilled coffee on the old shag carpet. Carrie and I busied ourselves cleaning up the mess in silence, our thoughts occupied until Carrie said, "Are you all right?"

"I'll be fine."

"That's why you stayed away? You think your father knows why the Martins disappeared?"

"Yes." Her question sent chills up my spine. I selected my words carefully. "Initially, I thought his dog story might be true."

Carrie scrutinized me from head to toe. Slowly, her arms relaxed. "What dog story?"

We stood silent for what felt like an eternity.

"I'm glad you're alive," she said and hugged me, sobbing.

"I'm glad I'm alive, too." I returned her hug. We cried and the tears turned to laughter. Then, I made a fresh pot of coffee and we sat in the kitchen talking.

"You never had a dog. What's the dog story?"

"The morning after seeing the Martins and Dad together, I asked him about it. He told me some woman was searching for her kid's dog and to mind my own business. I did until I found the necklace wedged in Dad's chair and grew suspicious. I stewed for a week. Remember Mr. Whatshisname? He lived next door, owned a red convertible … always teased us."

"Of course, Mr. Cuccinelli. The guy wore a skinny sleeveless undershirt he called an Italian dinner jacket."

I stared hard into the past, remembering Mr. C's performance. In the first act, he'd soap up his Mustang and hosed it off. The white suds swam across the lawn. In the second act, he scrubbed the grill work and hub caps. The finale? He whistled and danced around the car drying it with a chamois.

"Is he still alive?"

"He died about ten years ago." Carrie's green eyes turned sympathetic. "So, you thought your dad was lying?"

I slid over the question and focused on the memory.

"I waited for Mr. C to wash his car and went outside. He said, 'Hey cutie pie, what's up?' I lied and told him I was headed to Main Street. Sure enough, he cautioned me not to hang with the wrong crowd in the wrong part of town. When he did, I said, don't worry, I won't go missing like the mother and daughter searching for their dog in our neighborhood. He wrung the chamois out and said, 'Where did you hear that?'"

"But you did go missing." Carrie unfolded her arms. "Did you consider how hard it would be for us?"

Her voice expressed the burden I had left behind.

"Shit, Joy. You saw your dad with the Martins. You were a witness and had evidence to confirm he lied. Why didn't you tell me?" Carrie sighed and seemed to stare at a distant memory.

I thought about all the nights we spent together, fussing with each other's hair, and applying mascara, and wished I had. Truth pushed at my lips like hot lava ready to erupt. The pregnancy and adoption were secrets I had sworn to take to my grave.

Carrie snapped out of her trance. "Let's get out of here. Clear our heads. We'll take my Harley."

"Really?" The years apart adopted less significance and my mind relaxed into thoughts of regaining our friendship.

"You have a Harley?"

"Yeah, I bought it after my divorce, nothing fancy … not a bike week hog, just for cruising. Let's go for a ride … grab a beer. Like old times, when all we thought about were boys, and hung out in Flagler."

She pulled me out the door. An hour later we sat outside at The Funky Pelican in Flagler Beach, watching the whitecaps jump a high tide dance and smelling the salty air. It was one of a few beachside places in Flagler County. Families parked on A1A and carried babies and coolers across the sand to swim at their own risk, free. The pier next door was dotted with people who paid a small fee to fish. We sat at the bar watching surfers wait to ride a decent wave.

"Remember the night we went to the Stones concert in Jacksonville and ran out of gas?"

"Remember? Who could forget? Dad screaming the phone woke him, calling us stupid and hanging up." Carrie lit a cigarette. "We were stranded and then this guy showed up with a gas can. Like something from the TV show with Michael Landon. What was it called?"

"Right, I remember," I yelled over the bar noise. "Like it was yesterday. Only you didn't call him Dad. When did he become your dad, Carrie?"

"Well," said Carrie, leaning back in the bar chair. "Probably five or ten years after you went missing. Maybe 1990? Don't be a jerk. You'd disappeared. Were presumed dead." She straightened her back and retied her hair with a stretchy band. "You think he's a killer. So, don't get all Daddy's girl on me. He's a good-hearted man. Sweet, in a gruff way."

"When sober."

Our loud voices drew attention as we stood and people turned as Carrie walked away. I motioned for the check. Ashamed of my jealousy. Reeling from this emotional outburst.

Outside Carrie put her helmet on and handed me mine.

"I could bum a ride or call a taxi."

"Shut up, get on the bike, and don't suggest we ride The Loop, because it's not happening."

The trip back to the hotel gave me time to cool down.

"I hope I'm wrong. I'm being childish. Let me make it up to you, if possible. How about dinner, not at the Maverick?"

"Are you apologizing? I'm not going to call him Frank.

"Yes, I'm apologizing. You could call him Mr. Webb?" I laughed. Carrie did not.

"Right. He'd give me the shark stare ... You remember the shark stare?"

I did remember his stare, appropriately named because the threat of doing it again would mean death. My father would never say a word, but we knew what to expect. His look kept us in place.

The Top of Daytona restaurant had spectacular views of both the Ocean and the River. Carrie ordered seafood linguini, clams, mussels, and shrimp tossed with a garlic white wine sauce. I selected the spinach salad and wild mushroom ravioli. Thirty years melted away and we resumed our friendship, as I had hoped.

Carrie talked about her marriage, divorce, and her two adult boys. From time-to-time interjecting, "Shit, Joy. I can't believe you're alive."

I shared my work as a nanny, talked about opening my agency, and didn't mention kids. After a few glasses of wine, we discussed Dad and his need for representation.

"I know a lawyer," Carrie said. She refilled our glasses. "My ex has had his share of trouble."

Chapter 8

The Arraignment

ص

In the courtroom the next morning, I sat behind criminal defense lawyer John Murphy. The room was heavy with the shuffling of feet. Dad entered the courtroom disheveled after spending the night in a jail cell. Seeing him filled me with remorse.

"How do you plead?" said Judge Goodwin after reading the charges of obstruction of justice, assault, and resisting arrest.

"Not guilty, Your Honor."

I shuddered with fear. Could he survive prison?

"Bail?" The judge nodded at the prosecutor.

"Your Honor," Murphy interrupted, "my client has lived and worked in the community his whole life. Mr. Webb is a retired teacher. These charges relate to a cold case and claims made by his daughter who has been conveniently missing for over thirty years."

The lawyer's voice was loud and clear as he glanced at his notes.

"The only charge of merit is resisting arrest. The arrest was in his home. No warrant. It's understandable a man of Mr. Webb's age upon learning his only child was alive may have resisted leaving. Detective Atwood's assertion of assault is biased. Your Honor, I respectfully request all charges be dropped."

"Biased … and the grounds?"

John Murphy cleared his throat. "Detective Atwood had a romantic relationship with his daughter years ago."

"Case dismissed." The judge slammed his gavel. "You are free to go, Mr. Webb. In the future, if you are arrested be nice and smile."

"Where's Carrie?" Dad asked, walking out of the courthouse.

"Working. We can stop by the Maverick for breakfast."

"Now you're going to be nice to a murderer? Just take me home. Then disappear back to wherever you were hiding from your terrible killer father."

"Dad, please. Let's not fight."

We drove in silence. When I parked in front of the house, he got out and walked up the driveway.

"God damn it! You locked the door?"

"Did you want it unlocked overnight?" I rushed to unlock the front door.

"You have a key? I've gone to bed for thirty years with the door unlocked, praying you'd come home. Fall asleep smiling about how happy I'd be if you were still alive. Now, my prayers have been answered. You're back but … I AM NOT HAPPY!"

"You're upset. Did you even sleep last night?"

"You bet your ass I'm upset. You disappear. Show up years later making wild accusations. Upset? Don't talk to me. Give me the goddamn paper and leave."

"You need to eat. I'll fix breakfast."

"No! Get out! I want nothing from you." He closed his eyes.

"You're still dead to me."

I busied myself by giving the kitchen a good cleaning. Mom's dolphin salt and pepper shakers were layered in dust, and the dust turned to muck as I soaped them. When the water stopped, I heard Dad snoring.

He was asleep and I climbed the stairs to my bedroom. My Betty Boop collection decorated a bureau. The same purple curtains draped the window. I recalled the night, thirty years ago. I had been sneaking a cigarette, blowing smoke out the window when the doorbell rang. Dad's voice diminished as the door shut behind him and I watched him unlock the car and get in. A young girl slipped in the back seat, and a woman got in the passenger side. They drove away. I figured it was a neighbor or someone from school wanting a ride. Maybe a battery went dead and they needed a charge. It was odd. Nevertheless, I brushed my teeth and went to bed.

Now, from the top of the stairs, I heard Dad talking and tiptoed down a few steps.

"Can you believe Joy is alive? All these years of hoping and praying, for what?" he cried.

I froze in place and listened to every word.

"Now she's making accusations and some of them are true."

His voice was almost a whisper. I shimmied down further on my butt to see him.

"I didn't want to hurt you, Mary Elizabeth," he said to an empty chair, "I fell in love with Diane Martin the first time I saw her and thanked God she married right out of high school. That night she told me Tammy was my daughter. When they disappeared ... I decided to let sleeping dogs lie. You didn't need to know."

He had confessed to an affair and not wanting Mom to know. I walked down the stairs dizzy; my thoughts scattered.

"Dad. You, all right?"

"Shit. You scared the bejesus out of me."

He looked older than he was – older than the young man in the wedding picture gathering dust on the bookshelf – older than the retiree in an anniversary photo displayed above it – and much older than I had recalled when I left in 1984.

"You damn near gave me a heart attack coming down those stairs. Aren't you dead?" His jowls sagged in defeat as his shaking hands wiped his eyes with a cloth hanky. "Now, wait, wait. Don't tell me. News flash, Missing and Presumed Dead Woman, really is ALIVE."

His gun cabinet stood in a corner. The key was in the lock.

"You think I murdered a woman and an innocent child?"

I wanted to say, *undeniably yes, I think you killed them.* Instead, I said, "I'm sorry."

"Sorry? Sorry, you left? Sorry, you came home?" He shook his head. "Sorry, you think I'm a killer? Sorry doesn't change squat. Shit, for a smart gal you are VERY stupid." He blew his nose. "You're never going to prove diddly because I'm innocent."

The hate in his voice made my skin prickle.

"How many times do I have to tell you? Get out! ... Now!"

I glanced at the gun cabinet and wondered if any of the rifles were loaded, then moved cautiously past him, and out the door.

Chapter 9

The Cold Case Squad

⤬

Ray returned to Daytona Beach PD as a drug arrest was being processed and a crazy person in the holding tank created a ruckus by throwing shoes. He slapped Baumgardner on the back, "What's he unhappy about?"

"Fancy Pants?" Baumgardner, known for nicknaming detainees, looked up. The detainee wore a pair of Levi's with metal studs running down the side. He continued, "Fancy Pants claimed to need medical attention. He was taken to the hospital, where he assaulted the doctor and fled."

"I guess he didn't get too far." Ray smiled.

"A helicopter picked him up out at Tomoka Park."

"Anyone here yet?"

"You got the full squad, Bobby, Danny, and Joe."

Bobby Smart, on the job for twenty-five years in South Beach, retired to Palm Coast in 1998 and got into land sales at Grand Haven. After ten years, he started a volunteer cold case unit in Daytona and recruited Danny Egan and Joe Bucci as assistants. Danny retired from NYPD, and Joe from Jersey City. They had been working cold cases since 2008. The men huddled in Conference Room B, a file and photos scattered on a work table.

Ray shook hands with Danny and Joe. Then stood next to Bobby.

"Thanks for coming in. Tell me what you got."

"The latest?" Bobby asked.

"Get us updated, and then we can talk about new developments."

Bobby moved beside the table of photographs, picked up one featuring human bones, and sighed.

"These remains were found in 1996 in Georgia, twelve years after Diane and Tammy Martin went missing. There were no leads or connections to them. The technology wasn't there on old bones. So, the remains sat in a cardboard box. Recently a forensic anthropologist decided to examine them again. The second examination determined the bones to be from a girl between ten and fourteen years of age, Tammy went missing at ten. We figure it's a possibility."

"I inspected the site photos earlier. Nice work. It's a theory we need to follow."

"The National Center for Missing and Exploited Children is interested in Tammy's case," Danny said. His voice was raspy from years of smoking.

"We need DNA. Nothing's on file…The whereabouts of Diane Martin's ex-husband are unknown. His name is on the birth certificate." Bobby paused then added, "We're looking to locate other family members."

"We could canvas again." Danny shrugged his shoulders.

"Okay." Ray considered telling the group there may be a connection between the Martin and Webb cases. "We wait. Anything else?" he said instead.

"Rumor has it the Webb case is no longer cold," said Joe. "You want to tell us about it?"

Ray glanced at Bobby, Danny, and then back to Joe. The men worked on Joy's case for six years. He owed them an explanation; one he was reluctant to subject himself or Joy to. A potential media shitstorm, with sideway accusations coming at them a strong possibility.

"Right." Ray cleared his throat. "There have been some new developments. Joy Webb has surfaced. She was a runaway."

"Are we celebrating?" Danny smiled. "Does old man Webb know? He must be ecstatic."

He looked around the room as the others joined in relief. Bobby slapped Ray on the back. "It's unbelievable. Where the hell has she been?"

"Living in New York City," said Ray.

"Weren't the two of you an item way back when?" Joe asked.

"She married some wall street accountant. It's complicated. Give me a little space, guys."

"Complicated? Give you a little space?" Danny repeated. "Talk like that will jeopardize the case."

"She came back bringing evidence that implicates her father in the Martin disappearance."

"Evidence? What possible evidence could she have?" asked Bobby.

"A necklace. The peace sign necklace Diane Martin wore in the newspaper picture." Ray tossed the necklace on the table.

"Those necklaces were a dime a dozen, it proves nothing." Bobby searched the papers on the worktable until he found the newspaper clipping.

"She ran away? Sounds like a spoiled brat seeking revenge." Joe blurted out.

"Yeah, but for what?" Danny raised his brows.

"The way to find out is to bring them both in for an interview," said Bobby. He stared at Ray.

"Why don't you guys take this one? I'm too close to both parties," said Ray. He shoved his hands into his pant pockets.

The men nodded to each other. Frank Webb was cantankerous, a difficult man but a loving father. The room grew quiet. They sat at a table as though sitting in a boat about to push off, not talking. Were the two cases linked?

Bobby broke the silence. "Ray, recusing yourself may not be the way to go. It took Joy Webb thirty years to come out of hiding. She may open up to you."

Ray moved his hands to his hips and listened.

"Frank likes all of us. Let's not make anything official. I'll stop by and have a long overdue chat with the old man," Bobby said. "Danny and Joe, recanvas the neighborhood. And, Ray, talk with Joy. Find out what's going on."

Chapter 10

Maverick Hotel

ॐ

I n the hotel room, a thirty-year sadness descended upon me. Knowledge of my father's affair with Diane Martin confirmed my suspicion and sat on my chest like a ten-pound flour sack. My head was spinning.

I heard a knock and opened the door to see Ray. I rubbed my eyes and pretended I had been sleeping. Then suggested he sit on the couch while I slipped inside the bathroom. Behind the closed door, I wrestled with my feelings and washed my face. Then fluffed my hair, applied lip gloss, and opened the door to face the man with whom I had secrets ... and had never stopped loving.

"I'm glad to see you," I said and put on a cheery happy-to-see-you smile.

"Glad? Me, too."

Ray's comment was flirtatious and he relaxed his straight-as-a-board posture. My fake cheery smile followed suit.

"I have good news. The Martin cold case has been re-opened."

He was quick to notice I stopped smiling.

"It's what you wanted. Right?" Ray shifted his weight from

hip to hip.

"Yes and no ... I was going to open a bottle of wine. Will you join me or is this an official call?"

I opened the refrigerator and took out a chilled bottle of Chardonnay. Ray peeled back the seal and removed the cork.

"Your being alive doesn't change the facts," he said, filling our glasses. "Both you and your dad withheld information. Legal talk? Obstruction of justice. A prosecutor might question your motivation in concealing evidence. You waited a long time to come forward."

How could I explain and not tell him about our son? I had made decisions for his sake. Assumed our love was not strong enough. What if Ray would have been happy to be a father? I didn't want him to know about Dad's confession. My father might be innocent and me wrong.

Ray shortened the distance between us. I felt the heat on his clothing and smelled his day's end scent.

"Your dad isn't a bad guy. He loves you."

I recalled spending time with my father. We played stickball in the street. Boogie boarded at the beach ... Until I was eight years old and then things changed. His attention went elsewhere. Now I know. His absence had nothing to do with me. He was spending time with Diane Martin. Maybe Ray was right, maybe he loved me.

"You ran away. Didn't want to be found. Now ... You show up." He probed. The softness in his voice made my shoulders relax and stripped away my defenses. I began to cry.

Ray held me longer than I wanted. I was afraid to tell him Dad was Tammy Martin's father. The truth festered in my mouth. I couldn't tell him, unless — I told him the whole story, we had a son I'd given up for adoption.

"Thirty years is a long time to be away from someone you love. I thought I would never hold you again."

Ray paused as he stared deep into my eyes.

"Where have you been? Why didn't you contact me? Let me know you were alive?"

Memories of our love filled the room. My inability to answer created a deafening silence. Our embrace became the calm before the storm.

"It's not a hard question." He held me at arm's length. "I know the answer." His voice grew in volume. "You went to New York City, and married a good-ole-boy Florida politician's son? Did you meet him before you left?"

"No. It's not what you think."

"Okay, what should I think?"

I wanted to say I was pregnant and did not want to force him into marriage. Scared my father was right ... I was his summer fling. I felt like Cinderella watching the carriage turn back into a pumpkin and the footmen mice again. I could explain Ben and I met years later but feared if I told him there would be no turning back.

"Be honest ... or maybe ... you just didn't care." His lips gripped shut with emotion.

"Of course, I cared."

I felt like that immature nineteen-year-old again and wanted to flee. The thought of what our lives may have been crushed my chest and I braced for the next tidal wave of anger and sadness ... which kept coming. Perhaps telling him about our son would be better. "You never missed me. I thought you didn't love me."

"Joy ... that's silly."

"My father ..." I pulled away and wanted to say ... *was*

Tammy Martin's father, but couldn't. "I've ignored my feelings for you for thirty years … seeing you wasn't planned."

I feared if he knew about the adoption he would want nothing to do with me. "Help me clear my father of involvement in the Martin case first!"

"Okay, if that's what you want." He dropped his arms. "We both need time to think."

He resumed the straightness he had arrived with and left. I closed the door behind him.

* * * * *

A walk on the beach did nothing to keep my emotional tsunami away. I paced the shoreline and regretted not telling Ray I was pregnant, but at the same time relieved. I was ill-prepared to deal with these buried feelings for Ray — not yet anyway. My head swam with what-ifs. I got in my car and drove aimlessly then found myself knocking on Carrie's door.

"Come in," Carrie said smiling.

The stained Maverick work shirt had been replaced by a flowing caftan; her hair piled high. I followed her into an open-plan living room.

Framed watercolor paintings hung on the wall. Their soft hues flattered the butter-colored hall. There was no TV, recliner, or sofa. Instead, four chairs in geometric fabric upholstery provided seating. Lighting and modern pole lamps set the mood for conversation. The kitchen countertops were granite. The island, surrounded by stools, faced a backyard laced with flowers and shrubs.

I recalled my father holding Carrie's hand. Me dangling the necklace.

"I love your artwork."

"Thanks, I'm an artist. My studio is upstairs. The outside of the house needs work I can't afford. Besides, in this fringe part of town, you don't advertise something nice might be inside. How's your father?"

"The charges were dismissed. Did he call you?"

"No. He's your dad, Joy. We're not attached at the hip. Ray told me. You want red or white wine?"

Lucky stood at her side, wagged his tail, and appeared to smile as she talked.

"Whatever's open." I laughed, wanting to hide my jealousy. "Well at least someone's talking to you. Ray's not happy with me and Dad threw me out."

"Dad ... You know how crabby he can be. Have a seat and chill," she said and handed me a glass of wine.

The dog – a puppy really – ran around fetching toys, until he leaped onto my lap, and licked my face. "Yuck," I said and laughed.

Lucky's coat was tricolor, with brown markings running up and down its ears, and instantly became my new best friend when I scratched him under his chin. "How did he get the name Lucky?"

"I was driving down Beach Street. Almost hit the dog, who was running from a woman holding a broken leash and ranting about being late for work. The woman said, 'This worthless dog is going back to the shelter.' We exchanged phone numbers. And the dog came home with me. But luckily, I never heard from her."

Lucky gave Carrie a puppy dog look and traded my lap for hers. She rubbed his belly.

"He's my best buddy. I told you the other night that my sons are grown. Derrick is married and lives in Tampa. Kevin and his girlfriend share a house here in Daytona. He's a trucker, like his dad."

I sighed a big jealous sigh filled with regret. She had more wrinkles and less money, but I came home to an empty apartment. Not even a dog. My mouth puckered as if filled with sour grapes. My father wanted nothing to do with me and once Ray learned the truth would more than likely feel the same.

"How about you? You haven't talked about children," she said.

"Stepkids – Bryce and Scarlet. I don't see them much." My heart pounded. "After Ben died, well, their mother, Jackie, put a wedge between us." I changed the subject. "Your backyard looks incredible. Can we sit outside?"

"Sure, I'll grab a smoke."

Crisp air complimented the sky as the sun disappeared. Wicker chairs surrounded a fireplace. She dangled a cigarette from her lips, lit it, and blew smoke into the night.

"We missed the sunset." I made idle conversation, stalled, and hoped for the courage to tell my secrets.

"Not really," Carrie said and refilled our glasses. "The houses on Rockefeller Drive block the view. I get the afterglow. Besides, I've missed many a sunset ... turned my head at the wrong time and poof, the sun disappeared, vanished."

"I know." I stuffed an empty feeling. "Things happened too fast. The years are gone. My mother's dead, my father's old and tired."

We talked in the reserved tone of strangers.

Carrie nodded and barked, "This is bullshit. I've got a bucket load of anger over you coming back from the dead. Treating me to dinner didn't erase the hurt." She snubbed out her cigarette.

"You disappear … and show up … after a long, long time. Why?" Carrie folded her arms under her breasts and sighed. "Spit it out."

"I was pregnant." The secret I thought I would take to my grave slipped out.

Carrie's jaw dropped. "No way. You were on the pill."

She blinked several times and trembled as though a bug had been dropped down her dress.

"Let me get this right. You ran away and let us believe you were dead because you were pregnant and had suspicions about your father?" She swallowed hard. "Did you consider abortion?"

She kept shaking her head in disbelief. Her eyes deepened to the emerald green of her youth and her lips produced her signature smug giggle.

Flushed with embarrassment, I wanted to run out the door.

"You find this amusing … It's not funny." My voice quivered. "No. I never considered abortion. My mother believed it to be murder. Which would make me no better than my father." The words spilled out between tears.

"I'm sorry, Joy." Carrie embraced me. "That was insensitive of me. Please forgive me, are you sure she wouldn't have understood?"

"Positive. Mom … kept white gloves in her handbag, attended Mass every Sunday, wore an apron in the kitchen, and never owned a pair of slacks."

"She did after you were gone. My mom drove me to Planned Parenthood."

"You had an abortion?"

I remembered Mrs. Heller ate chocolate cake for breakfast and danced barefoot after dark.

"The summer you went missing, my life was a mess. A one-night stand with a biker, I would have trouble recognizing. It seemed foolish to burden the dude."

I cringed realizing how little I knew about the people left behind.

She paused and looked me in the eyes. "I think about the child every day," she sighed.

Carrie's honesty and knowledge of her heartache melted the years of silence. It made the moment poignant. The lasting connection we experienced in kindergarten ... unexplainable ... we were friends.

"Carrie, I believed Ray would've married me out of obligation, not love, and I didn't want that. Do you regret the abortion?" It was bold of me to ask, but I wanted to know.

"At the time ... it was the right decision for me." She fidgeted with a bracelet on her wrist. "Don't confuse Roe vs. Wade with a moral decision. The ruling is based on privacy laws. Big Brother can't tell us what to do with our bodies. You can't be prevented from an abortion unless abortion's murder." Carrie's voice came down hard on the word prevented.

"You're a feminist?"

"Not really. I still wear a bra." She laughed. "What did you do?"

"Adoption." I regretted telling her as the words tumbled out.

"You had the baby and never told Ray?"

"I didn't want Ray to feel trapped. The doctor said the pill wasn't foolproof. Anyway, Ray would have insisted on marriage, a marriage surrounded in doubt."

"Doubt?"

"Dad said I was Ray's fling ... I gave birth to a son."

The words lingered like closed caption dialogue on the television and I felt my sadness aloud for the first time.

We sat with the grief until Carrie said, "I'm confused. You criticize your father for keeping secrets but won't tell Ray he has a son you gave up for adoption? Aren't you being hypocritical?"

I lowered my voice and whispered, "Yes. Very hypocritical."

There was tension in the air, again. A hurt entered my chest, a deep long-ago sadness. I studied Carrie's face looking for answers, and wanted to tell her Dad confessed to having an affair and Tammy Martin was my half-sister. However, it's motive for Dad to have killed them both.

I had returned to put my suspicions to rest. Instead ... things were more of a mess. Carrie was right. I had to tell Ray about Jason, but first I had to confront my father face-to-face about what I overheard.

Chapter 11

Get Out!

ॐ

The sun was setting when I parked at Dad's late the next day. An orange glow penetrated the late day. Rain was in the air and dark clouds appeared from nowhere. A gust of wind swept across the lawn and stirred the trees, creating a trumpet sound reminiscent of my father's love for music.

In the mid-1970s, he worked weekends at the Flamingo playing piano and singing in the band. He never appeared happier or more intoxicated. Perhaps the intoxication was Diane.

On Saturdays, Mom kept a red lipstick in her housecoat pocket, often applying color to her fading beauty. We thought he had stopped loving us.

Hearing my father's confession, *"I fell in love with Diane Martin the first time I saw her,"* danced in my head and added another piece to the puzzle.

The affair provided a motive. Diane Martin may have threatened to tell Mom, and he wanted them out of the picture. Was my father guilty? I could not imagine him doing so, but thought of other discovered murderers who passed as normal. I wanted to hear the truth.

A heavy downpour forced me to rush inside without knocking.

"What do you know, back-from-the-dead-Joy is here. Hope you brought dinner," said Dad.

His red eyes watched a March Madness game. His tone revealed the emptiness alcohol had carved into his life. It was a sarcastic reception.

"As a matter of fact, I did. KFC." I headed to the kitchen.

"Great, bring me a beer." He held the remote, switching channels.

I fixed plates, grabbed two beers, and returned to the family room.

"Who are you cheering for?"

"Boston," he said. After a long stare at the tube, he sighed and added, "Listen, I'm not unhappy you're back. Be happier if you had amnesia or been abducted, not that I want those things for you. How can I be happy? I'm happy you're alive. It's just ... Shit, I can't believe you think I'm a murderer."

"I could apologize."

"You put us through hell ... Two weeks missing before we knew. The case was already cold when an overdue tuition notice from Stetson showed up in the mailbox. Every time I get the mail, I think of you. An apology would be nice if you're sincere."

A string of smoker coughs interrupted his words. He wiped his eyes.

Outside, secured in the ground by a bent pole, was the army green mailbox. It had a curious angle. The numbers on the side were faded. The memory of him opening his car door, and Diane and Tammy Martin getting in completed the picture.

"Your mother phoned the dorm. Your roommate, Cheryl, said you left two weeks ago. Ray came to get you because your father had a heart attack. Lies, you lied!"

He flung his head back and chugged the beer.

"Dad, did you have an affair with Diane Martin?"

He ignored my question. "But Ray hadn't picked you up."

"Dad did you have an affair with Diane Martin?"

His eyes fired with hate. A hate I remembered and I ducked to avoid the emotional shrapnel. Then took a seat across from him, determined to learn the truth.

"Always the nosey body, poking into other people's business." He yelled and turned red in the face. "What's it to you? It was forty years ago." He clenched his fists. "Leave it alone, will you?" His anger disappeared. He shrunk in the chair and sighed like a deflated balloon. "Okay — I did. You happy? Now you know."

I did not feel happy. There was no pleasure in hearing my suspicion had merit.

"This Martin thing was your excuse for running away ... there's got to be more to this picture. The hell you put us through."

"Dad! Why did you lie about knowing them and having an affair? The police were seeking information about them. It was on TV, in the newspaper. You never came forward. Why?" I studied his face and waited for an explanation.

He got up from his chair, his face distorted with anger, and pointed his finger at me.

"How come you get to ask all the questions and never have to answer any? Who do you think you are on your high horse, better than me, better than everyone? Where were you for thirty years? Did you ever think about anyone other than yourself? Living the rich life in New York. Guess Ray Atwood wasn't good enough for you."

We stood nose to nose.

He poked my shoulder. "Add this to your need-to-know list. The night Diane Martin came to the house, she told me Tammy

Martin was my daughter."

The smell of beer and tobacco dominated the air. He wore a drunken smirk of satisfaction, leaving no doubt about why I left and stayed away.

"Did you kill them?"

He sat down and moved the snack tray holding a plate with chicken in front of him, picked up a double breaded deep-fried leg, took a bite, licked his fingers, and with a full mouth said, "Get out!"

Chapter 12

Who's Guilty?

"Mary Elizabeth, can you imagine Joy thinking I killed someone? Remember the day she was born? You wanted to name her Frances Elizabeth. I insisted on Joy." Frank's smile faded. "I wish you were alive to see her. I've wished she were alive for years, and she is. But holy crap!"

Frank Webb drank a cup of coffee and talked to his wife wondering how important it was he remembered the smidges of last night. He recalled licking his fingers, but little else. When he heard a knock on the door and yelled. "The door is open. Come in, whoever the hell you are."

Bobby Smart wandered in carrying a crumb cake.

"Look what the cat dragged in. How've you been?" Frank got out of his chair and gave the man a sideways hug.

Bobby shifted the cake to one hand and embraced him. "I'm good."

"You should've phoned. I'd have cleaned up. You brought my favorite though. It'll earn you a few points. I'll make a fresh pot."

The two men sat at the kitchen table and talked.

"To be honest Frank, you don't look so good. How are you feeling?"

"Lousy. I was just talking to Mary Elizabeth about what's going on."

Bobby squelched a laugh, scratched his head, and looked around. "Frank, she didn't go shopping. She's dead. You're not suffering from dementia or the other one?"

"Alzheimer's. No, I have my wits about me. It's stress ... You heard Joy's alive."

"Yeah. One of the reasons I stopped by. Thought we'd celebrate."

"Cut the crap, Bobby. Everyone and their mother knows there was an incident here at the house. You dropped by to interview me, rather than bring me in for questioning."

"I'm here to talk. We go back a few years, Frank."

"Then put yourself in my shoes. Who has the necklace?"

"I do." Bobby took the peace sign jewelry from a pocket and handed it to Frank. "Tell me what happened."

"How Joy happened to find the necklace? Or how I happened to kill them?" Frank twisted the chain in the air to reflect the noon light. "Damn. This was why I didn't come forward at the time. It would've made me a person of interest, and as interesting a person as I am, I couldn't help then and can't help now. My involvement with Diane Martin was and always will be a dead-end waste of a cop's time, and would've destroyed my marriage. Get out your notepad, or record what I say on your goddamn cell phone because I've got nothing to hide."

Bobby pressed the record button on his phone, rested the phone on the kitchen table, and helped himself to a second piece of crumb cake. "What do you remember?"

"I don't remember the day of the week. Might have been a

Sunday late in May or early June. Ask Joy. Evidently, the night has been seared in her brain. It was late, around ten o'clock. I was watching TV. The wife was in bed. Joy was upstairs and supposed to be sleeping. The doorbell rang. It was a former student and her daughter. She was Diane Taylor when we had the affair. I took a second look at her young child and knew we had to talk. So, I got my car keys and closed the door behind me."

Bobby made a mental note; Frank might be Tammy Martin's father. He wiped coffee off his lips, and asked, "Did you see them after that night?"

"We planned to meet later in the week."

Bobby studied Frank's face, pressed a wet finger against the few remaining crumbs fallen on a plate, and licked it clean.

"Diane was wearing the necklace I'd given her way back when that night. I thought it would be nice for the kid to have one like her mother's. A keepsake. The next day I went down to the shop on Main Street and bought one for my new daughter."

Frank played with the necklace in his hand. Looked up and locked eyes with Bobby, deliberately. "I never saw them again."

"They were last seen in the morning walking to the bus. You have an alibi?"

"Come on Bobby, you're asking me for an alibi? For the record, I was at school and never left the building, not even for lunch. I'm not sure when they were reported missing. The story appeared in the newspaper a few days later."

"Right, asking the public to come forward with any information. You didn't."

"What would you have done? Destroy your home life with a news flash of infidelity making you a serious suspect. Coming forward would have opened Pandora's Box, and for what? I'm innocent. And if not, it's between me and God Almighty!"

"And the evidence? You said Diane was wearing the necklace the night she came to the house."

"The necklace I gave her, not the one I bought the day after."

"Can you prove it, Frank?"

"Do I have to?"

Silence filled the room with doubt.

"Guess my word isn't good enough. Look, I bought the necklace for Tammy. I'm guessing it fell out of my pants pocket while I was sleeping in the chair. Ask Joy about where and how she found it. She's hiding something. I see it in her eyes. Maybe she's the killer in the Webb family."

"Frank, that's crazy."

"You know what's crazy, listening to these accusations. I'm trying to be nice while dodging grenades."

"It would help if someone could verify you were at school that day." Bobby stood and rinsed his coffee cup in the sink.

Frank thought back to that time in his life. The brief affair with a student had been a mistake but when he learned he had another child he was happy. How anyone could imagine he'd harm or kill another human was unfathomable. Now thirty years after the facts he had to prove his innocence.

"You can ask Teresa McGee. I had perfect attendance my last ten years."

"Really."

"Yeah. I thought they would pay out my sick time in retirement."

Bobby grabbed his notepad. "You got an address?"

* * * * *

Bobby Smart parked on state road A1A in Daytona Beach and searched for the historic marker for Seabreeze High School. He found the plaque in front of the new convention center and imagined many students and teachers would have had a difficult time attending class in a building sandwiched between the ocean and river.

Sea gulls circled above and he smelled the sea. At 11 a.m. the March sun was hot but the humidity was low. He was dressed in a golf shirt and golf shorts, figuring to play nine after talking with Teresa McGee. He walked west toward the river, carrying his favorite crumb cake. The neighborhood was holding its own. The house a few doors before Teresa's looked abandoned, but showed no sign of drugs or squatters.

Pots filled with colorful flowers hugged the side of the house and the roof was new. The inside door behind an old-fashioned wooden screen door was opened. He rang the bell and a woman yelled. "I'm coming. Give me a minute."

Teresa dried her hands as she walked to the door.

"Ms. McGee, Can I ask you a few questions about Frank Webb?" Bobby held up his badge.

"Frank Webb. What's this about?" She hesitated, tossing the towel across one shoulder. "And you are?"

"Bobby Smart, Daytona Beach Cold Case Unit." He shifted the cake in his hand and showed his badge.

"Please come in, Mr. Smart. That hot sun might dry the cake up," she said and smiled. "I imagine you'd like coffee with that. Call me Teresa, please."

"If you call me Bobby." Bobby set the cake on the kitchen table.

Teresa talked as she made coffee and by the time the coffee perked, he had a history. She had been the school secretary and had considered herself a welcome ambassador for the school with a sand crab as its mascot. Teresa and Frank Webb started at Seabreeze the same year and retired a few years apart. He still phones her from time to time.

"Oh my God. This is delicious. Where did you buy it?" she said, with crumbs in her mouth.

"A bakery in Palm Coast."

"Too bad, that would be a trek for me. So, ask me what you came to ask."

Bobby liked her direct approach and fired back. "We need to verify Frank's work attendance in connection with a cold case. I thought you might've kept some records."

"Diane Martin?"

"Yes. How did you know?"

"The reporter, Doug Dillon. You just missed him."

"He inquired about Diane Martin? What did you tell him?"

"Not much. Diane and Doug were both Frank's students. They graduated in 1974. She went missing long after. Can't recall the exact year."

"Ten years later, summer of 1984," Bobby said and pulled out his notepad. "What was she like in school?"

"Attractive, popular, prom queen and in the marching band. She had an adolescent crush on Frank."

"And did he reciprocate?"

"Be serious, of course not. Frank teased all the girls. He made everyone feel special. Named teacher of the year several times."

Bobby pressed the crumbs lingering on his plate together then licked his finger clean.

"Frank bragged he had perfect attendance. Can you confirm or deny it?"

"He never took a sick day."

"Did he ever leave the building after clocking in?"

Teresa stood and cleared the table. With her back to Bobby, she said, "That, I can't confirm or deny." She turned around to face him. "If he did, I didn't know about it."

Before Bobby could ask more questions, she put her hands on her hips and said, "It's time for you to leave, Mr. Smart. You want me to talk badly about a man I've respected for a long time. It's not going to happen."

Bobby walked himself out.

Through the screen door, Teresa said, "You may want to talk to Doug Dillon. He had a big crush on Diane Martin."

Bobby came back up the steps.

"He acted like a sick puppy following her around the school. At the time it wasn't called stalking, but today it would be. He was disciplined for chasing her into the locker room. An odd guy. A real loner. I felt sorry for him."

* * * * *

Joe Bucci and Danny Egan got out of the car and slammed the doors simultaneously. The two-bedroom house on Annabelle Avenue in Holly Hill had been where Diane Martin lived in 1984.

"You're wearing the same shirt," Danny said.

"What difference does it make? Only you know that. This will be the first time any other dudes see it. Does it smell?"

"No."

"So, what's your problem?" Joe shook his head and yanked his pants up.

They had canvassed the area six years ago when Bobby Smart first formed the Cold Case Unit, and several times since. Neighbors always had different versions of the same thing, no one saw or heard anything the day Diane and her daughter Tammy went missing.

Today a dog barked. The sound got louder as they followed it around the back of the house and through an empty lot to where a German shepherd was in a dog run, yelping and leaping.

"You think anyone's home?" Joe asked Danny.

Before he could respond a screen door slammed.

"Can I help you with something?" said a man who wore a gun in a holster.

"Yes." They both yelled holding up their badges.

Come to find out the guy was a retired fireman. Joe and Danny were invited for sweet tea on the front porch. When Mary Smith, his wife, joined the men on the veranda, she brought the tea and homemade lemon drop cookies. Passing around napkins she said, "People were still talking about the Martins' missing when we returned in October." She turned to her husband and said, "Remember, Alan."

The couple were snowbirds and stayed at their Maine camp from May through October, sometimes November if the weather was mild.

"Were either of you here when it happened?" Joe wanted to confirm what Alan had already told them.

"We were at Yellowstone Park with the grandkids," said Mary.

"Right," said Alan. "As soon as I heard about the ten-year-old missing, I thought of Jeffrey the pervert."

"You mind if I take a few notes?" Danny said and found a

notepad and pencil in a pocket.

"Does this Jeffrey have a last name?"

"He didn't need a last name. Everyone knew Jeffrey."

"Tell me about no-last-name Jeffrey."

Alan explained the guy was a cousin of the neighbor who lived next door to the Martins.

"He wasn't homeless. To be kind, more a free spirit. He would show up at Lydia's uninvited, work a few days or a few weeks then leave. People in the neighborhood locked their door when he was around."

"Why was that?" Joe asked and popped another lemon drop in his mouth.

"I'd put a money envelope out for the newsboy and it'd be empty. Spare change in car consoles would disappear. Jeffrey had a creepy way of studying girls from behind."

Mary shuddered. "He gave me the willies."

Joe stood. He was ready to leave. "And this Lydia, she still in the neighborhood?"

Chapter 13

Racing's North Turn Restaurant

ဆ

Carrie was right. I needed to tell Ray. He answered on the first ring and suggested dinner when I asked if we could meet.

"You look nice, Joy," Ray said when I got in his truck. He smiled checking out my legs.

"Thanks. A dress is cooler. I haven't adjusted to Florida's humidity."

"Give it time ... Kind of like my adjustment to your return, Joy."

"Adjustment? That's a nice way to put it. It feels more like a death trap amusement park ride."

"We thought you were dead! And the accusations you've laid on your father. He's not a young man... Well."

"Where are we dining?" I asked to change the subject.

"Dining?" He rolled his eyes before continuing. "My favorite, Racing's North Turn, you know, in Ponce Inlet."

"Heard of it, but I've never been. Had to be legal or have proof. Besides I was ..."

He completed my sentence, "Studying. It's on the beach and one of my favorites. You'll love it."

My mind drifted off, lost in the past, confused about the present, and surprised about my feelings for Ray. I wanted to tell him about our son, that I had confronted Dad about the Martins and been thrown out again.

Our conversation was easy, but I thought it best to wait until after dinner. When we parked at the restaurant, I smelled the sea air. Ray greeted the hostess by name and embraced her. We followed her through the bar area into the blinding sun and a deck sprinkled with white tables holding large red umbrellas. Ray pulled out a chair for me as Michelle dropped plastic menus on the table.

"A margarita, lots of salt on the rim,for you, Ray? And for the lady?"

"The same." I adjusted my large framed sunglasses for a better look at her.

Ray nodded yes, then flashed a big smile. "Michelle, this is Joy. Joy, this is Michelle."

"Joy. Your Joy, Ray?" she said, her eyes widening.

"Yup. My Joy ..."

"You're not dead," she laughed. "Nice to meet you! I'll get your drinks."

Ray called after her, "And some Bang-bang Shrimp." My eyes followed her.

It was low tide. The sand extended far into the ocean. Its smooth flat surface glistened with red and orange hues, and the sound of flapping sea gulls was heard as their formation dominated the sky. Ocean waves rolled across the beach and created background music for conversation.

Ray put on sunglasses and exclaimed. "What a view, I never tire of it."

"The waitress or the ocean?" With my arm on the table, I

supported my chin with my fist. My mood had changed. I felt jealous. Ray obviously had some sort of relationship with the waitress.

"The ocean. You must agree this beats city heat, dirty pavement, and tall buildings. What was city life like?"

Apparently, Ray's mood had changed along with mine. He brushed his wavy black hair off his forehead disinterested in my answer.

"When you went missing, I fell apart. Sure, on the outside I was a young police officer who held up nicely while looking for his girlfriend. The media called you, my girlfriend. I loved you. We were serious, weren't we?"

Michelle brought our drinks before I could respond, although it was obvious, he didn't expect me to. He glanced toward the perfect sky and continued, misty-eyed.

"Your dad and I filed a missing person report in DeLand, while your mom sat in the car. You'd been gone two weeks. The only lead was a phone call from a gas station to your dorm room."

"Thanks," he said when Michelle brought the appetizer. He winked at her, then turned his attention to me. "Bang-bang Shrimp is spicy with the right amount of heat."

I picked up a fork, but had no appetite,

"You know what has me hung up?" Ray paused, shook his head, and looked me in the eyes. "Is why you never said good-bye?"

"You want the truth? The truth can be damning."

"Or it will set you free." Ray stared at the water. "The Daytona 500 was held here until 1958." He pointed behind him. "Drivers taxied out onto A1A from the restaurant driveway, drove two miles south then drove back on the beach. You know we're sitting at the finish line."

My heart raced. I closed my eyes and prayed for courage to tell him, and the right words to convey the emotions of a scared nineteen-year-old.

"You're right I should have said goodbye. It was complicated. Still is."

"A simple question deserves a truthful answer. I know you, Joy. It's obvious you're hiding something. It could be you know more about the Martin disappearance than you're saying."

"Why would you even think that? Of course not."

"Why didn't you come to me then with the necklace?"

Michelle approached the table, "Are you ready to order?"

Ray forced a smile at Michelle. "The ribeye, my usual sides."

Ordering and eating were not on my mind. Michelle must have picked up on my lack of appetite.

"If you're not real hungry, the clam chowder and mandarin orange salad make a nice choice," she said.

I nodded yes. She did not write anything down and walked away.

"Michelle and I met at the Speedway."

"Michelle, our waitress?"

"She's, my ex-wife. She worked for the France family as an event planner."

"She's attractive." I was jealous, although I had no right to be. I wanted Ray to be in love with me more than ever.

"After five years, your mother still waited for a Red Cardinal to visit. So, we agreed to a vigil, a candlelight service at St. Paul's. It was time to end the search." Ray studied the sky, then continued. "I started dating. Found Michelle two years later ... But she wasn't the one, you were always the one."

The tenderness in his voice proved the love I questioned years ago, worried I was the fling Dad warned me about, and I felt foolish, and realized, I had nothing to lose by telling him and everything to lose if I didn't. However, the words refused to come out of my mouth. I loved him and did not want to lose him, or worse hurt him more.

"Ray, please I can explain."

"Yes, explain. There must be more to this story."

Live music started. The lead singer grabbed a microphone to welcome the crowd. The timing was horrible. I would have had to shout I was pregnant to be heard. I secretly cursed the band and said, "Let's enjoy the music and our meal. I'll tell you after dinner." And we did. We talked, laughed, and joked. Ray shared a few stories about the founding fathers of NASCAR.

As the music stopped, Michelle arrived to clear the table and asked. "You want coffee?"

"No, the usual." Ray smiled.

"Irish coffee for me," I said.

"And the rest of the story ..." Ray said after Michelle walked away.

Like a criminal all alone in an interrogation room, I blurted. "I was pregnant."

Michelle brought a large brandy and Irish coffee to the table. He responded slowly and deliberately, gulped the brandy, threw a credit card on the table, and headed for the beach.

I studied his back. One shoulder drooped as he shook his head from side to side.

Michelle joined me at the table and said, "He'll be back."

* * * * *

Ray didn't come back. After the band packed up, Michelle drove me to the Maverick and suggested Ray probably walked to her beach house to watch TV. Her house had been their house before the divorce.

"We went to a fertility specialist, nothing happened," she said at a traffic light. "We both wanted a family and the strain of trying to conceive destroyed things." Her long blonde hair bounced to a country western song playing on the radio. "We're still friends. I can talk to him about anything."

When she dropped me off the song, *I Can't Make You Love Me If You Don't*, was playing. She turned to me, gave me a hug, and said, "I couldn't make Ray love me. He's always been in love with you, Joy." The song played as she waved goodbye.

She was a nice person. More Ray's type than I had ever been. Ray and I were both introverts. Michelle was extroverted. I wished I had asked for her advice; how to tell Ray the rest of the story. Tell him all the things he didn't know yet.

My insides felt like they were stuck in a cassette player, rewinding an old Johnny Cash tune about regret. I believed the Dolans would provide a better life for my child, and went to work as a nanny on the Upper East Side, knowing they lived there. I saw him in the park and felt part of Jason's life, vicariously. I told myself it was the right thing for all of us. What did I regret more? Not telling him then or telling him now. It was a hard choice.

I powered up my laptop and logged into Facebook. A wedding picture of Jason and Alison was displayed on the home page. He had Ray's black hair, eyes, and smile. I had attended their wedding at St. Patrick's Cathedral and watched Jason walk Sara Dolan, his adopted mother, to her seat; and then take his place alongside his best man, Matthew Dolan, at the altar. I recalled applauding with everyone else ... green with envy.

I clicked open the message box and wrote:

Dearest Jason,

*In 1985, I gave a son up for adoption. I believe you
are my son.*

This was silly. The Dolans had the original birth certificate
and had agreed to tell him if he asked. I erased the words and
started over.

*This will come as a shock and I apologize but I don't
know how else to let you know I am your biological
mother.*

My hand shook as it hovered above send. Then I came to my
senses and hit delete.

Chapter 14

Main Street
March 2014

ॐ

In the morning, a housekeeper knocked on my door and inquired if I wanted the sheets changed. It was after eleven. I had slept in my sundress.

I brushed my teeth and went downstairs, and told Carrie everything. She tried to console me to no avail. I was devastated and thought my fears had become reality. Ray had walked away as I imagined he would have thirty years ago. I'd been in Daytona less than a month and thought about going home.

Home? Where was home? What was I doing here? Chaos surrounded me and those I loved. It was selfish to come back. I recalled my father's words, *let sleeping dogs lie.* But I hadn't.

"When was the last time you had fun?" Carrie asked as she wiped the table. "Don't look at me! It's not a trick question."

I smoothed out the wrinkles in my dress and wondered if I had combed my hair.

"We're going to Main Street when I'm done here," said Carrie. She checked her watch.

"You're taking the Harley?"

"Of course not! We're going people-watching."

* * * * *

The Budweiser Clydesdales pounded down A1A and turned right on Main Street. The sound of hooves delivered a cadence I remembered and had missed. Thoughts of Ray were dismissed. A stream of bikers dressed in leather attire swarmed the sidewalk, their Harleys parked diagonally in the street. The women wore chaps that exposed their bare butts, and hats saying, "We're Hot!" Heavy metal bands accompanied by wet t-shirt contests, as strangers cheered and called, "Take it off, babe."

I relaxed despite the conflict I had created by staying away for years, never contacting Ray or Carrie about my fears. Unchallenged, the suspicion surrounding my father had formed its own reality.

Carrie interrupted my thoughts.

"Remember the night we brought Larry and Gary home?" She paused. "They were drunk and couldn't find their bikes. You let them sleep in the shed."

"Thank God, they'd be dead. When Dad found them hung over, he made them mow the lawn and called their mother in Ohio. Are you sure it was Bike Week?" I smiled.

"It might have been Spring Break." She lit a cigarette.

"You know smoking causes cancer."

A woman wearing a tutu crossed the street in stilettos. We both laughed and stopped to chat with a biker who held a Chihuahua named "Dazzle" and sat on a bike decorated with fifteen thousand Swarovski crystals next to a Harley on which the Last Supper was painted.

Fifty thousand folks would descend on Daytona Beach for Bike Week. Locals holed up, got a little cranky, and complained about the noise, but I loved Bike Week.

Carrie and I stopped to eat and were finishing up a beer when Ray called.

"He wants to talk," I said.

"After last night, now he wants to talk?"

"He wants me to come down to headquarters. He doesn't sound happy."

"You want me to go with you?"

"No. I'll be okay."

I drove to the Daytona Beach Police Department filled with dread, parked, and took note of the security cameras. Baumgardner greeted me at the front desk. "Ms. Webb?" I nodded yes.

"Have a seat. I'll tell Ray and Bobby you're here."

A creepy-looking guy sat on the only available bench, so I stood and wondered who Bobby was. A few minutes later Ray opened the door.

"Thanks for coming in Joy," Ray said. He looked at me as though we were strangers.

The man on the bench said, "Joy, Joy Webb?"

"Not now Doug." Ray turned away from the guy and ushered me through the door.

"Who's that?" I asked.

"Doug Dillon. He's looking for a story. Ignore him." He walked quickly through a corridor and I hurried to catch up as he entered an interrogation room.

Ray pulled out a chair. "Have a seat. We need to gather some information to close your file." His manner was curt, almost rude. There was no mention of our dinner last night and I could only guess what was going through his mind.

"Start with the night you went missing. Bobby will take notes." From a corner of the room, Bobby appeared.

I felt like the nineteen-year-old I was then, scared, alone, and fearful of letting people down. I bit my lip, exhaled, and said, "I worried Dad would go on trial for kidnapping, murder, or something, and I was pregnant. I wanted to disappear." The words tasted sour in my mouth.

"I'm Bobby Smart. I've been working on your case for the past ten years, welcome home. Yes, tell me what happened that night." He smiled and joined us at the table.

When he sat, I closed my eyes and forced my shoulders to relax.

"There was an advertisement in the newspaper." The words dangled through my mind as I spoke. "A New York City couple seeks to adopt a newborn child. Call collect." Their long distance exchange, two-one-two, flashed in my memory. "I did and explained my situation. One month later, they drove to Florida and picked me up outside my dorm in DeLand."

"The phone call you received the night of January 9th from a gas station in St. Augustine, was it from this couple?"

"I don't know – probably – they said they stopped for lunch at Flagler College cafeteria. Mrs. Dolan wanted to see the Tiffany stained glass windows."

"Your roommate said you got a call saying your dad suffered a heart attack. She thought I picked you up. Instead, you got in a car with a couple of strangers," said Ray. "What were you thinking?"

His face turned red.

"I was thinking they were nice."

I stared at the ceiling for a moment. My voice was younger reliving the events. Emotionally transferred back in time.

"I fantasized you would look for me." It was the truth but the wrong thing to say.

"Joy, how the hell was that going to happen if I didn't know you were gone?" His voice got louder with every word.

Bobby put his hand on Ray's shoulder. "Calm down, partner. Let her talk."

"Well, Ray. I phoned you every day. When I didn't, did you miss me? Did you phone me? No! Didn't ... miss me ... enough to phone me."

I had waited a long time to ask why he never missed me.

"Neither did my parents, nor Carrie. Nobody thought to phone me for weeks. Nobody noticed I was gone until the tuition wasn't paid."

Now I was yelling.

"The bursar missed me."

Bobby said, "Why don't you get Ms. Webb some water?"

Ray left the room.

"Let me get this straight. You went knowingly with them," he said.

I shook my head yes.

"This couple's name and address."

Bobby took a pen from behind his ear.

"Sara and Matthew Dolan, they still live in Manhattan. I don't know the exact address."

Reliving the events was harder than I expected, but continued.

"We drove to Hilton Head. Mrs. Dolan said it was a chance to get to know each other before we went too far. After a few days, we left for New York City. I got to see Washington, D.C. lit up at night."

Ray re-entered the room and joined in the conversation.

"Sounds like a vacation."

He slammed a bottle of water on the table.

"Not exactly, but I got a glimpse of the life my child would have."

"Our child," Ray whispered.

I heard the sadness in his voice and made an effort to explain.

"The apartment was on the Upper East Side, the seventies, with a servant's suite. You know a Murphy bed and kitchen all in one, its own bathroom, and walk-in closet. The doorman lets you in."

I examined his face for recognition of my pain. The confusion I felt then and now. None was there.

Ray shook his head in disbelief.

"No I don't know, Joy! You know that life, a more affluent life."

He pounded the table with his fist.

"It was never about me or money. It was a better life for Jason and you."

"Jason? My child's name is Jason?! I have a son named Jason?"

Ray leaped up and gripped both my shoulders. His nails pinched my skin. I grimaced. Bobby pushed Ray to the floor.

I was stunned by Ray's reaction, clutched my handbag, and ran from the room. The first door I saw was an emergency exit. When I pushed the bar, it triggered a screeching sound and I paused. The alarm pulverized my ears, as I fled to my car and drove away.

Chapter 15

Tell the Truth!

The emergency exit alarm sounded. Baumgardner checked the security monitor and viewed the exits. Joy Webb was exiting the rear emergency door.

Baumgardner buzzed the conference room. When Bobby answered he said, "Joy Webb exited the building and is coming around the front. You want me to grab her?"

"No. It's best to let her go. She's late for a hair appointment."

He had just been helped to his feet by Joe and Danny who entered the room as Joy had left.

Danny said, "A hair appointment, what the hell is going on?"

"You don't need to know," said Ray.

Ray's reaction was out of character. Bobby had never seen Ray lose his cool. A silence as wide as the Grand Canyon settled in the room until Bobby spoke.

"Joy had to leave in a hurry. She was late for a hair appointment."

"Late enough to set off an alarm?" Joe asked sarcastically. "Like the rabbit in Alice in Wonderland (he studied his watch), 'I'm late. I'm late for an important date.' That explains something, but why were both of you on the floor?" Joe shook his head from side to side in disbelief.

"Bobby was tipping his chair when she bolted and the alarm went off. He slipped and we all went down."

Ray got off the floor and brushed some dust off his clothes.

"She probably didn't realize it was an emergency door. The sign says exit."

Awkwardness surrounded the four men as they straightened the desk and righted the chairs.

Bobby's next question. "What happened when the two of you recanvassed? Find anything new?"

It was an effort to pretend things were normal.

"Well evidently there was a relative of a neighbor who visited erratically, and created quite a stir when he did," said Danny.

They supplied each other with their findings.

Bobby shared that Frank Webb bragged he had perfect attendance and therefore an alibi for the time the Martins went missing. He had visited the school secretary to verify the information.

Bobby said, "Teresa McGee pointed a finger at Doug Dillon. She felt sorry for him and said he'd had a thing for Diane Martin."

"Has Doug Dillon ever been questioned?" Ray asked.

"Well no. But it's easy enough to do. He's probably sitting outside right now," said Joe.

Ray buzzed Baumgardner and asked, "Is Doug Dillon out front?"

Baumgardner checked the waiting area. Doug was not there. He scratched his head and then scrolled through the security camera footage. "He ran after Joy Webb."

* * * * *

I drove to Morningside shaken and stunned by Ray's behavior. Then sat and cried, and searched through my handbag for a crumpled tissue I knew was in there, somewhere. When I stepped out of the car, I stood face-to-face with Doug Dillon.

There was nothing attractive about this man. Years of Florida sun were carved into his face. He had a long nose, narrow eyes, and drooping ear lobes. His arms were disproportionately longer than his torso, and his hands were chunky. He dropped a pen and bent down. His pudgy fingers retrieved it. On the way up he said, "Joy Webb, I'm Doug Dillon, reporter for the News-Journal, do you have a minute to answer a few questions?"

"No!" I locked the car and hurried into the house listening to him shout. "Where have you been for thirty years? People want to know."

My father met me at the door. "Deep Digging Doug found you. He's like a dog with a bone. He will not leave you alone until he gets answers."

"I'm going back to New York." I was frazzled by Doug Dillon's pursuit of me and the upheaval surrounding Ray, there had to be a better way.

"Surprise, surprise, when the going gets tough, Joy gets going ... out of town."

"Don't you think you're being unfair?" I wanted to tell him what happened with Ray, but couldn't.

"Unfair? Not one bit, you appear after years of missing, explain next to nothing, except that you were a scared little girl who thought her dad was a killer, and when a reporter asks questions, you're ready to jump ship and return to a mysterious life in the Big Apple. A life you don't want to talk about."

"It's not that I don't want to talk about things, I just don't know how to tell you the truth."

"Damn it, Joy! Just spit it out! You're forty-eight years old. Tell me the truth!"

I took a deep breath and said, "I was pregnant."

The color drained from his face. He limped to his chair and whispered, "Holy crap, are you trying to give me a heart attack?" He sat holding his head in his hands. "Thank God your mother is dead. Why didn't you come to us? We would have done anything for you," he said.

It felt like I was sinking in quicksand and thought back to that time.

"Except give up alcohol, you were having a great time jamming and drinking at the bar and Mom's depression was chronic. I was on my own. Besides, you never loved me."

"Never loved you?" He shook his head and rolled his eyes. "Your mother is to blame for this. She spoiled you rotten. Thirteen years old, and you told her not to talk to your friends. You hated her teased hair and asked her to wear flip-flops like Carrie's mom."

He threw a Stephen King paperback he'd been reading at me.

"She never let me set you straight. Why, when I was thirteen my brother died, and Dad left, never to be seen again. I became the man of the family."

I had heard the story many times. His words bounced off the walls and landed on deaf ears. His mother got a job with the NYC Subway System. He looked after his sister until she got home. On weekends, starting at 3 a.m., he sold newspapers. I ducked in time as his words droned in the background but felt like the spoiled brat he spoke about.

"Your mother and I were living our dream when we bought this house," he said.

I regained my hearing of his tirade.

"NEVER LOVED YOU? I volunteered for years … YEARS teaching you and your friends how to play softball! And NOW you say you didn't feel LOVED? It would have been a dream come true if my father had been alive to teach me the game and watch me play."

"That's the problem. It was your dream, not mine. I felt like a trophy," I said through gritted teeth, no longer able to hold back the resentment and anger brewing for years.

"When were you dropped on your head and stopped thinking straight, Joy? Do you need to twist your childhood to justify your behavior? You probably had an abortion. How could you have had an abortion? I hope your mother, God rest her soul, can't hear you. You know she believed abortion is murder, you murdered my grandchild? Abortion, how could you?"

"I didn't. I couldn't. I gave the baby up for adoption."

"Now you tell me I have a grandchild that I'll never see," he said incredulously.

"His name is Jason"

"You know, your mother wanted you named after me, Frank Jr. for a boy. Fran for a girl. However, the moment we saw you, we felt joy. But now, you're no longer a joy." He gritted his teeth.

Somehow, he reminded me of the Witch in the Wizard of Oz and a voice in my head said, "I'll get you my little pretty."

"Go back to your fancy life in New York City," he said and pushed me out the door.

Outside Doug Dillon leaned against my car trunk and grinned. "How was the visit with the old man?" He wiped beads of sweat from his receding hairline with his shirt sleeve.

Cobweb clouds filtered a hot orange sun and weaved light streaks across the Florida sky. It was a far contrast from the gray New York skyline I would return to, and feel the last raw winds of March.

"Great – he compared you to a dog with a bone. Said you wouldn't leave me alone until you had answers. So, what do you want to know?" He looked like a dog chewing a bone.

I unlocked the car doors and slipped in. Doug Dillon opened the passenger door and jumped into my vehicle. We sat side by side.

His squinting eyes framed a sarcastic smile. "The public wants to know how and why you disappeared."

"Good questions. But I can ask questions too. Are you going to get out of my car or do I dial 9-1-1 and have you arrested?"

Doug Dillon countered the threat. "Arrested, that's creative." He continued to ask his questions. "Did you know your dad was the music teacher at Seabreeze High School my senior year? Why was your father brought in for an interview? Is he a person of interest?"

"Why not ask him?"

In an adversarial mood, I got out of the car, and pushed lock on the key fob, knowing Deep-Digging Doug would be trapped inside. I smiled and decided not to dial 9-1-1, but pondered leaving the locked car and walking back to the Maverick.

"Hey! What the hell, I can't get out! Are you crazy or something?"

"Crazy," I said and unlocked the car.

Doug Dillon jumped out of the vehicle and gave me the finger when I drove away.

* * * * *

Breathe, I repeated the words as I checked over my shoulder on the entrance ramp to I-95. Doug Dillon's sun-bleached vehicle was not in sight ... But, could I be certain the creep had not followed me? NO!

Frazzled, I exited in Savannah. The first hotel I saw was a historic tavern on the square, where I met Charles.

After checking in and sending Carrie a text, I powered up my computer, and sent Jason a friend request. He had been on my mind the entire ride.

Within minutes a musical sound signaled Jason was online and had accepted my friend request. Dizzy with shock, I considered not responding ... but with my heart pounding ... started a chat.

"Thank you for accepting my friend request. I know your parents."

"You're Bryce's stepmother, Bryce introduced me to my wife, Alison."

"Yes, Bryce and Scarlet. I haven't seen them since their father, Ben, died."

"I'm sorry for your loss, Mrs. Gardner. They'll be at our Gender Reveal Party this summer. Why don't you come? I'm sure they would like to see you, and I haven't seen you since high school. Send me your address and I'll mail you an invite."

I typed in my address and got a thumbs-up emoji back. Ray and I were going to be grandparents. Jason's enthusiasm was sweet, but a sad reminder of how fear kept my pregnancy a secret.

My head spun with happiness, and I savored the joy. Then I threw myself across the four-poster antique bed and fell into a deep sleep. The highs and lows of the past months were taking a toll on me.

An hour later, I woke and dressed in a black sheath and pearl earrings. I had dropped ten pounds since Ben died, last November, and suddenly ravenous, ready for a big steak.

The fight with Dad, telling him I didn't feel love, I felt loved like an object. A trophy awarded to make a person feel good about themselves, Doug Dillon hounding me, countered with the bittersweet news Ray and I would be grandparents. Never fitting in, although I did everything to appear like I did.

Downstairs, in the dining room, the maître d' asked with a wilted British accent, "Do you have a reservation?"

"No."

"Will someone be joining you?"

His question triggered the sadness in me. The day-to-day reality of my life was that I would be eating alone.

"Regrettably, Madame, there are no tables for one, at this time."

His face acknowledged my disappointment and he perused the seated crowd, paused, and said, "However, a regular is dining alone, and welcomes company. Would you care to join him?"

He nodded in the direction of a silver-haired man sitting at a table for two. He appeared harmless.

"You sure about this guy?"

"Yes, Madame. He stays here often."

I was hungry and had nothing to lose, so I said, "Okay, lead the way."

"And your name, Madame?

I stood taller and practiced a smile, "Introduce me as Mrs. Joy Gardner." I did not want to be Joy Webb any longer.

At the table, the maître d' said, "Mr. Dunmore, may I introduce Mrs. Joy Gardner? She's a guest at the hotel and ..." Before he could explain further the man stood.

"Splendid, Jacob, of course, I'd be happy to have her join me." He took my hand in both of his and with a slight bow of his head. "Pleased to meet you, Joy. Call me Charles."

His hands were soft and warm, nails polished like those of a diplomat. We were about the same height.

The maître d' pulled out the chair and unfolded a cloth napkin with a flick of his wrist. The napkin found its way to my lap.

"And Jacob, please bring the lady a drink," Charles said as he took his seat. "What would you like?"

"I'll have what you're drinking."

"A mint julep."

I felt happy to have company and not dine alone. Like an actress playing a part in an impromptu skit. I said coyly, "Charles, thank you for letting me join you. I haven't eaten all day. How is the filet minion?"

"Excellent, served with cheese grits, caramelized onions, and stuffed mushroom with a side of collard greens, my choice for tonight." He smiled and his Paul Newman eyes came to life. "Thank you for joining me! I dislike dining alone, as well, especially in Savannah. I am here on business. Antiques, and yourself?"

"I'm on my way back to New York. I've been visiting my dad in Daytona Beach." Suddenly tired of hiding from life, I blurted out, "We hadn't seen each other for thirty years. He didn't know I was coming."

With a Mister Rogers quality to his voice, Charles said, "A surprise visit?"

In the silence, I imagined him singing *It's a Beautiful Day in the Neighborhood.*

The waiter brought my drink and then asked if we needed

menus. We ordered and Charles selected a red wine.

The situation became awkward after the waiter left. Perhaps it was the stress of the past month. I inquired of Charles who was clearly my senior.

"How was your day?"

"My day? Lonely ... and you? Thirty years is a long time. What caused the riff?"

"The riff? Families are complicated."

"I never had the luxury of knowing. I never married or had children. I feel the loss today, but as you said, families are complicated. Why come back now?" There was a twinkle in his eye.

"I'm tired of living a lie."

"Do you love your father?"

"I'm not sure." It was a bold question, but something that had been on my mind. "When I think about why I left, well?"

"Joy." He paused and hesitated. "Love isn't a thought. Love is a feeling, an emotion, and life is what happens as we manage our emotions."

Damn! His insight lit sparklers in my mind, and I decided that this just-met stranger was a sage.

"My father said I was dead to him."

"Those are harsh words for a daughter to hear. When did you stop loving him?"

I played with my napkin, rolling the corner back and forth toward the center as he gave me more to think about.

"I didn't. He stopped loving me, first," I mumbled.

I came out of the trance when our waiter held a pepper grinder over my salad. "Black pepper, Madame?"

"Yes." I looked across the table. "Do people ever call you Charlie?"

He laughed. "Never. I was born in Asheville, North Carolina. The South and people are Christian and have Christian names. Have you been to Asheville?"

"With my husband, Ben, Benjamin, we did the Christmas tour of the Biltmore."

Charles raised his eyes and readjusted his neck and shoulders. "Your husband?"

"He died last November, a sudden heart attack. My shoulders shook to conceal the tears, resulting in sobs that transitioned into nervous laughter. I was crying over Ben and everything else.

Charles reached across the table and touched my hand. "I'm sorry. We can skip dinner if you prefer. Death is a life-changing event."

I composed myself, blotted my eyes, and sighed. "No kidding, I was hoping to pretend life is normal. Will you help me pretend, Charles?"

Charles patted my hand in a gentleman's fashion and resumed our conversation.

"The Biltmore? I've been there many times, as a tour guide in my younger years. A docent. Now I'm a consultant and recommend antique pieces and floral decorations for holidays. I hope you went on the kitchen tour."

"We did. It was a history lesson, for sure. There was an Olympic-sized pool in the basement. Is Savannah as interesting?"

Charles wiped the corners of his mouth, then cleared his throat. "Well... I could give you a tour of Savannah. History and architecture are of interest to me, too."

"Deal. I'll pretend you're a docent."

* * * * *

In the morning, Charles waited for me in the dining room. He wore what my mother called Bermuda shorts (impeccably pressed), a plaid shirt under a cashmere sweater, and the closest thing to penny loafers on his feet.

Mom died four years ago, but losing Ben had opened the floodgates for all my life's losses. I decided not to go home when I learned of her death. The thought of seeing my father then created a sound like chalk, scratching a blackboard, in my head. Nothing had changed, his outbursts were the same.

"Good morning," said Charles.

"What's for breakfast?" I asked once we were seated on the veranda.

"I'll order Eggs Benedict, orange scones, and half a grape-fruit."

"You have no doubts?"

"None. It's my favorite when I travel."

"Then I'll have the same."

I admired his certainness. The feminist movement had done little for women. I debated what to eat, wear, and buy. The list was endless. And questioned the choice throughout the day. The aroma of the rich coffee permeating the room opened my senses. The year was 2014! I was 48 years of age. This is the lifestyle that fits me, even if it is a land of make-believe.

"I'll show you around Savannah. We can walk. Visit St. John's, Forsyth Park, and of course the Mercer House. I need to be back around 1 o'clock to meet a client."

"That works for me. I've already packed."

Charles looked into my eyes. "You could stay and have

dinner."

I knew the implications and struggled with my thoughts. Delaying could propel me in a new direction. I looked past the flowers on the veranda and listened to reason. It was much too early for a relationship. "Dinner would be lovely if I didn't have unfinished business in New York City."

"I travel frequently to the city … perhaps we can have lunch there."

"That would be nice. Although I may return to Daytona, my life is complicated. But yes, let me give you my number.

Charles quickly added my number to his address book using the microphone. Once again something was enticing about his voice. I had a good feeling about Charles and wondered if I would see him again.

He stood. "Why don't we talk, while we walk? It's much better for digestion." He nodded to the waiter; we were done.

The morning air was cool. I searched my handbag for a pair of sunglasses and we strolled toward the river. Ornate metal gates protected a house decorated by pink bougain-villea; the unique scrollwork revealed the home's personality. Live Oaks lined the streets. Moss hidden among their leaves created a veil of mystery.

In the distance, the spars of John the Baptist Cathedral pierce the sky. I chose my words with care. "Are you Catholic?"

"Raised Christian. Sunday church and ladies' hats were a part of my childhood. You?"

"Big-time Catholic upbringing. 'The one and only true reli-gion,' to quote my mom. She believed abortion was murder. Both she and Dad considered sex before marriage a NO NO!"

Charles studied the cathedral. "It's French Gothic." Then glanced at his watch. "We can go inside if you like."

I sat on a bench staring at the historic building. Charles joined me and continued. "The Cathedral was built in 1876, but burned to the ground, shortly after. It's been rebuilt and renovated several times. The latest renovation was in 2000. The murals have never looked more vibrant." He paused and repeated my words. "Sex was a NO NO in your house. Abortion, too?"

"Yes." The stained glass windows prevented a clear look inside and my memories felt like I was being stabbed in the chest. We sat quietly until Charles said, "So you're running away from a fire?"

"Is that what I'm doing? You tell me... Are we far from the Mercer House? That house in the movie, Midnight in the Garden of ... something."

Charles finished my sentence, "Good and Evil. We'll go by Mrs. Wilkes Restaurant."

We walked along East Harris passed Lafayette Square, turned left on Whitaker, and paused at Joan Street to peek at the cafe. We admired the Mercer House on Montgomery Square and then headed to our destination.

Versailles Square ... where we said goodbye. He took my hand and smiled. "It's been a good morning. Are you sure you want to leave?"

"Thank you, Mr. Dunmore." I shook his hand. "You've opened my head to new thoughts, Charles. But, yes, I must go. I have a long ride ahead of me." I kissed his cheek.

* * * * *

Leaving Savannah, I was distracted and found myself in Lewes, Delaware. It's the oldest American fishing town on the Bay. The salty air was reminiscent of the North Shore of Long

Island and triggered my lingering doubts. Daytona had been a tight-rope walk. I was running away from problems with my father. But what was I rushing back to?

So, I spent the night and didn't cry myself to sleep, but sobbed needlessly over a parking ticket, in the morning. People laughing made me grind my teeth and the sea breeze attacked my face, on the ferry ride to Cape May.

In the 1800s, once rail service was completed, Philadelphians flocked to the area. The wealthy built seaside summer homes. Many of the Victorian houses, painted in lollipop colors, had been restored and became bed and breakfast inns. Charles would have shown me around and known the history and nuance. Instead, I heard the details from a tour guide; my brain was on pause. I was less stressed rather than refreshed when I left Cape May and headed to New York.

Chapter 16

Call a Realtor

ℒ

Carrie arrived at Morningside Drive to find Frank Webb asleep in his chair. The television was still on. Lucky licked Frank's face. He woke up and pretended he had been watching the morning show, and continued to bellyache about fake news.

"Good morning Old Man, have you heard from your daughter? Want coffee?"

"Make it strong. If you're talking about Joy, she's dead to me. Did you know she was pregnant when she went missing? Thank God Mary Elizabeth isn't here. You're my only daughter."

Lucky finished licking Frank's face and sat at his feet.

"Joy phoned me last night from Savannah," said Carrie from the kitchen. "She's going back to New York City ... wants to check on things. She's worried a water leak might damage her designer handbags."

"Carrie, we both know that's a cock n bull story. She left because I'm not the perfect father she needs for her perfect life. I'm not surprised, actually ... I'm relieved! Now I can stop romanticizing about how my life would have been if she hadn't gone missing. She's doing me a favor. We didn't get along then and don't now. Especially after giving my grandson, Jason, up for adoption."

Carrie brought two cups of black coffee into the room, handed one to Frank, and sat opposite him.

"You're right, I don't think there's a water leak."

"You know, when Joy went missing Mary Elizabeth and I teamed up, and worked on what was important, finding our daughter. When Joy was a kid, we were never on the same page. Mary Elizabeth spoiled her rotten. Bribed her for affection. I wanted Joy to be tough. Life is tough. Carrie, you know that. Mary Elizabeth was jealous of our father-daughter relationship. When Joy went missing, we pulled together and what followed were probably our happiest years. When Mary Elizabeth died, I felt sorry for myself. Sitting here, alone, drinking beer late into the night is not the life I want. Joy's return has given me that, I have my life back."

Carrie did not know what to say, because she too had spent years feeling sad about things that happened long ago.

"I am too old to continue feeling sorry for myself. I'm done being angry, sad, lonely, and depressed. I'm putting the house up for sale and moving to a retirement community. Do you know a realtor?

"I do. A woman named Roxanne."

* * * * *

A week later, Roxanne Hart knocked on Frank Webb's door.

Frank stood at the entrance dressed in pink shorts and a tropical shirt with a collar. "Hi Roxanne, you're late."

"Very funny, Carrie told me you had a great sense of humor."

She talked to his back as he flipped-flopped into the living room, a price tag dangled from the shirt armpit. When he turned around, Roxanne extended her hand.

"Nice to finally meet you, Mr. Webb. Your daughter has told me so much about you."

"Call me Frank. Mr. Webb makes me sound like someone's grandfather. You spoke to Joy?" He plopped into his recliner.

"No, your daughter, Carrie, and aren't you a grandpa?" Roxanne chuckled. Natural curly blonde hair caressed her makeup-free face.

"Carrie – right. She's my daughter but not really, and yes, I'm a grandfather, but not really. It's complicated."

"I know, Carrie told me." Her smile broadened, as she said, "I have six sons and fifteen grandchildren. I don't get to see them much. They live on Long Island."

Frank smiled but not with his eyes. "That's terrific, but you're here to talk about houses. Tell me what you think."

Her casual chatter about sons felt like salt in his wound. If he'd had a son his heartache with Joy would be less.

"I like a man who cuts to the chase. Why don't you show me around? The comps show this house would sell in the $130,000 to $150,000 price range."

"You've got to be kidding." Frank sounded annoyed. "A house four streets over sold for $250,000 and was a teardown. This house is in move-in condition."

"Honestly Frank, I gotta tell you, that house has a view to die for. It's riverfront property." Roxanne walked into the kitchen and on tippy toes stretched over the sink to look out the window. "Your yard has lovely, beautiful trees, but the view of a falling down fence won't get anything close to that."

"Damn, Roxanne, you think I could only get $150,000 for this place?"

"To be honest Frank, the carpet and appliances need to be replaced. You'd be lucky to get that. How eager are you to sell?"

"The carpet was replaced when Mary Elizabeth died, and the appliances are better than anything new."

"I'm sorry for your loss. My husband passed six years ago. Carrie said you and your wife adopted her after Joy went missing." She glanced at the dated knickknacks. "I gotta tell you, no one wants carpet, buyers want tile or wood, and fresh paint. Gray is the new color."

"I gotta tell you, Roxanne, gray may be the new color, but gray is an ugly color."

Roxanne sat opposite Frank in Mary Elizabeth's chair. "A home inspection will reveal the condition of the roof. When was it replaced?"

"Replaced? The roof doesn't need to be replaced. Not one leak, drip, or blown-away tile. Quality, we're talking quality. Something this younger generation hasn't a clue about."

The age lines highlighted Frank's face, now red, as he spoke.

"Honestly Frank, I gotta tell you, that is an excellent selling point. Quality. We'll run with that and like you said move-in condition."

Roxanne scanned the family photos decorating the living room, the dark window treatments, and pink walls, and sighed, relieved to hear a knock on the front door.

Carrie opened the front door. Lucky scampered in, jumped on Roxanne, and ran in circles like he was trying to bite his tail, then made his way to Frank's recliner to lick his face while Roxanne's and Carrie's laughter was background music.

"Did he offer you coffee?" Carrie asked.

"No." Then she whispered, "But he's wearing pink shorts and a new shirt with the price tag still on."

"I'll make coffee." She rolled her eyes. "I bought crumb cake. Did you notice Doug Dillon is parked outside?"

Roxanne followed Carrie into the kitchen asking, "Why is Doug Dillon, a reporter for the News-Journal, outside?"

"It's complicated." Carrie brewed the coffee. "Frank has strong feelings about this property. How much do you think he can get for it?"

"It's unlikely he wants to make any changes, not even paint and carpet. I think the house could sell as is if priced right, but pricing it low fuels the idea there is something wrong. Roxanne cut the crumb cake and said, "I'll recommend an owner inspection, and if everything holds up, list at $150,000. Affordable for first-time buyers. You never know."

"Did you talk about signing papers?"

"I was getting to that, but first let's get him thinking about where he'll move to."

Carrie put three cups of coffee on the kitchen table along with cream, sugar, and the coffee cake. Called out, "Dad, come and have some cake and coffee."

Frank sat at the kitchen table and listened to the two women debate where he should live, the best list price for the house he has lived in since 1967 and paid $27,000 for, and which home inspector they should call. When Frank finished the second piece of cake, he wiped his mouth with a paper towel, stood, and said, "I'm too old for this crap. Doesn't Marshal's son-in-law, Kyle, do inspections? Phone him. List the house at $150,000. I'll be in the bathroom and when I come out, Roxanne and I are going for a drive. The Riviera and that place you live at – what's it called – Crane Lakes? I'm getting on with my life."

* * * * *

"Like I said, you'll love Crane Lakes. It's a friendly community." Roxanne told Frank as she drove on South Nova Road toward Port Orange. "We'll pass The Riviera on the way, and stop if you like."

"I've been thinking about that. Been there! The crowd was not only old but decrepit. A bunch of sad, sorry saps. Let's go straight to Crane Lakes. I heard they have a dance event monthly." Frank realized a price tag hung off his shirt, and yanked it off. "You have a last name, Roxanne?"

"Hart. That's why those red hearts are dancing over my head on my business cards, lawn signs, and the side door of this new Honda CRV you're riding in."

"It smells new." Frank ran his hand across the dashboard. "Roxie Hart. Wasn't that the dame in the play Chicago?"

"And the movie. Boylhart's my married name ... My husband shortened it to Hart, for business purposes. Russell was my maiden."

"Aye, a bit of the blarney in you."

Roxanne laughed, "I gotta tell you, Frank ... I like your humor."

"Great. But I gotta tell you, I don't like having a dame drive me around town. Don't take your eyes off the road." He emphasized gotta. Her constant use of the phrase was getting on his nerves.

"Now you're gonna tell me how to drive? In case you haven't noticed, I'm a woman, not a dame, or girl."

"Oh, I noticed, Roxanne." He smiled and dug a deeper hole for himself. "So, tell me, what do I call you people?"

She stopped for a red light and smiled at him. "Oh, Frank ... it's simple. You call me Jane, and I'll call you Tarzan." When the light changed, she continued. "Now, what are you looking for in a new place?"

"I always wanted a pool table." Frank's voice was low and slow. Almost subdued. "Mary Elizabeth said, 'A pool table in the living room is uncouth. Pool tables belong in a basement. There are no basements in Florida.' So, I forgot about it." He paused. "The living room must be large enough for a pool table." And sighed.

"How long has Mary Elizabeth been gone?"

"She died in 2010. Pancreatic cancer. She ignored those stomach pains, and by the time she went to the doc, it was too late. The chemo, well, was a lot of pain for nothing."

"My husband died in 2008, he'd just turned sixty-five and retired. A stroke."

"My age."

Roxanne parked near the community center and they got out of the car.

They walked around the pool area, tennis, and bocce ball courts. Then checked out the restaurant, and got in a golf cart to view houses. She talked non-stop, explaining the association fee included, water, taxes, and internet service. You own the house but rent the land. Frank's head ached by the time they sat poolside, under an umbrella, and ordered Margaritas.

"I showed you three houses today. Which is your favorite?"

"The turtle house didn't have shade trees, so it's out. I liked the carport on the one with all the flags twirling about, but it had a dog smell. The last one was terrific if ... a pool table would fit in the living room."

"A pool table will fit. I measured the room."

"Barely, our butts would be too near the walls to shoot a pool stick."

Numerous people stopped by their table to be introduced to a potential homeowner and chat with them.

"Holy crap, Roxanne, you know everyone and their mother," said Frank, on his second drink. "Does anyone call you Roxie?"

"Never."

"How about Annie? That's a nickname for Roxanne." He brought a paper napkin to his mouth to distract a belch.

"Never! My ex called me that, just to infuriate me."

"Ex? I thought your husband died from a heart attack?"

"He did. This was Mark. Not-too-long-ago-Mark. I discovered he gambled, just in time."

"How?"

"I Googled him."

"You Googled him? You can Google? Gee whiz, have you Googled me?"

"Not yet, Frank."

* * * * *

"Mary Elizabeth, I wish you were here, but I'm glad you're dead because this would have killed you. Could be you're a fly on the wall... maybe even a spirit, and you already know the crap that went down in this house, today. But I need to tell you; your daughter, Joy, the girl, now a woman, you cried your heart over ... is alive. Guess what? She was pregnant when she ran away, thirty years ago."

Frank was working on his second six-pack, after returning from Crane Lakes. A bag of chips sat on his lap and in between belching he crunched on a few.

"You better sit down, or lay down, whatever is more comfortable ... Jason was born in 1985 and you passed in 2010. I'm too drunk to do the math, but it's a hell of a lot of years we could have enjoyed being grandparents."

He closed his eyes and nodded off for a bit, then awakened by his loud snore, said, "I'll be back. I gotta pee."

He came back with one last beer and settled into his recliner.

"Mary Elizabeth ... I've met someone. A real dame, named Roxanne. You'd like her. She's one of us. A New Yorker, likes music. Likes to dance. She'll never replace you, Mary Elizabeth, but I'm lonely. For all I know you could be getting it on with another ... resident. Last year, I learned Bobby Pacer died. He was always sweet on you. Isn't that what heaven's about? We can't even be sure I'll make it up there. I wasn't the best husband, and will probably be sent to purgatory. So, I might as well be happy here in hell on earth."

Chapter 17

April in New York City

૭

New York City didn't take a back seat to Paris in April. Central Park's azaleas were blooming. Bright yellow daffodils lined the garden paths. The air was crisp and the sky sunny. The kind of weather that puts a smile on everyone's face.

The doorman greeted me and once upstairs, I sorted the mail, ripped up the junk mail, and thumbed through magazines, when the house phone startled me.

"Officer Atwood is asking to see you. Are you receiving guests?"

Ray was in the city? I wondered, why? The incident at DBPD, came to mind... this was hardly the time to tell Ray, we were going to be grandparents. Perhaps he came to apologize. The doorman wasn't going to wait forever... I said, "Yes."

I searched the apartment for my handbag, combed my hair, applied lip gloss, and opened the door on the first knock.

"You have every reason to be angry with me."

"No kidding." Ray brushed past me. Once inside, he stood quietly taking in the view. But quickly broke the silence he had created and said, "What do you want, Joy Webb, or is it Mrs. Gardner?"

His voice was harsh, almost a growl as he looked directly into my eyes. Bobby Smart was not here to protect me, and I stepped backward as Ray came toward me. My fear multiplied. How was I ever going to tell him Jason's wife was pregnant?

"I know I've made a mess of things."

"A mess of things?" he yelled. His fists were clenched.

"Are you going to hurt me?"

"No. I'm not going to hurt you." He unclenched his fists and stretched his neck from side to side.

"You had me worried for a second," I said, relieved to see his demeanor change.

"Joy, I thought you were dead but ... you knew I wasn't," he said sarcastically. "You show up unexpectedly with a story about Frank, and never mention ... YOU GAVE JASON UP FOR ADOPTION ... You're messing with my head!" He walked out onto the balcony and stood at the railing.

I joined him outside in the sun and fresh air. The view was remarkable and serene. But a prediction of rain caused me to fear the sky would become cloudy and black once again.

"You knew I wanted a family," he said with his back to me.

"After we were married! After we bought a house! After you made detective! The pregnancy was a mistake and I planned to take my secret to my grave."

"Well, you didn't." He turned around and faced me.

"Yes, I did, for years." Tears ran down my face. "Now that you know, do you wish you didn't?"

"No, of course not. Jason's not a mistake. He is our son." He glanced toward heaven and sighed.

"Ray, remember when we met?" I experienced a flashback to that night.

"How could I forget?" He closed his eyes and said, "Flag Day, June 14th. The streets were lined with American flags. Your dad was drunk. When I drove him home you opened the door wearing your pajamas."

"Baby dolls."

He opened his eyes, smiled, and said, "I fell in love with you."

He cupped my face in his hands and kissed my tears.

"I still love you, never stopped loving you."

His lips found mine. The attraction was strong, and foolishly we stumbled our way to the bedroom.

In the morning, Ray sat on the balcony. I thought he was enjoying the early morning breeze.

"You made coffee," I said and smiled. My body relaxed recalling our lovemaking.

"Good morning," he said and walked toward me. "What happened last night?"

"You tell me," I said flirtatiously. "Have you been up long?" He was already dressed.

"Before sunrise. I've been thinking about us, and love."

It was like a scene in a bad romance novel. I sensed something was wrong but didn't know what.

"I'm confused, Joy. Last night you didn't express your great love for me. In fact, you spoke more of loneliness and proving your dad's guilt or innocence. Who do you love?"

"You! I love you." In his arms I physically surrendered, but emotionally struggled with the past, and our future.

"It's a strange definition of love, Joy. When people love each other, they do anything to be together, not apart."

"You were the one who didn't want to be together, Ray. I

made sacrifices for you. I gave my child up for you, to shield you from a loveless marriage … from responsibility. Keeping the pregnancy and adoption a secret, I believed was in everyone's best interest."

"Well, it wasn't. Listen to yourself! You knew I was alive! EVERYONE thought you were dead. Thirty years is a hell of a long time."

He emptied his cup of coffee in the sink and stormed into the bedroom.

"You were right to give Jason up. You'd make a lousy mother."

He grabbed his wallet and cell from the nightstand and headed to the apartment door.

"Regardless of what you feel, think, or do, Jason was not a mistake and needs to know I am his father."

I'd make a lousy mother. His words stung me all over, as if I had stepped on a hornet's nest. I raced in front of him.

"No Ray, don't go! You have got it all wrong. Jason doesn't know I'm his mother. It isn't a good time, wait until after the gender reveal party, please."

Ray slowed as he approached the door, closed his eyes, and asked, "What's a gender reveal party?"

"We're going to be grandparents, Ray … please wait. There are so many what ifs."

"What are you talking about, and how would you know that?"

"We're Facebook friends." I smiled reliving the few moments I'd experienced a grandmother's happiness.

"You're fucking Facebook friends with my son!"

"He knows my stepchildren. He doesn't know I'm his

mother. I'm talking about our lives. What if we can be happy together? What if Jason wants us in his life? What if we can be a family?" I hugged my robe around me.

"Grandparents? Family? Dammit, Joy! What if I find Jason, tell him I'm his father, and never come back?"

"No! Please don't go!"

He twirled around to face me. "You know what your problem is, Joy?" But did not wait for my response. He said calmly, "You don't want to be alone."

The door slammed behind him. I pressed my back against it, closed my eyes, and let the tears escape. He loved me last night and hated me this morning. I thought about phoning Carrie, however, explaining the latest ... would hurt too much. I locked the door, crawled into bed, and fell asleep. It was silly to talk, or think, about a relationship that was never meant to be.

* * * * *

I had been crying but pretended not to be, when Charles phoned.

"Are you following me?"

"Mercy me, Joy. Like a stalker? Don't be silly. In Savannah, we spoke about having lunch when I was in town. I called to invite you to Tea at the Plaza Hotel. But if you're going to bite my head off ..."

"Forgive me, my re-entry hasn't gone well. I'd be happy to have lunch."

Ray hit the nail on the head. I was lonely. This whole return to Daytona to resolve my past had backfired. Charles, at least, was a good companion.

"Great. You'll join me then. I can have tea sent up to my apartment, or meet you downstairs, in The Palm Court. High Tea is from 10:30 until 4 p.m. Do you have a preference?"

"Let's meet downstairs at noon." I didn't want to give Charles the wrong impression. He was winning my affections, and his timing was perfect. I felt unhinged.

"I'll call ahead for a table. I look forward to seeing you, Joy."

Ray's threat to never come back was similar to my father's declaration, "You're dead to me."

Inside the Fifth Avenue entrance of the Plaza, the iconic chandelier sparkled and light bounced about Charles, creating an image that he had come from heaven, and not the eighth floor, to greet me. His reference to his apartment implied he was staying in one of the private condominiums.

People were waiting to be seated for High Tea. However, the maître d' acknowledged Charles, at a distance and said, "Good afternoon, Mr. Dunmore. Your table is ready."

He unhooked a velvet rope and ushered us in. Maybe Charles owned the condominium.

Outside it was raining and gloom descended as though the lights had been turned down. Two hot whiskeys and tea sandwiches arrived. Charles said, "I hope you don't mind. I took the liberty of ordering ahead."

I didn't mind. The simplest decisions were becoming difficult, besides I felt cared for.

"What brings you to New York, Charles?" I wanted to get the low down on his whereabouts, after all, I'd heard of many lonely widows who had been charmed.

"New York is my permanent residence. However, I travel and have several apartments. One is in Hammock, Florida."

I played with a napkin before saying. "I stopped in

Lewes, Delaware and Cape May on my return and missed having a personal tour guide."

Charles appeared flattered, and said, "Joy, I enjoy your company as well."

I interrupted him. "Charles, I don't want to mislead you. Things are complicated." I started to cry.

"The story is more than I was pregnant thirty years ago and fought with my father. We were not estranged. I've been missing for thirty years. It wasn't planned. I thought the father of my child, Ray, would look for me, and when no one did, I stayed in the city and got a job. Ben was newly divorced and needed a nanny for his kids. We fell in love and married so his ex-wife wouldn't get full custody."

It was almost a rant.

Charles signaled the waiter for another drink.

"This may be more information than required to have another lunch date."

I laughed. "Right! But you need to know ... Ray showed up yesterday and we made love. This morning when I told him about being invited to the gender reveal party, he said he never wants to see me again."

It felt good to get Ray's latest rejection off my chest.

"Joy, this situation needs professional help." He raised his hands as though surrendering and smiled.

"Does that mean, you never want to see me again, too?"

"Now you're being silly, again. Let's go for a carriage ride."

Chapter 18

Dolan & Dolan

ॐ

Ray Atwood stood outside the sleek glass modern building on Park Avenue looking up, impressed. He entered the lobby and was told to take the elevator to the thirty-sixth floor. When the elevator doors opened, a huge Dolan & Dolan sign behind the reception desk filled the room. Ray rubbed his sweating hands as he read the tagline, Best in Business, scripted beneath it.

The office, decorated with real plants and leather furniture, reeked of money and was intimidating. Ray closed the button of his sports coat, approached the desk, and showed his badge.

"I'm here to see Jason Dolan."

The woman behind the desk was about Ray's age, not thin, but attractive.

"Your name, detective?"

"Atwood, Ray Atwood, out of Daytona Beach."

"Daytona Beach, Florida? Then you have no authority here."

"Right, I'm with the Cold Case Unit and hoping for verification on a thirty-year case."

"What could Jason Dolan possibly verify about a case that old? He probably wasn't even born," she snarled. "Dolan &

Dolan, one moment please." She quipped to the next caller. Her eyes studied Ray.

"Is he expecting you, Detective Atwood?"

"No Madam, he isn't. I was in the area and took a chance."

"Take a seat, I'll see if he is available, and please, don't call me Madam."

Ray picked up a Wall Street Journal from a mahogany table, sat, and pretended to read. The office lobby was active. People hurried in and out nodding and greeting each other with a monotone, Good Morning.

A grandfather clock chimed eleven thirty when his name was called. Ray stood and walked to the desk. The receptionist said, "Jason is tied up until noon then having lunch with his father. You can leave your cell number or come back. Although there is no guarantee he'll have time to see you this afternoon." She pushed a notepad toward him, punched a button, and said, "Hold please."

Ray scribbled his name and cell number on the notepad, laid the pen on top of it, and pushed them back toward the receptionist as she said, "Good morning. Dolan & Dolan. How can I help you?"

* * * * *

Outside the air was polluted with cigarette smoke and car fumes. Ray mingled with pedestrians on the corner and crossed to the other side when the light changed and waited. As he did the temperature rose higher with the noon sun.

Shortly after twelve, the Dolans exited the building. There was no doubt Jason was Ray's son. They were the same height and stature. They even walked with the same long stride. Jason's hair was thick, black, and as curly as Ray's at his age. In contrast, Jason's adoptive father was much shorter, his hair was light and thin, and his stride was erratic.

The two men walked south on Park Avenue. Ray followed. He stumbled and bumped into people as they wove between the crowds headed toward Forty-second Street. On Vanderbilt Avenue, Jason Dolan opened the heavy door of Grand Central Terminal and then cradled the senior Dolan's shoulders as they entered the station. After passing The Oyster Bar Restaurant, they slipped into a food court. The laughter was loud, and the smell of food was promising. Ray got on the elevator instead. One flight up the doors opened to The Campbell, and Ray found a seat at the bar. The early afternoon sun streamed through the huge leaded pane glass window behind the bartender who asked, "What will it be, sir?"

"A Bud Light and a menu."

"The Campbell only serves locally brewed beers, sir and you can't eat at the bar," said the bartender. He handed him a parchment paper menu. The prices, printed in small cursive writing, started at $16 a pint.

Ray stretched his neck from side to side and said, "Better make it a double Absolute. No, a triple, on the rocks with a couple of olives." He placed a fifty-dollar bill on the bar.

When the bartender brought the drink, he placed two singles on the bar.

"Holy shit," said Ray. "I could have bought a bottle. Were the olives extra?"

"No, included." The bartender laughed. "You're paying the cost of renovation. You're sitting in what used to be John Campbell's office. He was a wealthy financier who liked to work from home, a 3,500-square-foot apartment, in 1923."

Ray looked around at the art deco wall sconces and the

stone fireplace, "Damn, it's beautiful, the whole building. It's my first time in New York."

"What brings you here?"

"Searching for the son I never knew I had."

The bartender stopped wiping a Martini glass and listened.

"I'm sure you've heard the story before, a woman you haven't heard from in forever, shows up to announce a pregnancy way back when." He left out the part about Joy missing and accusing Frank of murder upon her return.

"The one-night stand? All the time." He polished a glass with a cloth.

"It wasn't like that. She disappeared. Gave our baby up for adoption."

"That has got to be rough. You married? Have other children?"

"Once. That didn't work. No children though." Ray played with a coaster embossed with the Campbell Bar logo. "And you? You have kids?"

"Twins, two boys, happiest day of my life, the day they were born and what's keeping me sober."

"I said goodbye to the dream of a family long ago. It was just me and my mom." Ray removed the large green olive from his drink, popped it in his mouth, and drained the glass.

Several businessmen pulling briefcases took seats and signaled for service. Ray absorbed the indoor noise below, people hustling as departures and delays were announced and he relaxed into his anger.

The bartender returned. "Ready for another?" He picked up the empty glass and wiped the bar.

"Give me one of those locally brewed beers."

"So, have you found the son you never knew you had," he asked while filling a pilsner glass.

"Sure did. They're Facebook friends!"

"Who, your ex, and the son she gave up? They know each other? That's complicated."

"More than complicated." Ray scratched his head and sighed. "His biological mother is the stepmother to his friend." He sipped his beer. "Spin that around in your brain a few times, and bibidy, bobody, boo, what you get is me in a sports coat, attempting to persuade a Dolan & Dolan secretary to see my son."

Under the influence of alcohol, Ray talked freely.

"Dolan & Dolan on Park Avenue and Fiftieth?"

"You know the firm?"

"Everyone knows Matthew and Jason. They're regulars. They're big on pro bono, and community service. Holy crap, I see the resemblance."

The bar was getting crowded with men in business suits and women in spiked heels and tight dresses. Ray looked around to see if one of them was a Dolan. Then downed his beer and said, "What do I owe?"

The bartender said, "It's on the house." Then leaned in to say, "Don't do anything stupid."

In the main terminal, the afternoon sunlight filtered through four large windows and created shadows that drew attention to the ceiling. He looked up. The star-studded ceiling mural was amazing. He studied the Baroque interior until the sudden crying of an infant reminded him of what his life might have been if Joy had told him about the pregnancy. He exited the building and walked across 42nd Street to Fifth Avenue, buying a hot dog stuffed with red onions along the way. He chatted with the guy and asked to be pointed in the right direction. On Fifth Avenue, he headed uptown past Rockefeller Center, St. Patrick's Cathedral and The Plaza Hotel then found a bench in Central Park. By the time he returned to Joy's apartment, she was gone but had left a written note with the doorman, which he stuffed in his pocket to answer his phone.

"Detective Atwood?"

"Speaking"

"This is Jason Dolan. You wanted to talk. What's this about?"

"Can I explain in person, Jason?"

"That might be easier said than done, detective. I'm booked solid for the next few days and am told you're from out of town."

"Florida, Daytona Beach. You tell me what might work."

"Okay, I have a meeting at the Small Business Association tomorrow morning. Meet me at 8:30 outside. The address is 26 Federal Plaza."

* * * * *

The sun was bright at 26 Federal Plaza in the morning. Television cameras and reporters swarmed the sidewalk. Protest signs poked the sky and defended Gay Rights. Honking car horns and jaywalkers polluted the atmosphere.

Ray arrived early, and asked a jogger, "What's going on?"

"Sweet Treats by Margie," he said and sprinted away.

"Sweet Treats by Margie?" Ray repeated.

"A small bakery that refused to decorate a wedding cake with a gay couple. The case is going to the Supreme Court," said a bystander.

Ray studied the crowd and realized; he was looking for himself. A limo pulled up, and Jason exited the vehicle. The media descended on him. They thrust microphones and cell phones at him, and blocked his path to the building. The protestors chanted louder and created a flurry of activity. Ray instinctively held his badge high, rushed into the mob, and heard a reporter ask Jason, "What position will the Business Bureau take on the Sweet Cakes ruling?"

Jason shouted over the noise. "That's an important issue and the topic of this morning's meeting."

"We're done here," Ray said and flashed his badge.

"What are you doing?" Jason asked once behind closed doors.

"Protecting you," Ray answered.

"Well, you just blew our free media coverage. Who the hell are you?"

"Ray Atwood. You said to meet you here, and that we'd have a few minutes to talk."

Jason studied the man. They were the same height; their hair and eyes were the same color. Both their noses were straight and not pointy. The only thing that did not match was their accent.

"You're Ray Atwood from DBPD? You wanted to talk about a cold case."

"Yes, I thought you could verify some information."

Jason turned pale and asked, "Are you, my father?"

Chapter 19

House for Sale

Viewing Daytona Beach from the sky relaxed me. The clear water sparkled in the noon sun, and the gentle push and pull of waves toward the shoreline mesmerized me as the plane descended over Daytona Beach. I looked out the plane window and saw International Speedway. As we taxied to the gate, I sent a text to Carrie.

When the seat belt sign turned off, I stood and disembarked. Carrie had phoned to tell me Dad was putting the house for sale and she needed my help. It was the perfect excuse for me to leave New York City and return to Daytona. I had spent the week alone in my apartment.

The airport walls were lined with artwork capturing the beauty of the Tomoka River and the changing skies of Florida. I took the down escalator and got in the car rental line.

"If you want anything from the house you better hustle back here." Carrie had said on the phone. Roxanne sold your dad on Crane Lakes and he is ready to sign papers."

"Who's Roxanne? And why would I want anything from that house?"

"Are you joking? You don't want anything? A high school yearbook? Your baby pictures or wedding pictures of your parents? Roxanne's the realtor."

"I have lived without that stuff for years. Besides, who would I leave those things to?"

Pandora's Box had been opened and dormant emotions circled the room. I was alone. The blow-ups with Ray and my father were reality checks. I could not put the wheels back on this bus. And the icing on the cake, Charles hadn't phoned.

"Carrie, Dad threw me out."

"He threw you out because you accused him of murder. Your dad said that once Doug Dillon was parked outside the door, you'd flee. You did."

"Is the creep still parked outside?" Carrie hung up.

On Morningside Drive, a landscaper's truck blocked the driveway, and the annoying sound of weed whackers and leaf blowers dominated the air as I parked and locked the rental car. A for-sale sign picturing the realtor, Roxanne Hart, decorated the lawn. Red hearts appeared to dance over her head.

A new doorbell had been installed. Instead of ringing the bell, I opened the front door. Carrie was in the living room cursing and flinging clothing into boxes. She looked up and said, "What the hell are you doing here?"

"I felt guilty after you called me a brat and said I was having a pity party. So, I'm here now to help. Didn't you get my text?" I tossed my handbag and a jean jacket on Dad's chair.

"Put your stuff in the kitchen, there's enough crap in here already. No, I didn't read your text, I've been busy."

"Look, I'm sorry, I should have said that I would come back right from the start. He's my dad and my responsibility. It was wrong of me. I don't want to fight. I'm sorry, really, sorry."

"Sorry, you're sorry! Sorry doesn't cut it, Joy. Sorry is a word people say to make themselves feel better. Really, sorry? Be as sorry as you like, but you never cooked a meal, cleaned a toilet, took out the garbage, drove anyone to chemo, or comforted the dying. You don't want to fight, well I do.

"I want a big blow-up ... maybe even slap-you-in-the-face fight. I have been cleaning up after you forever, from the first time you slept over because your parents were fighting. You threw up in my bed. Remember? Who cleaned it up? Me!

"Thirty years later I'm still at it sorting your mother's clothing. You came back to help? What do you want to do with this? Throw it out or give it to Goodwill? Decide back-from-the-dead-designer-girl!"

Carrie held up my mother's wedding dress in a garment bag. She unzipped the bag and tossed the dress at me. Pearl buttons secured by crocheted silk loops adorned the long dress sleeves. The waist was narrow, and the neckline V-shaped. Shoulder pads gave any woman more stature.

After all this time it hit me, I would never see my mother again. Her wish that I get married in her dress invaded my thoughts and the memory of being pregnant and too afraid to tell anyone crippled me again. But this time I wasn't going to be sick.

I grabbed the dress and said, "The Goodwill! What else you got? You want to fight, I'll fight. Designer girl is a survivor.

"All the people who said they loved me, Mom, Dad, Ray, and even you – did anyone miss me? Wonder about not hearing from me for two or three weeks? Ray never noticed I was gone. I phoned Ray routinely, every night from the dorm. Mom or Dad, and you, every couple of days. Routinely!

"Not one of you thought things were wrong or questioned why I didn't call until Dad was notified the tuition hadn't been paid. At least two weeks after I stopped phoning!

"I fantasized for months that Ray would come to New York

City and rescue me. He could have put two and two together. He was a cop trained to question and look for patterns. If he missed our nightly phone conversations, why didn't he call me? He was just not that into me.

"My father lectured me about men and convenient sex, how they use women and he was right. I would not, could not give him the satisfaction of being right!

"You think it was easy giving up a child, not having a family to lean on, lying to everyone I ever met about who I was and why I stayed in New York City for the next thirty years?

"What kind of life would my child have with an uneducated single mom? You think I traded Jason for a good life? The trade I made gave him a good life. The trade I made set Ray free from a life of obligations. He never wanted to marry me.

"Now you throw my mother's dress at me as a reminder of the disappointment I was. Don't pretend, we both know they would have disowned me and put the house in someone else's name.

"Oh, and now that the words are out of my mouth, who could that person be? Who else could it be, Carrie, not me, but you?"

"You are losing it, Joy, of course, the house is willed to me. We thought you were dead! A house can't be left to a dead person, but I get it you never thought of yourself as dead because you weren't.

"So, you get the house?"

"When your dad passes."

"You think that's fair?" I raised my hand to slap Carrie but she ducked and I spun around, tripped, and fell.

"Okay! Let's slap it out, Joy. I am so in the mood," she yelled.

We swung and missed each other as Roxanne and my father walked in. Dad carried a bakery box into the kitchen and said, "You're back! What the hell is going on?"

Roxanne held a small dog in her arms who yapped loudly. She pressed the pet to her breasts, kissed its face, and said, "No worries, everything is fine, just a little squabble, nothing to be upset about."

The dog was white and fluffy, with inviting eyes, and somehow looked like Roxanne who extended her hand and said, "I'm Roxanne, and you must be Frank's daughter, Joy. This is Laptop."

She held up the dog's paw for me to shake. I smiled, and the smile rolled into laughter as I pictured the dancing red hearts above her head. Laptop jumped into my arms, and licked my face.

Carrie joined in the laughter and said, "You can put her down, Roxanne. Lucky didn't come today."

From the kitchen, Dad yelled, "She's not my daughter, my daughter's dead to me."

Roxanne watched my laughter fade, and said, "Don't listen to that. He'll come around. Now, what's the ruckus about?"

Carrie held up the dress, "What to do with Mom's wedding dress."

"I'll take it." Roxanne put Laptop down and returned the dress to its garment bag.

"A woman's group at Crane Lakes uses the fabric to make Christening gowns. They'll be happy to have it. The satin is in good condition, enough for three or four infant dresses. A gift tag is attached to each dress naming the wedding couple. In this case, the card would say gift from Mr. & Mrs. Francis Webb. Sometimes the tag is in the bride's maiden name because her family originally bought the garment."

I nodded yes in response and watched her actions.

"What was your mother's maiden name?"

"Lynch." I felt a sense of peace in knowing the dress would be put to good use.

"Don't let me forget the dress when I leave."

Roxanne smiled and laid the garment bag across the couch. I took an instant liking to the woman and how she handled the situation.

"I'm glad you came to help. Carrie has been amazing. Now, I smell coffee and crumb cake."

I felt like the shepherd had gathered her lost sheep as she pushed me and Carrie into the kitchen

"You're taking Mary Elizabeth's wedding dress? Does that mean you changed your mind about marriage?" Dad said with a big smile.

His smile changed into a frown. "And you ..." he pointed toward me ... "I'm not talking to."

"Move your stubborn self over," Roxanne said, kissing him. "No, I've not changed my mind! I'm never getting married again, Frank, ever. We've had this discussion."

Dad lifted a big bite of cake to his mouth, and said, "Stubborn? Deal, I'll come around when you come around."

Chapter 20

Persons of Interest

The next morning, rain flowed across the car windshield on the drive to Carrie's. The wipers swished back and forth with a vengeance. At International Speedway I slowed as the water puddled, and cars moved around me creating splash, after splash, after splash. I was parked in her driveway waiting for the rain to let up when Ray phoned.

"Jason texted me. If I come to his office again, security will throw me out."

"You went to his office?" I rested my head on the steering wheel.

"Last week. The following morning, I caught up with him outside of some federal building."

"And you told him you're his father?"

"He figured it out."

"And you're blaming me?"

"Of course, it's your fault. If I'd known you were pregnant, he never would have been adopted."

I hung up.

I wasn't about to say sorry. I'd said it so many times before and it had never helped. Sorry was a word that had not changed anything. The wind rustled the tree leaves, and rain dropped on me as though I'd been through a storm when I got out of the car. I was trying not to get wet when I discovered Doug Dillon stood in my way.

"Leave me alone." He jumped every time I moved to avoid him like we were playing a game.

"You think your old man's guilty, don't you? That's why you left town."

"Get out of my way." I attempted to slip around him. He blocked me.

"Rumor is he's Tammy Martin's daddy and you've been hiding the evidence."

When I hopped around him, he followed, and I kneed him in his crotch. As he fell to the ground his yellow teeth glowed against the black driveway. By the time I got to Carrie's door, my blouse and hair were saturated, and I was emotionally drained.

Carrie and Lucky answered the bell. "Thanks for inviting me to stay with you," I said and rushed inside.

"Roxanne shamed me into it after hearing we'd been best friends," said Carrie.

Roxanne's influence on my behalf was welcomed, and I was thankful for Carrie's softening attitude, although she did not look happy. While Lucky nuzzled up to me, she headed to a bedroom and returned with a terry robe.

"Strip and put this on," she said. "Was that creepy Dillon outside?"

My wet clothing decorated the foyer. I nodded yes. "I hate that man. He asked if Dad was Tammy's father. How would he know that?"

"It's speculation. Ignore him. How about a hot toddy?"

"Sure, whatever that is."

"Whiskey, tea, lemon, and honey or sugar, your mom's favorite on a good cancer day."

"Charles calls this hot whiskey." I countered. Carrie had more knowledge of my mother's likes and dislikes than I did. It hurt.

"Who's Charles?"

"The gentleman I met in Savannah." I followed her into the kitchen and watched her fill the kettle with water.

"I just spoke with Ray. He saw Jason while he was in the city. What was I thinking not telling him, not telling you? I feel terrible about what I've put everyone through."

Carrie squeezed a lemon silently. The seeds tumbled into a strainer and remained there as the pale liquid drained into a fragile tea cup. I realized my return had brought nothing but heartache.

"So, Jason knows Ray's his father." Carrie dumped boiling water onto the tea bag she had placed in the cup and watched it steep.

"Evidently. Jason sent a text warning him not to come to his office again. Ray blames me."

She listened intently and gave me a bitter look.

"You should feel terrible. Ray's not through being angry with you, and neither am I."

She clenched one fist, and smacked it into the other, like a prize fighter warming up for a fight.

"I'm so angry I could smack you."

"Are we going to get physical again?"

She dropped her arms as though the end of the round bell

had sounded.

"You're right. Roxanne asked, 'What good will anger do anyone?'"

Neither one of us had an answer.

In Florida it might rain every day, but usually not all day. It can start hard, stop abruptly, and the sun will come out. Then the sky clouds over and it can rain again. Some days the sequence repeats itself, again and again.

Today was one of those days. Carrie and I listened to the rain and sipped our hot toddies.

"If only I'd not accused Dad of murder."

I was being pulled in opposite directions. My younger self, frozen in time by the image of him with the Martins; now mature enough to be embarrassed by my foolishness. But, not enough to admit I was wrong.

"Things couldn't be worse between Ray and me. He said he never wants to see me again."

"Call Ray. This on-again, off-again is normal for you two. Try listening to his side without getting angry."

"What about Doug Dillon? I can't prevent him from hounding me about this mess."

"To get rid of Doug Dillon you need answers. Did Ray mention the Martin case?"

I shook my head, no, and worried our personal lives would be a newspaper headline. I returned to learn the truth and thought my emotions were well in check. My life of secrets was bound tightly with a pretty bow.

Now, things were unraveling, and fast.

"Jason guessed Ray is his father, but does he know I am his mother?"

My mind raced furiously into a foreign land of possibilities.

"That Dillon creep is the least of my worries, Carrie." The words stuck in my throat as I started crying.

"Joy, I've never seen you this upset."

Carrie put her hands on her hips and sighed. "Come here, girlfriend."

She quietly folded me in her arms. I listened to the rain, thankful for her kindness.

"I've been uninvited to the gender reveal party. And if I don't go ... I'm sure Ray will think it's an attempt to sabotage their relationship. "

"Joy!" Carrie said sternly. "Everything's going to be all right."

I wasn't sure and shuttered to think about Jason's reaction. He was going to find out.

"Now tell me about Charles."

Chapter 21

Who is the Killer?

ର

Doug Dillon waited in the Daytona Beach Police Department for days to catch Ray Atwood returning.

Ray Atwood wore a scowl when he came back, kept his head down, and said to Baumgardner, "Is Bobby in the back?"

"Where've you been Ray?" Doug yelled as Baumgardner buzzed him in.

Ray had not been heard from since his outburst.

"I'm glad you're here. Did you get a hold of Jason Dolan?" Bobby asked. He greeted Ray with a handshake and assumed Ray had gone looking for his son because that's what he'd have done.

"Kind of, but I need to keep my personal life out of this, it's not professional. Can you help me?" Ray said as they walked down the hall surrounded by awkwardness.

Outside the door, Bobby put his hand on Ray's shoulder. "No problem, I've got you covered."

Bobby opened the conference room door to find Joe and Danny at the table.

"Hey guys," said Bobby. "Look who's back from vacation."

"Cut the crap, Bobby. We're not going to pretend Ray took a few days off. He looks like shit, not rested," said Joe.

"It's personal. And none of your damn business," said Ray.

"None of my damn business? You took off, to do what? Pursue an old love interest? Leaving us canvassing in one hundred-degree, scorching, blistering, sweltering, and sizzling, weather! And now you want to pretend it rained on your vacation?"

Joe was red in the face and breathing jaggedly.

Ray faced Joe with clenched teeth and wanted to knock him out. Instead, he imagined he was a matador twirling a red cape to distract a bull, and rather than straighten the Jersey boy's nose, circled him and said, "Take your seats."

The four detectives looked at each other and then sat back down.

"This old girlfriend is not only a subject of one of our cold cases, but she also has information on another cold case. I pursued her for information. We all agreed I should get more information from Joy Webb. I thought it was a conflict of interest then, and still think so."

"He's right," Bobby interjected. "Ray was upfront about his relationship with Joy Webb, or Joy Gardner, and wanted to stay out of this. Now, I see his point, and from this point on it's by the book."

Ray was the first to speak.

"Let's get started." Ray laid out the facts and reviewed them. "Joy Webb is alive and it's safe to say we can close that case. But we need to make some determination in the Martin case and give the family closure. So ... what are the possibilities?"

"The bone forensics indicate the remains might be Tammy Martin's, but the DNA on the paternal side doesn't match. If

Frank Webb's her father, we'll need his DNA. He might be the killer," said Danny.

"If Doug Dillon's her daddy, he'd have the motive and might be the killer. We'll need his DNA," added Joe. He looked around the room for approval.

Ray interjected, "You're assuming the killer is the father... out of jealousy, revenge or to keep them quiet. Doug Dillon's a stretch but a possibility."

Ray stood and gathered his papers.

"I'll phone Frank Webb. Doug Dillon is probably sitting outside. Tell Baumgardner to have Dillon join you. We will need both DNA samples."

After Ray left the room, Danny said, "Holy crap ... He looks God-awful."

* * * * *

Doug Dillon was all smiles when Baumgardner motioned him to sit in a conference room. He probably thought he was getting an exclusive.

"Have a seat, Doug," said Baumgardner. "Bobby will be with you shortly."

When Bobby opened the door, Doug said, "Hey man, what's happening?" He was permanently stuck in the 80s and would probably say cool and rad throughout the interview. Although right on brother was another strong possibility.

"We're looking into the Martin cold case and wondering where you were when they disappeared."

Doug squirmed in the chair. "Me? Are you crazy, man?" He shot Bobby a killer look and his beady eyes retreated further inside his head.

"Yeah, you! You had a thing for Diane Martin," said Danny. He had entered the room and taken a seat alongside Bobby. "Why don't you tell us about it?"

"If you must know, I had a crush on the girl, but that was years before she went missing. May 10, 1984, I worked at the New York Times. I worked in the mail room. Occasionally I was asked to write an obituary."

Beads of perspiration formed on his forehead despite the frigid air conditioning.

"You remember the date so clearly. Like we remember where we were when Kennedy was shot and on 9/11." Bobby turned to his partner and said, "Isn't that a little strange, Danny?"

"Not really, if the date has significance."

"Give me a break! I'm a reporter. We remember time and date. I was in New York City."

"So, maybe you took a few days off and drove to Daytona."

"I didn't own a car. I traveled on the Greyhound bus."

"Let's not squabble about details. Did you kill Diane and Tammy Martin?"

Doug Dillon's face turned red.

"Answer the question, Doug. Although, a DNA sample will clear things up," said Bobby.

"We're done here," said Doug Dillon and he stormed out of the room.

Danny smiled when he picked up the water bottle Doug had left behind.

* * * * *

Frank Webb's wife had been dead one thousand four hundred and sixty days, and his no longer missing daughter had been gone ten thousand nine hundred and fifty-eight days. But Joy was back. It had been a long heartache. He was expecting Roxanne to phone and picked up right away when the phone rang.

"Mr. Webb, it's Ray Atwood from DBPD."

"Just say good morning, Ray. You think I'm so old and decrypted I can't recognize your voice? And suddenly, I'm Mr. Webb. What's going on?"

"You need to come down to answer a few questions."

"Must be a communications problem, Bobby already paid me a visit, and recorded my version of what happened."

"It's more complicated, Frank."

"Right, an invitation. I would be stupid to refuse."

"How about I pick you up in an hour?"

"Great, that'll give me time to shit, shower and shave."

* * * * *

When Frank got in the truck, Ray said, "You clean up well."

"Very funny, but I'm not laughing."

Ray remembered how they met. Swerving while under the influence, Frank was stopped, and the rookie cop recognized him, as a teacher of the year, and drove him home. They probably would have been father and son-in-law.

"Joy told me about Jason."

"Let's focus on the Martin case."

"So, you think I'm guilty too."

Ray did not answer. The accusations had taken a toll and Frank looked old.

Baumgardner greeted them at the front desk and followed them to an interrogation room. Ray sat opposite Frank and Scott alongside Ray.

"Baumgardner will do the interview."

"Why so official, Ray?" Frank scratched his head. "Damn. This feels like a TV police show. Are we rehearsing or is this the real deal? Spit it out, suspect or person of interest? Either way, I have nothing to hide and don't need or want a lawyer. I want you clowns to get the monkey off my back."

"It's not that simple, Frank," said Ray.

"Does that mean I can refuse to answer?"

Baumgardner tapped a pencil on the table.

"New evidence opened the case, cold or not. That's Joy's doing, holding on to a necklace for this long. And then the remains found out of state got a second look. Well, if there is a match it will give the family closure."

"What do the remains have to do with me?" Frank cracked his knuckles. "I've explained the necklace."

"You're not overjoyed your daughter is alive. Perhaps it's because the evidence points at you and you're guilty. Now is your opportunity to come clean."

"This is ridiculous. I had nothing to do with their disappearance. Ask away."

"The night in question, the night Diane Martin came to your door. The night Joy watched from her bedroom window as the three of you got in your car and drove away. What happened?"

"I explained all this to Bobby."

"Well explain it one more time for me, please, Mr. Webb," said Baumgardner.

"Drop the Mr. Webb." Frank shook his head from side to side. "Diane was a student of mine, graduated class of 1974, married Tommy Martin right out of high school. Tommy enlisted in the army that summer. He came back to a New Year's Eve baby girl, named Tammy.

"The marriage broke up when he learned the truth and jumped ship. I had no clue. We hadn't seen each other in years. She came to tell me that night. We dropped Tammy at her friend's, then got coffee at Dunkin Donuts, and sat in the car talking. I wasn't about to leave Mary Elizabeth but gave her rent money, three hundred dollars cash."

"That's a lot of money. Where did you get three hundred dollars, Frank?" Ray asked.

"Working with Glen Ritchey's band, The Mustangs. We performed Saturday nights at the Best Western Aku Tiki Inn. I was on keyboard, did some singing." Frank grew distant from the memory and smiled. "The cash covered the extras a teacher's salary couldn't."

"You mean the Best Western on A1A with that huge Tiki God head statue in the front?"

"That's the place."

Ray took the peace necklace out of its pouch, put it on the table, and said, "And what about this? The necklace Diane Martin was known to wear."

Frank shook his head.

"It was a rough time. I was having an affair and drinking heavily. I knew it was wrong. Joy thought the worst of me, I could see it in her eyes. Yeah, I gave that necklace to Diane."

His tone grew angry.

"Yeah, she always wore it. So, I bought one like her mother's, for Tammy, but never gave it to her because they went missing. I told Bobby, it must have fallen out of my pants pocket and landed under the chair where Joy found it."

"Sounds plausible, Mr. Webb, however, you had motive."

"Call me Frank. We've been talking on the phone for years and didn't you have me arrested? What possible reason would I have to want them dead?"

"Perhaps Diane Martin threatened to tell your wife and was going to blow up your world."

"That isn't true."

"So, you said, but you could be lying."

"I'm not lying. I did not kill Diane and Tammy Martin, and I wasn't the last person to see them alive. They were seen the following morning while I was teaching."

"You said that too, but you still could be lying."

"But I'm not. What do I have to do to prove it?"

"Give a DNA sample, Frank. That'll make everything easier."

Frank looked at Ray and then back at Baumgardner and said, "You got it! Do I spit in a cup? You can swab my cheek, stick something up my nose. If proving I'm Tammy's father proves I'm innocent, go for it."

"A cheek swab is the most reliable," said Ray.

When Danny left the room to get a kit, Ray followed out to the hall.

"Frank Webb says Diane Martin never wore this necklace, that Joy is wrong about it being evidence. Send the necklace to be checked for Diane Martin's DNA. Let's find out if the experts think it's as clean as Frank is touting."

Ray cracked his neck from side to side.

"Send Doug Dillon's water bottle left in the interrogation room, too."

"Don't we need his permission?"

"I don't. Do you?"

Chapter 22

Meet Me at Betty's

With Carrie's encouragement, I phoned Ray and he agreed to meet at Rockefeller Gardens. When I arrived, Ray opened my car door, got in, and handed me a beer.

The temperature was above one hundred and we sat in the vehicle with the air conditioning blowing loud enough to discourage conversation, not that it mattered, Ray was not talking. After a few minutes, he said, "Let's walk." I bit my bottom lip, as a reminder to follow Carrie's advice and not say a word, listen.

We walked along the river like so many times before. Except this time there was no hand-holding and no laughter. I forced images of our recent reconciliatory lovemaking out of my mind.

"I hate you, Joy. When you asked to meet today, my first thought was there was nothing left to say. It has been one belly punch after another."

His eyes met mine, and he looked away quickly.

"First it was, you're alive and your dad's a murderer. You forgot to mention you were pregnant! Oops … correction … the baby was adopted, and guess what? We're Facebook friends. And then … the icing on the cake … 'Ray, you're going to be a grandpa.'"

I squelched the urge to defend myself and yell, "How was I to know Jason and his wife were pregnant?"

He drained the beer and crushed the empty can in one fluid motion.

"I hate you, but sometimes I don't."

His rant ended with silence. I listened to the crunch of pebbles under our feet as we walked and embraced the slight breeze that filled the void, but desperately wanted him to hold my hand, to suggest we might work things out … but he didn't.

"Tell me about the gender reveal party," he said.

My heart leaped with hope, but I was stunned to hear the words repeated behind us, like an echo.

"Tell me about the gender reveal party," said Doug Dillon.

A photographer with a bazooka-size long lens had an elbow on the hood of a car as he recorded our every move from across the grass in the parking lot. With his notebook in hand, Doug persisted in his questioning.

"Are you pregnant?"

With a prize fighter's skill, Ray delivered a punch to Doug's chin, then stepped over his body and grabbed my hand. As the photographer raced toward us, Ray yelled, "Tell your buddy to lose the story!"

When we got to our cars, Ray held me close to his chest. I absorbed the slight scent of moisture on his neck, pleased he had come to my defense.

As we caught our breath, he said, "Are you all right?"

I was better than all right. I was hopeful. Although Doug Dillon was a thorn in our sides, he had brought us together.

"Meet me at Betty's."

* * * * *

When I saw Ray sitting in the restaurant, I felt young and in love. Checkered tablecloths and plastic bread baskets still decorated the place. Nautical hats and life preservers hung on the walls. Toothpicks were available in a large conch shell by the cash register. Nothing had changed.

As I approached the table his eyes suggested I looked attractive while his lips said, "I ordered." Which meant, I was having a medium-done burger on a bun with lettuce and tomato, no onion and coleslaw.

"Do you think Doug Dillon will follow us?" I said and took a seat facing the window.

"If he does, I'll see him," he said and moved a cold beer onto my paper placemat.

With his back in the corner, Ray could see the entrance and the kitchen door.

"Why is he tailing me? It's spooky." I checked around to be sure the creep was not hiding somewhere.

"You went missing, were presumed dead, then showed up unexpectedly and accused your father of murder. He's going to ask questions."

Our food arrived. He squeezed ketchup on his fries, smiled when I stole a few, and said, "He's looking for a story and you provided one by dangling a necklace."

"Do you think he knows about Jason?" I asked, stealing another French fry.

His smile faded. Way back when our relationship had been playful, today it was fragile and I returned the fry to his plate.

"How could he? I just found out about Jason." He paused. "We were interrupted before you told me about the gender reveal party."

"Right, I've been invited but only because Bryce and Scarlet, my stepkids, will be there and we haven't seen each other for a while."

I bit into the hamburger and the mayonnaise fell into my lap. I thought about all the times I pretended not to be his mother when he hung out with Bryce or slept over. Their friends called me mom, rather than Mrs. Garner or Joy. I teased the boys, gave advice on how to get a date, and made a heart-shaped cake on Valentine's Day. We had rubber glove fights and when other friends asked about them, Bryce simply said, "You had to be there."

"Oh … we're not going together?" he said, sounding surprised.

I sensed a sometimes-I-hate-you moment coming and became cautious.

"I assumed I'd go alone. Jason doesn't know I'm his mother," I used a paper napkin to remove the tomato that had followed the mayo to my lap.

"Well, I just assumed you were going to tell him. He knows I'm his father." He emphasized assumed and crunched down on a dill pickle.

"Ray, people in New York don't know we were romantically involved and have a child. This event is to celebrate a pregnancy and announce the sex of the child." I spoke as compassionately as I could.

"Celebrate a pregnancy like you did?"

He shifted in the chair, and I thought he would leave, but he did not. I remembered the doctor confirming I was pregnant and me crying. His nurse handed me booklets for abortion clinics and told me things would be fine. She knew a pastor if I wanted spiritual guidance.

"I'm sorry," I said. Sorry flew out of my mouth without a thought. "You were focused on your career, not ready to be a father. I was alone."

"It's no longer about you, Joy." He pushed his plate aside. "Damn it! I have a grown son who isn't talking to me and it hurts."

Our conversation had become heated and heads turned in our direction.

"Maybe we need to ask for the check." I signaled for the waitress.

Ray threw his napkin on the table as though he agreed and was ready to leave but, instead leaned back from the table, sighed, and said, "Let's not do this, Joy."

"How's everything?" The waitress asked. "You need a to-go box?"

"No, we'll have two more beers," said Ray.

The sun softened in the sky. "I was wrong. I had made assumptions and never allowed you to prove otherwise."

It was as though I ripped off my bulletproof vest. Ray sat quietly, and I continued.

"It was wrong not to tell you. Perhaps I was the one not ready. I don't know... But how can we move past this?"

His eyes scanned the room and I wondered if the answer was out there. His cheek bulged as he rubbed his tongue inside his mouth.

"We need to go to the gender reveal party together."

Chapter 23

The Letter

Jason Dolan sat at his desk with the office door closed and studied the newly created file. Most staffers shared the opinion that Connie, the receptionist, often overstepped boundaries. However, Jason did not feel that way. Connie had been the first hire at Dolan & Dolan and was considered family. She had clipped the New York Times photo of him and Ray Atwood and filed it discreetly. He was thankful she had and understood why. She knew Officer Atwood was Jason's biological father.

Jason more than resembled Ray. The similarities were shocking, and more than likely the reason for Jason's reaction. But, texting Ray not to come to the law office again, well that was impulsivity that he'd been warned about.

He didn't know why he overreacted. He powered up his personal computer and searched Google. Officer Atwood, originally from California, settled in Daytona Beach, Florida after being discharged from the Air Force in Jacksonville. He had been married briefly. There was no mention of children. Several pictures of the International Speedway popped up as Jason read. He imagined a younger Ray and pondered contacting him when there was a knock on his door.

"Jason, have you got a minute?" said Matthew Dolan as he

entered the room. "I thought we'd talk strategy for the Sweats Treats case."

Jason sighed and gestured to his adoptive father to take a chair.

"We can do this later if something else is on your mind," commented the senior Dolan.

Jason hesitated, "Actually, there is." He shut his computer down.

Matthew was a great father, the kind Jason hoped to be. But what if Ray Atwood had raised him? An image of Ray Atwood holding a toddler's hand and walking on a beach flew across his mind.

"An officer came to see me." Jason leaned back in his chair.

"Connie mentioned it, an inquiry about a cold case in Daytona Beach. You've never been there, or have you?" Matthew removed his glasses and polished them with a cloth he found in a pocket.

"Is he, my father?" The room became quiet as the question settled and waited for Jason to continue. "I know my mother didn't want to be a single mom but what can you tell me about my father?"

"Not much. It was a private adoption. We dealt with your mother exclusively."

"You know who my mother is?"

"Of course, she stayed in our house in Montauk until you were born. She left a letter for you if you ever asked about her. To be honest, I thought you would have asked long ago, but you never did."

Jason tipped his chair back, sighed, and closed his eyes, emotionally confused by his father's earnestness. Of course, he wanted to know but was afraid to ask. Matthew and Sara were wonderful parents. He had a charmed upbringing, every advantage coupled with deep love and understanding had been afforded him. He had never wanted to imply otherwise by suggesting they hadn't been enough. That something was missing, something only a biological parent could provide. So, he had never probed. One year on Father's Day, Jason almost inquired about his biological dad but didn't.

"Well, I'll ask now. Who is my mother?"

"The letter is in my safe," Matthew said and stood. "I'll get it."

When his father returned, he placed the letter on Jason's desk and said, "I'll give you some privacy. I'll be in my office."

"No, Dad. Stay."

The letter expanded in importance as Jason searched for an opener and then labored to break the seal.

Dearest Jason,

Close your eyes and feel my arms surround you with a love that will never let go. I hold you and pray I'm making the right decision. The Dolans are good people. When I put you in their arms, they checked for my hesitation, but I could not waiver, as I believe my certainty is a gift, I can give you both. My heart is breaking. If circumstances were different, I would raise you on my own. I hope someday you'll want to meet. Ask your parents where to find me.

Your loving mother, Joy Webb

Jason closed his eyes and felt his mother's love in the present, as though a cocoon enveloped him. "Joy Webb?" he asked. He opened his eyes. "Why is her name familiar?"

"You know her as Mrs. Garner," Matthew said.

"Bryce's and Scarlet's stepmother is my biological mother?"

Jason felt like he'd driven into the eye of a storm. He stood and circled the room many times, confused.

"And, you kept this letter in your safe for ... thirty years ... never thought to tell me I was sleeping over at my real mother's house. Did Mom ... know about this?"

"Of course, we had a legal agreement. Joy thought it best. None of us predicted you'd become friends with her stepchildren."

"If she was happy to have Bryce and Scarlet as her children, why wasn't she happy to keep me?"

"Joy was nineteen years old and thought you'd be better off. You are better off, aren't you?"

Jason slammed the door on his way out.

Chapter 24

The Rest of My Life

June 2014

ঽ

The overgrown hedges in Dad's yard were being yanked out, and the driveway power washed. His insistence the house be sold as is, had been revisited. The door was open and I let myself in, repeatedly checking for Doug Dillon's whereabouts. The walk from Carrie's was a mile but a better choice than parking out front.

I called out several times wondering if anyone was home. No one answered. I climbed the stairs to my bedroom to pack my Betty Boop collection. Carrie was right, my childhood mementos needed safe storage. The room opposite mine had been my mother's sewing room, and I peeked inside. Fabric organized according to the rainbow was stacked on open shelves. I ran my hand across a bundle and found a layer of dust, a reminder I should have come back sooner.

I was downstairs sorting things when Carrie surprised me with her new look. Her long grey hair was gone. It was now the chestnut color of her youth and styled in layers that framed her face.

"You cut and colored your hair!"

"Roxanne made me do it – said I looked old. She was right." She pirouetted around and her hair bounced. "Just had it done and why I'm late," she said with a big smile.

"You look great."

"Thanks, I feel great. So great, I'm thinking of dating, and finishing my art degree."

"What?" Her enthusiasm was obvious. "How did all this come about?"

"Roxanne had breakfast at the Maverick this morning and went on a rant about life expectancy. How someone my age will live to be eighty years or more, said I was halfway through my life. She asked if I planned to spend another forty years waitressing. I started thinking about the rest of my life while getting my hair done."

"The rest of your life?"

"Yeah, the rest of my life. Truthfully my life has been about getting by... my kids, you missing and more than likely dead. Now I have closure. The mystery is solved."

I studied Carrie's face. The hardness was gone.

"So, you forgive me?"

"No! I'm still angry. I'm furious you're alive and hate myself for feeling this way. I'm outraged that your mother never knew she was a grandmother, and died calling for you. And now thirty years later, thirty bleeping years, you dare to show up and expect things to be nice."

Carrie was out of breath from yelling and I wondered if she would forgive me, ever, but said nothing.

"Don't give me that sorry face," she said and continued. "You resent Dad leaving me the house like you were never dead. It's hurtful."

"I apologize. It makes perfect sense that you get the house. I hardly need the money."

"There you go again. Hardly need the money!" Carrie stood up and put her hands on her hips. "How condescending."

"I only meant you'll be in good shape. You own your house and Dad will leave you his," I said trying to defend myself.

"Shit Joy, you haven't a clue." Carrie shook her head. "I've re-financed so many times I owe more now than when I bought the rundown shack. What if Dad needs a reverse mortgage to get by? You must have been living in La La Land, not New York City."

Our slapping incident was fresh in my mind. I wanted to say, what if he's guilty, and spends time in jail, but didn't and was relieved to hear the front door open.

"Are you two at it again?" Dad said as he carried groceries into the kitchen.

Roxanne was behind him and said, "I love what you've done with your hair, Carrie."

Laptop peeked out of her handbag and yapped as though he agreed. I watched them squeal with delight and explanations of what the new hairdo had done. Their laughter changed the atmosphere, and I found myself in the kitchen, the three of us having a glass of wine and discussing dinner. My suspicions about Dad slipped away.

Dad searched in the refrigerator for another beer, popped the can, and said, "I bought a house in Crane Lakes. The closing is in a few weeks."

"We were just talking about houses, weren't we Carrie?" I desperately wanted to put the hurt behind us.

"Yup, Joy understands why you willed the house and anything else to me."

My head spun from the highs and lows. I felt as though my return was being paved with hot tar; over and over, a roller pressed the past into a pavement. I was at a breaking point but hoped to soothe the wounds.

I said, "I do."

The words rang out as they do during a wedding ceremony.

Roxanne chopped a carrot, celery stalk, and small onion feverishly.

"This is called the trio in cooking circles, and the base for many sauces."

She dumped the vegetables in a heated fry pan and they sizzled.

"Joy may understand, but I don't Frank," said Roxanne.

"We thought Joy was dead," Frank said

"Dead? What made you think that?"

"Miss Smarty-pants assumed I killed Diane Martin and disappeared," said Frank.

"I thought you were estranged over her pregnancy?" Roxanne deglazed the pan with wine.

"Nope, Joy came home to accuse me of murder. I told you about being arrested."

Roxanne straightened her back and repositioned her hips as she stirred the pot.

"You did. I thought it was a joke. We laughed about it."

"It is a joke and the DNA will prove I'm innocent."

He brushed Roxanne's cheek with a kiss. "Holler when dinner's ready, I'll be watching the game."

I pressed my lips together and stepped aside as Dad left the room.

Roxanne said, "Are you free for lunch tomorrow, Joy?"

"I am," I said, a little surprised by her request.

"Great. How about the River Grill at noon? We can get to know each other better."

* * * * *

The following morning, Lucky lapped water from a bowl while I listened to a voicemail message from Matthew Dolan. I was surprised by what he said.

"Hope you're well. Jason read your letter and is in shock. He phoned Bryce and Scarlet and told them you are his biological mother."

His long sigh prepared me for what came next.

"I've been asked to uninvite you to the gender reveal party." He sighed again. "I'm sorry, Joy, but it would be awkward."

His hang-up lingered in my ear as I hurried to shower and dress for lunch with Roxanne. The disappointment clouded my thoughts and confusion as to what to tell Ray. I was holding on to the notion we would attend together and things would work out.

A realtor sign magnetized to the car door meant Roxanne had arrived at The River Cafe. I parked alongside her hoping she was early and I wasn't late. Her bold animal print dress and large sun hat drew my attention and I hurriedly joined her at an outside table.

"Thanks for asking me to lunch," I said and hugged her.

"I wanted to hear your side of the story." She removed her sunglasses as two Dirty Martinis arrived.

"My side of the story?"

"Yes. Why do you think he's guilty of something? Frank

swears he's innocent."

"Dad lied about being with the Martins, and when I found myself pregnant, I fled to New York City. No one noticed I was gone until an unpaid tuition bill arrived in the mail."

"Oh, my," Roxanne commented several times.

"Frank jokes about going to jail. Do you think he's guilty?"

"I did at the time, but now I feel foolish about the suspicions. I guess my pride needs DNA proof. I don't know what to think. My dad's not the only person of interest. Ray's not talking about the case."

On my second drink I shared how Ben died, my decision to come back, Ray's plea to be an active grandfather, and most recently, being uninvited to the gender reveal party.

I chugged the last of my drink. "And then there's Charles."

A freight train traveling the tracks along the Halifax River blew its horn as she said, "Let's order something to eat. Who's Charles?"

"A gentleman I met in Savannah."

"Are you in love with Ray?"

"Yes. I love him, but he's angry. Things are worse than ever and I don't know what to do. Are you in love with my father?"

Roxanne cleared her throat, and said, "Have you thought about the rest of your life?"

"People don't usually kiss their realtor, even friendly ones."

"You're what? Forty-something? You could live another forty years."

Her comments smacked me. "No! My life is pretty much over. I have no future with Ray."

"We can't predict the future. You don't know that. Get Jason to talk with him."

"How would that help?" I said, wiping my tears and laughing at the same time.

"Ray is happy he has a son and wants a relationship with the young man."

"Roxanne, Jason's not talking to me either. I have so many regrets."

Roxanne removed her sunglasses. "Joy, that's a victim's mentality. Try imagining your life without regret. Call Matthew Dolan, and see if he'll help."

Her words were a lightning bolt. The sun came out from behind a cloud, blinding me.

"What would I even say?"

"Start with the truth."

She put her glasses back on.

We ordered coffee and apple pie alamode and talked some more. She never answered my question about my father. I mulled that and everything else over while driving to Carrie's, prepared to have a good heart-to-heart. Instead, I found a note and Lucky. When I unloaded my worries on him, he gave me his puppy dog look and licked my face.

* * * * *

In the morning, I phoned Matthew Dolan and told him the truth.

"Ray never knew I was pregnant and, being as young as I was, I believed he was better off not knowing. Please ... talk to Jason, persuade him to meet with me. Ray's not the one he should be angry with."

Matthew said, "I'll do my best and get back to you."

When his number flashed on my cell screen, I answered before it could ring twice.

"Jason will meet with you, but it has to be a public place."

Chapter 25

Tyrannosaurus Rex

ↄ

The Museum of Natural History was an odd place to meet, but when Matthew Dolan suggested the location, I agreed. Florida's heat was becoming bothersome, and the kids were out of school.

City schools would still be in session, the museum not crowded, and the weather cooler. I told Dad I needed to attend to a few legal issues with Ben's estate, and asked Roxanne and Carrie not to say otherwise.

Matthew said to wait for him by Tyrannosaurus Rex. I had been there a zillion times with my stepkids but, the huge dinosaur still astounded me. Thousands of fossil bones had been reclaimed and wired to form the creature that had once roamed the United States. I felt like a nervous spectator looking up at King Kong on top of The Empire State Building.

My thoughts were interrupted by Matthew and Jason Dolan walking toward me. The last time I saw Jason was at his wedding. His growing resemblance to Ray was striking as he came closer. I had pretended he was not my son for so long, when he addressed me as, Mom, the room whirled as though I was gliding across ice. The next thing I remembered was sitting on a wooden bench.

"There's a café downstairs. Perhaps we should get something to eat," said Matthew Dolan.

His voice sounded distant. "Fresh air might be the best medicine; can we walk outside?" I asked, but felt unsteady on my feet.

We went down on the escalator, passed the floor-to-ceiling aquarium, and stopped to see the large fish, so I could regain my balance.

During his teen years, Jason called me mom, an alternative to Mrs. Garner, as all the kids did. Things are different now. He knew I was his biological mother and hurt and confusion appeared in his eyes.

Outside, Jason slipped his arm through mine and commented. "We don't want you to fall."

"I'm sure you both have a lot to talk about," said Matthew curbside and explained he would get a taxi. I was surprised but grateful. Jason was receptive to being alone with me. I waited for him to start the conversation, and he did once we found a bench.

"I read your letter."

The heartache of writing the letter came back to me. Every word had been carefully chosen, and the deep-down pain of saying goodbye to him surfaced with a vengeance.

"You know, all of Scarlet's and Bryce's friends liked you." He smiled. "Especially me. You were cool. It's spooky that you watched me grow up and never said a word. Why?"

Needing a moment to find the truth, I searched my handbag for a tissue.

"Fear."

Although I wasn't positive that was the truth.

"You had a good life. I wasn't going to be the one to change things."

Now that was the truth.

"Why did you give me up in the first place?"

The memory of placing Jason in Sara Dolan's arms washed over me and I didn't answer the question.

He continued. "You've heard about open adoption – I'm sure."

He didn't appear as patient as he had been a few minutes before.

"Now this Ray dude shows up and claims to be my father. What's that all about?"

Ray's appearance outside of Federal Plaza had been the equivalent of dropping a hand grenade in Jason's lap.

"Ray never knew he fathered you until recently."

I worried any explanation might be more damaging and selected my next words cautiously.

"If he'd known, he would have married me because he had to." I paused. "I didn't want that. Supporting you on my own? Well, I was young and thought adoption was a better choice. I was wrong."

I watched his face absorb the argument, as a lawyer would, so I struggled to find another way to emphasize the point.

"Imagine you're a freshman in college, and your girlfriend gets pregnant. What would you or she have done?"

"I don't know. I don't ... know."

A mother doesn't want to tell a child they were an accident or simply a mistake, but I did.

"I was on the pill."

I left out all the complications of my father's involvement with the Martins. His eyes appeared sympathetic.

"I'll understand if you don't want a future relationship with me, but ... please don't punish your father for what I did. Allow him to know you."

Jason shook his head.

"Put yourself in his shoes. Is it possible you have a child you don't know about?"

He appeared to give the notion thought before he said, "I'll think about it."

The Dolans had raised Jason to be a fine young man. I hoped Ray and I would have a relationship with him in the future. When he walked away, I noticed his left shoulder drooped slightly, just like Ray's.

The uninvite to the party was not discussed. The reaction of Ben's children and their mother, Jackie, to learning the truth appeared in my mind like a twenty-one-gun salute. There was no more pretending.

On the plane ride back to Daytona Beach, I thought about Carrie's plans for the rest of her life. What would the rest of my life be like? I fantasized Jason and his wife would vacation with Ray and me in Daytona. We would build sand castles. Visit the art museum where Carrie's work was displayed, and have dinner at Racing's North Turn Restaurant. All of us together, including Dad and Roxanne.

Then, I bumped into Doug Dillon leaving the car rental desk.

"Are you still following me?" I demanded.

"No. My car was stolen, and this is the closest rental spot. Chill, Joy."

Mud stains covered the knees of his khaki slacks. His eyes were bloodshot. He seemed surprised to see me, and I felt sorry for the jerk. My cell phone pinged. I pulled it out to discover a message from Jason.

> *My wife and I discussed the situation, and have de-*
> *cided not to pursue a relationship with you or Ray At-*
> *wood. We don't need any drama at this emotional*
> *time.*
>
> *Regards, Jason*

I was devastated and dizzy. A blue color blurred my thinking. The memory of Sara Dolan bringing that blue baby bunting to the delivery room and insisting it replace the handmade quilt I had made stabbed me, I called out.

"Is everything all right? You don't look good," said creepy Doug.

Doug Dillon was the last person with whom I was going to share my pain.

"It's a leg cramp," I said and stumbled to a chair, feeling lightheaded.

"If you think you have problems, think again. Not only did my car get stolen, but your boyfriend wants my DNA to rule me out of the Martin case," he said in a way-too-loud voice.

He wiped the sweat from his forehead with a dirty handkerchief, like I'd seen before. Referencing Ray as my boyfriend brought me to my senses.

"Boyfriend? You don't know that."

"It was in the archives. Joy Webb, fiancée of Officer At-wood."

He morphed into a reporter as if he'd had a caffeine jolt and was on the hunt. I let him fire away.

"Your dad must be a person of interest, too. They wanted his

DNA, and he gave it willingly. Big mistake, he'll be in the system, and all kinds of shit can happen."

I thought about his beat-up car and assumed he probably had to work. But then I reminded myself that my assumptions about people's lives had turned out wrong. Perhaps he was a millionaire and had money in the bank. I didn't know whether he was married or had children. Perhaps he had nobody to go home to and was just waiting around for a Pulitzer Prize story. I wondered what he was going to do with the rest of his life. But I knew I wanted Jason, Ray, and my dad in mine. There would be no regret.

Chapter 26

Frank Tries to be Nice

ॐ

Outside the Morningside Drive house things looked different. The house had been painted a cheery shade my mother called lemonade. The door had a fresh coat of another favorite, robin's egg blue. The walkway stains, dead shrubs, and weeds were gone.

But dreariness, like a hangover after seeing Jason and Matthew, lingered. Reconciliation seemed like a fantasy. Roxanne's advice to call Matthew, hoping he could persuade Jason to meet, worked. But Tyrannosaurus Rex? It was ironic; the size of the dinosaur indicated the challenge ahead. It was a miracle Jason met with me after reading my letter. I had betrayed and deceived both father and son.

My life was a mess. I wanted to phone Charles. His was a dependable love, and I hadn't deceived him ... yet.

I turned off the car engine and went into the house. Dad came into the living room towel drying his hair. His snappy appearance caught me by surprise. I suspected Roxanne had taken him shopping.

"Well, look who's back," he said and gave me a peck on my cheek.

I smiled, "Are you going out? I can come back."

"No. Roxanne is coming by. I'm going to sign the papers to put the house for sale. How was your visit to New York City?"

There was no sarcasm in his voice. The circles under his eyes seemed less dark. I did not mention Matthew and Jason, and being uninvited to the gender reveal party. The conversation would require more explanation around him becoming a great-grandfather and I lacked the energy to do so.

"You cleaned up the outside and painted. I thought you were selling as is."

"I didn't do a thing. Blame Roxanne. That woman is quite a salesman, or saleswoman or salesperson. I never know what to call a girl today, pick the politically correct one."

He tossed the damp towel on his recliner before walking into the kitchen and said, "How about a cup of coffee? I have a crumb cake."

The Entenmann's bakery box on the table triggered a slew of forgotten pleasant memories. The family gathered after Sunday Mass, visiting aunts and uncles arrived with the bakery crumb cake during Bike Week or for holidays. I had forgotten the laughter, singing, and dancing the Lindy. I recalled doing the Cha-Cha with my father and teared up. Only a month ago he'd been alone in the house, drinking – a bitter aging man. Today he appeared to be sober and happy.

"Are you all right?" He sounded concerned.

"Why are you being nice?" His kindness scared and comforted me, simultaneously.

"You're my daughter and you're alive. I can be nice. You got a problem with that?"

I did, but kept quiet and brewed coffee while he set the table. He found the cream in the refrigerator and searched the cupboards for paper plates and napkins. It felt awkward.

Once we were seated at the table he said, "I've spent many years being angry and depressed – lonely years. I want to enjoy the time I have left." He choked up. "I just wish your mother were alive."

I felt the same way and remembered him talking to Mom's empty chair – a lonely man.

After clearing his throat, he said, "Joy, I forgive you for running away and making these crazy accusations." He stirred sugar into his cup of coffee.

My jaw dropped. "You forgive me?" I glanced at him sideways.

"Roxanne told me to say that," he said with food in his mouth.

"Roxanne told you to say that? You're not mad?"

"Damn it, Joy." He exploded. "This isn't easy for me."

His outburst was like an ignited firecracker going off, and so reminiscent of my childhood, that it made me jump. I leaned back in the chair with my eyes closed to compose myself as he continued.

"Of course, I'm mad. Mad as hell. People get angry with each other, Joy. People fight. They make up. Your mother and I fought." His clenched fist reminded me of how he would bang on the table. "It was wrong, and I'm sorry."

He unclenched his hand and reached for a napkin. "Your mother suffered from depression after you were born. Today it's called postpartum." He wiped the crumbs off his chin and sighed. "If she'd had some of those happy pills the doctor's got me on, things might have been different." He sighed again, heavily.

His acknowledgment of his poor behavior paled compared to mine. I gathered the courage to speak up, and as Roxanne cautioned, you're not a victim.

"Dad, I appreciate your apology, but let's be honest. It was screaming and yelling at the top of your lungs. You threw things and punched in walls. Mom hid in the bedroom, and I would escape to Carrie's guilty about leaving her alone." I sat up in the chair. "She didn't have the strength to leave you and withdrew into darkness."

He got up from the table and stood at the sink with his back to me.

"That was the alcohol," he paused, then continued. "I didn't know it affected you so badly. I don't remember much about that time in our lives, only that I was disappointed in myself. I betrayed your mother, and she knew it. I drank the pain away. It was selfish of me." He turned around with tears in his eyes, and said, "I forgive you. But can you forgive me?"

The validation felt horrible, like jumping from ice mass to ice mass in a thawing lake, while the sun warmed me. I stuffed my tears, afraid he'd call me a crybaby and taunt me like he did during my teen years. How could I be sure he was sincere? Ben had once remarked, "Joy, you're an adult child of an alcoholic." At the time, I glossed over it. Now, I realized what he wanted to tell me and put a hand over my mouth to stifle the sobs.

"I didn't associate your missing with Diane Martin's disappearance. I feared you had been snatched. Now you explained things... being pregnant and all, I understand. I had nothing to do with Diane and Tammy missing. The DNA results proved it."

"The DNA proved it?" I repeated his words.

"Yes. Ray didn't tell you? There'll be a taped TV press release. I'm ready to go on with my life," he said. "Selling the house... Meeting Roxanne, well I've got a different view on life. I'm too old to waste one more minute holding a grudge, and I want something good for you too, Joy – for the rest of your life."

He sounded like the father I always dreamed of. The father I remembered as a young child. The rest of our lives had been suddenly elevated and more important than the past. My life was going nowhere. I wanted to tell him about my troubles. Ask for his advice. But remembered his lies, the dog story, his never telling the police Tammy Martin was his daughter, and that he gave them money and drove them home. A voice echoed in my head: *Keep your mouth shut*. And I did.

The conversation ended when the doorbell rang and Roxanne let herself in. Laptop escaped from her tote bag and began to dance around the house, creating laughter and excitement. I wiped my eyes, went to the cupboard for another cup, then turned around, smiled, and said, "Roxanne, I'm glad you're here. Coffee?"

"Of course, and crumb cake." She greeted Dad with a kiss and said, "The house is the perfect shade of yellow. It shows much better on a sunny day. Mary Elizabeth called it lemonade, right? And the door color, perfect, too." She plopped a large folder on the table.

"Welcome back, Joy ... How are Jason and the gender reveal party invitation coming along?"

"What's a gender reveal party," asked Dad.

"When a couple is pregnant, they have a party to announce the sex of the expected child," explained Roxanne.

"My grandson is pregnant?"

"No, his wife."

"You mean, Joy is going to be a grandmother, Ray a grandfather, and me a great-grand whatever? And Roxanne will be great-grand significant other?"

He slapped his thigh and laughed.

"Let's get this party started."

I glanced at my mother's empty chair. Their wedding picture had been packed. The China cabinet emptied.

"It's not like that, Dad. Jason learned Ray and I are his biological parents recently and wants nothing to do with us."

"Don't be ridiculous. Everyone wants to know their roots. He'll be thrilled he has many aunts, uncles, and cousins living on the other side of the Hudson River. Give me his number, I'll set him straight."

"Dad he won't even talk to Ray. And Ray is barely talking to me."

"Then I'll talk to Ray. We were close at one time. Your mother and I attended his wedding to Michelle. After they divorced Ray came alone to Sunday dinner."

His comment reminded me of what I'd missed, and how my disappearance had changed lives. I imagined a photo of Ray, Jason, and me, framed on a shelf in the living room. If only I hadn't run away. The accusations I'd brought back with me melted away. My father gave me a heartfelt look.

"You'd do that for me?"

"For us, Joy," he said sincerely.

* * * * *

Roxanne smiled, as Frank kissed his daughter goodbye.

When Joy hugged her, Roxanne whispered. "Call me, I want to hear about New York."

After Joy left, Frank became serious and said, "Roxanne, do you mind if we sign the paper's tomorrow? Something else is on my mind."

"Are you getting cold feet about selling? I'm not going to marry you to close the deal."

"I'm selling and marriage isn't the only thing on my mind. No, can you teach me about Google?

"You want to Google?" She roared in a fit of laughter.

"What's so funny? All I hear about is Google this, Google that. Damn it! I want to Google Jason. See what he looks like and all that jazz.

"You'd probably find more pictures on Facebook. But do you own a cell, computer, or tablet?"

"Be serious, I thought a cell was for prisoners, and the only reference to a tablet I know about was in the movie, *The Ten Commandments*, starring Burt Lancaster."

"Tomorrow, we'll sign the papers and go shopping."

* * * * *

"It's been a good day, Mary Elizabeth," said Frank, after Roxanne left.

He reclined in his chair drinking a cold one.

"I wish you were here. Joy and I are getting along. She reminds me of you. But what I want to tell you is ... I put the house up for sale."

He waited for Mary Elizabeth's reaction, then powered through the silence.

"There's a big hullabaloo about the Cadillac Eldorado. Remember buying the Cadillac Eldorado when I retired? We'd accepted Joy's disappearance and you didn't have cancer yet." He sighed. "Remember the smell of a brand-new car, and driving west on Route 66 to California – Chinatown in San Francisco and Las Vegas."

He had his eyes closed and a smile on his face.

"I can still picture your screaming like a manic as the quarters came flying out.

"The realtor, Roxanne ... I told you about Roxanne? ... She says it's an eyesore," he mumbled and fell asleep.

Chapter 27

Case Closed

ঔ

"We did it. We closed the Martin case," Bobby said. Ray was startled by Bobby Smart's hand on his shoulder and turned to face him.

"Yes, nice work. Congratulations!"

Ray had reviewed the reports earlier and the DNA results confirmed Frank's innocence and that Diane Martin's DNA was not on the necklace. Thanks to new technology and the establishment of the National DNA database, a forensic anthropologist reviewed the Martin case and told the cold case unit they needed a DNA sample from Tammy Martin's father. Frank Webb had complied, and the results were back. The body had been identified and the squad knew who the killer was.

"Are we going to go tell Frank Webb?" Bobby inquired.

"Might as well," said Ray.

Ray parked his truck on Morningside Drive. A Camry with a realtor sign magnetized on the car door was in the driveway. He and Bobby walked to the door as Doug Dillon arrived in his beat-up car.

"What's he doing here? Does he know he's no longer a person of interest?"

"With his insider connections, probably. Dillon's a snake in the grass." Ray rang the doorbell.

Frank answered the door with a pen in his hand. "Hey Ray," he said, surprised to see the two officers. "What's going on? Must be something official since you brought Mr. Smart along."

Roxanne joined Frank in the living room, and he introduced her to the men.

"Bobby, we met years ago at a Chamber of Commerce luncheon. I was a lot thinner," Roxanne said and shook his hand.

"And I had a lot more hair."

Ray interrupted the pleasantries. "We can come back if this isn't a good time."

"No, not at all," said Frank. "I'm signing papers to buy a place in Crane Lakes. I'll put Morningside Drive on the market after I move, right Roxanne?"

The living room was filled with boxes. "That's why you're packing up. Danny Egan loves living there."

"That's what Roxanne tells me; everyone loves living there. You know a Danny Egan, Roxanne? He's a retired cop." He did not wait for her answer, "Take a seat. Roxanne needs to hear the news. We're talking about our future."

"The DNA came back a match," said Ray. "You are Tammy Martin's biological father.

"So, is that good or bad news?" Frank asked.

"Good news!" Bobby confirmed. "The teenager's remains were found in Virginia on the property of a known killer, the Martin's neighbor's nephew, Jeffrey. The DNA wasn't a match to the father listed on her birth certificate and therefore the forensics was inconclusive. They couldn't be certain."

Roxanne gasped and put her hand to her mouth then turned her attention to Frank. He appeared to be relieved. Bobby gave a nod to Ray who continued explaining.

"When it became known that Frank and Tammy's mother had an affair, the missing pieces fell into place. Frank willingly gave a DNA sample that matched. The remains were from Tammy. The Martin family will have closure."

"Now I'm a hero!" Frank said.

"Kind of," Bobby added.

"This DNA stuff is hard to understand." Frank sat down next to Roxanne. "I bought that peace necklace to give to Tammy, so she'd have one like her mother's. Joy thought it was evidence I'd done something wrong."

Frank held Roxanne's hand and looked at Ray.

"If spitting into a cup proved my innocence, I'm happy."

Roxanne smiled slowly as Frank asked Ray, "Can this insanity be put to rest? Are we free to get on with our lives?"

Ray glanced toward the couple and said, "As a matter of fact, Frank, you are."

He was happy for the couple. He and Frank had been through a lot over the years. Ray wondered if Frank knew his grandson, Jason, wanted nothing to do with them.

Frank gave Roxanne a tender look. The past thirty years had been hell, starting with Joy's disappearance, and then the effort to make a life without her. There were some good times pretending to be happy, followed by the fight to keep Mary Elizabeth cancer-free. After her death, Frank succumbed to depression. The search for Joy was over and his guilt over his affair was put to rest.

"Let me walk you to the door," he said to Ray and Bobby.

The men shook hands. Frank said, "Joy's coming home and this whole revelation about Jason is mind-blowing." Ray nodded in agreement. "Joy was here earlier and I told her I'd talk to you about it." Ray looked surprised. "How about we go for a drink?"

"Sure, I'll give you a call sometime," said Ray.

"Better yet, how about you pick me up tomorrow around 5 p.m. and we go to Billy's?"

"Billy's? I haven't been there in ages. Sure thing!"

* * * * *

Outside Doug Dillon was waiting and called to Ray and Bobby.

"Is Frank Webb being arrested? Was his DNA a match?"

The punch Ray had delivered to the reporter's chin was fresh in his mind and Doug Dillon kept a respectable distance, as Ray and Bobby slipped into his truck. They heard him lament their lack of response and watched him in the rearview mirror.

The overweight out-of-shape reporter chased after them. "I'll quote that as a no comment, officers," he said.

The following morning's headline read, Cold Case Unsolved? The article announced the return of Joy Webb, who had been missing for thirty years and presumed dead, and speculated about visits from the DBPD to the family home. Ray Atwood was quoted as saying, "No comment."

Ray sipped a hot cup of coffee and then buzzed Baumgardner.

"Call Doug Dillon. Tell him the Martin case has been solved. We'll announce details at a press conference. Tell him it starts at eleven o'clock. Call the local TV stations, too, and see if Bobby and anyone else can get down here."

At exactly 11 a.m., Ray Atwood and Bobby Smart stood in the Daytona Beach Police Department lobby ready to answer questions. Doug Dillon stood with the audience of reporters. He had shaved, patted down his hair, and may have even pressed his shirt.

The room was crowded. Television cameras from Orlando News and WESH News decorated the room. Reporters, from The Daytona Beach News-Journal, The Orlando Sentinel, and other papers, had pad and pencil in hand.

Ray Atwood tapped the microphone for attention.

"Thank you for coming. Today's announcement is the culmination of the efforts of the Daytona's Cold Case Unit. They are a volunteer force. Detective Bobby Smart retired from Miami, Joe Bucci from Jersey City, and Danny Egan from NYPD. Joe and Danny couldn't be here today. But Detective Smart will fill you in, and answer any questions."

Bobby raised his hand to the crowd and stepped to the podium. Reporters jockeyed for a position close to the officer. Doug Dillon lingered in the back.

Bobby took a deep breath and continued.

"Diane Martin and her daughter, Tammy, were last seen walking to school the morning of May 10th in 1984. It is hard to imagine how the Martin family coped not knowing what happened to them for the past thirty years. This old case has always been about closure for the Martin family. We now know who the killer was."

Heads turned when Doug Dillon called out, "Is Frank Webb the killer?"

Bobby maintained his poker face but stared at the weasel in the back of the room.

"Ten years after the mother and daughter went missing, remains were found in Georgia on property owned by a neighbor of Diane Martin's. The neighbor's nephew, Jeffrey Hicks, traveled between Florida and Georgia for work but was never a person of interest at the time.

"Jeffrey Hicks was previously convicted of other murders, a serial killer who died in prison."

Quiet occupied the room followed by a buzz similar to swarming bees.

Doug Dillon pushed his way to the front and was the first to raise his hand.

"What took so long, detective? It's 2014?"

Bobby ignored the barrage of questions that followed.

"Forensics, DNA, and new technology solved this case. The creation of the National DNA database in 1998 and the consolidation of non-criminal DNA indexes from all fifty states and the District of Columbia to include missing persons gave investigators a possible match, which we now have. Thanks to a benefactor, Tammy Martin's remains will be coming home."

"Who is Tammy Martin's biological father?" Doug demanded as he wiped sweat beads off his forehead.

Bobby glanced at Ray before responding. "Confirmation of the biological father…"

Ray stepped into camera view.

"The Martin family has asked all media to respect their privacy at this emotional time, and want to thank the Cold Case Unit for their hard work and diligence in bringing this case to closure. That will be all."

Like a bulldog chasing after fleas, Doug shouted, "What about the Webb Cold Case? Detectives visited with Mr. Webb on several occasions. Was Frank Webb involved in the Martin case?"

Ray turned and walked away. Bobby followed.

"What about the Webb Cold Case?" Bobby asked Ray as they entered the conference room.

Ray walked with his head down, hiding his annoyance. His business was his business and not for public disclosure. He imagined the headline, Cold Case Detective Atwood Is Hot. The article would embellish Ray's reaction upon discovering he had a thirty-year-old fancy lawyer son in New York City.

"Joy is alive. Do we need to know why she went missing?"

"I guess we don't, boss. What about Dillon, he's always looking for a story?"

"That nuisance? Eventually he'll shoot himself in the foot."

"Someone else might shoot him. He's made more than a few enemies."

Ray said, "You think."

Chapter 28

Billy's Tap Room

ॐ

The bar crowd inside Billy's Tap Room was three-deep. The mirrored back wall reflected all the different faces. A skinny woman with drop earrings, clearly on the make, dominated the scene with loud laughter. Dark mahogany paneling and woodwork enhanced the musical conversations that dipped and ebbed throughout the room.

The grill was famous for its food and old-time friendly atmosphere. A fiddler tuned his instrument and tested the microphone as they walked in. It was early and the owner escorted Frank and Ray to a table although they hadn't come for dinner. Frank ordered a Guinness and Ray a double vodka on the rocks and they toasted the solving of the Martin case and Frank's innocence.

"God, I miss this joint. Mary Elizabeth and I frequented the place in the eighties. Maybe I'll bring Roxanne here to propose, not that she'll say yes."

His foot tapped to the music.

Frank toyed with the words to start the conversation he'd promised Joy he'd have. So much had happened while she was gone and yet it was as if she'd never been away.

"Any chance you and Joy will get back together?"

"No! Joy's return has me in a tailspin and now this."

Frank smiled at the man he'd known for thirty-plus years and wished Ray was his son. He'd settle for a son-in-law. He assumed that "now this" was a reference to Jason and the fact that Jason wouldn't agree to meet with Ray.

"It's a dream come true for me, even if the kid wants nothing to do with us. He'll come around once the baby is born."

Ray drained his glass and motioned for the waitress. "You ready for another beer?"

"Things change ... sometimes quickly. Put yourself in Jason's shoes. How would you react if your perfect life was turned upside down?"

"My life has been turned upside down, too. I'm angry with Joy. Sometimes ... I hate her."

"Yeah, but your life was never perfect, and if you didn't love her, you couldn't hate her."

Ray pushed away from the table and leaned back in the chair.

"Let me give you some advice on the anger thing. It's a waste of time," said Frank.

Frank knew his anger with his wife and her postpartum depression precipitated his drinking and lack of understanding that spiraled out of control, resulting in the affair. He watched Ray stretch his neck, his head acting as a lever to reach his left shoulder.

"I just can't believe she ran away thinking I didn't love her."

Frank hesitated before he said, "I may have contributed to her thinking that."

It pained him to remember baiting her into a conversation about the teacup ride in Disney, chasing her up the stairs, and banging on her bedroom door.

"When I learned the two of you had been intimate, I said some mean things. In my day, a guy took advantage of the girls he wasn't going to marry."

Crisp white tablecloths matched the starched dress shirts of the wait staff as more people were seated. Leather-bound menus were brought with their second round of drinks.

"Why don't we get something to eat? Billy's is famous for their rib eye."

Frank opened his menu. He wanted to tell Ray not to let his anger simmer. To have a civil cold sober discussion with the people he loved. Instead, he said, "I'm having the steak, with a baked potato, sour cream, and butter. How about you, Ray?"

"I never took advantage of your daughter. We were in love. I'm still in love with Joy."

Ray stared at Frank silently. Frank returned his muted gaze.

"Then don't let her slip away. Give Jason time. Once he cuddles his flesh and blood, he'll phone."

"Gentleman, can we join you?" Roxanne said as she and Joy approached the table. Roxanne wore a bright yellow peasant dress and Joy was dressed in a black and white sheath.

"Certainly," said Ray. He stood, motioned Roxanne to take his seat, and pulled a chair out for Joy admiring her legs as he maneuvered his way around the table to the empty spot.

"Hey, babe! You came," said Frank. He signaled for the waitress. "We're ready to order, steak dinners around and whiskey sours for the ladies." Frank wore a huge smile as the waitress scribbled everyone's preference on wellness and sides. Before she walked away Frank said, "We'll have another round." His index finger pointed to the half-filled glasses.

"Well, we're here." Roxanne laughed. "And hungry." She looked at Joy who appeared pale in the face. "I know I am." No one was talking when the waitress brought the drinks. Frank raised his glass.

"This isn't a funeral," said Frank. "Let's celebrate ... I'm innocent, a grandpa and soon to be a great-grandpa ... and ... Roxanne and I are getting married ... right Annie?" He winked at Roxanne.

"Don't call me Annie, Frank. My ex called me that and we're not getting married."

"I know ... I know, not yet anyway. I have to sell the house first." Frank snickered.

"Your father ... always the kidder." Roxanne addressed her comment to Joy.

Joy rolled her eyes and studied Ray.

"You're surprised to see me."

Joy played with the cocktail napkin.

"I didn't want to come ... but Roxanne ... Ray, I want to clear the air." She wiped her mouth with the napkin.

"To clear the air?" Ray drained his glass. "Go ahead, Joy. Talk ... clear the air. Explain to me how you got to be part of Jason's life and I didn't. Is that what's called an open adoption?"

"Joy, was it an open adoption?" asked Roxanne.

"No, well kind of ... you see, I was a nanny after Jason was adopted by the Dolan's. Most of the children on the Upper East Side had nannies and went to private schools. So, Jason shared playtimes with my stepkids. I was at school plays, accompanied them on trips." She paused, then looked directly at Ray. "How would you know that?"

"What difference is it how I know? I know. Now I know."

"You watched your son grow up?" Roxanne exclaimed.

"Yup, she watched our son grow up and I didn't." Ray

sounded angry.

Frank intervened. "Ray, shit happens. Nothing can get those years back. But don't blow the opportunity to be part of his future – you love him – you love Joy. You just told me you did."

The waitress brought their salads to the table and there was a not-so-polite silence.

"I missed my grandson growing up, too. But let's focus on the future."

He raised his glass and the others followed.

"To the future," said Ray. He tossed back the drink and stormed out of the restaurant.

Chapter 29

Still in Love

ço

When Dad offered to speak with Ray on my behalf, Roxanne suggested we join them for dinner at Billy's Taproom.

"A public setting is best ... well ... if things become unpleasant."

"Are you sure?"

"Yes. People rarely embarrass themselves in public, and if things do get ugly, they can leave."

Well, things did get ugly and Ray left. I raced after him and jumped into the driver's seat of his truck before he could. He was drunk and I was not about to let him drive. Our lives were a mess but the last thing we needed was a DUI or accident. Hopefully, we could put the past behind us, and have a relationship. I loved him.

"Get out of the damn truck, now, Joy!" He yelled.

"I'm driving, Ray. Get in or walk to where you want to go."

A couple exited the bar and stared at him, he staggered toward the vehicle, sat in the passenger seat, and glared straight ahead.

"Take me home."

"Okay ... where is home."

"Turn left at the light, you know the way ... the house before Tomoka State Park."

I knew the way. It was the house we fantasized about buying. Our house. The house was within walking distance of the elementary school. A short drive from everywhere. The long driveway stopped at the Intracoastal Waterway. I could see the bridge and Rockefeller Gardens on the east shore and my heart pounded with regret.

It was dusk, the time of day when the water appeared to be a sheet of glass. The house was tucked behind shade trees, and the smoky blue sky created a surreal picture. Ray broke the silence.

"You coming in?

"If you'll make coffee."

The house had been renovated and was spotless. I wanted to know if he and Michelle had lived here together but did not ask. The view was like the one from the driveway, and better than my apartment view of Central Park. The coffee perked. The aroma comforted me.

"Look, your dad is right, I do still love you. I've never stopped loving you. But I loved you more when you were dead." He slurred his words.

"I loved me more when I was dead, too."

"Joy, be fair. You're peeling an onion, all the layers of loss and betrayal, right under my nose, and – I'm expected – what do you expect from me?"

He wiped his mouth with the back of his hand.

"Learning you were there at all the big events, and sports, I bet he played lacrosse."

"He did."

"You were there at his kindergarten and high school graduation ... his wedding … I was not."

"I was there but not as his mother. It broke my heart to watch. But ... I thought it best 'he didn't know.'"

"You thought it best! Stop, please stop – I'm the one who missed it all. You were there – don't you dare play the victim. This is my pain."

His voice grew louder.

"I want – you to hurt like I hurt, today – the burn in my chest, the explosion in my head hearing you watched him play sports – it's as though I'm going crazy. Why – why did you tell me thirty years later."

It seemed foolish to say it was never my intent. His speech was slurred and there was no consoling him. He pushed me away.

Behind the couch was a sofa table filled with photos. I picked up one of his brother's family, the resemblance was strong.

"Is this Allen?"

"About ten years ago." He was lying down on the couch. "They took the kids to Disney and stayed with me for a few days."

Everyone in the picture wore Mickey or Minnie Mouse ears.

"We had a great time."

"And this one?" I held up a picture of racing cars.

"That's the Daytona 500." He grinned remembering the event. "I managed security for the France organization after I retired from the police force."

A picture of him and Michelle laughing, I did not mention. He'd had a full interesting life but had no one to grow old with.

Ben was dead and my stepchildren were not talking to me, so neither did I.

When I turned around Ray was passed out.

* * * * *

Carrie picked me up from Ray's house, I did not want to spend the night.

"I guess this meeting in public didn't work out so well."

"He passed out. Roxanne said, there were no guarantees, and your just 'listen' wasn't much help either," I said.

"What did you expect, Joy? You're up against thirty years of heartbreak. Give it time."

"He's going to wake up with a big hangover. The more he thinks about the situation the angrier he gets. Tonight, his fury was about Jason's kindergarten graduation."

"Jason's probably angry about that now, too. His mother was present incognito."

I was sinking in quicksand and my cries were ignored.

"I'm calling Charles. He texted he was coming to St. Augustine soon."

"Charles aka Mr. Rogers from Savannah? What's he doing in St. Augustine?"

"An estate sale, or something financial. I didn't pay attention to the details."

Carrie drove while I phoned Charles. He was in Hammock Beach Resort, and insulted, when I asked, why?

"You think I'm following you, again?" I didn't answer. He continued, "A friend is negotiating to buy an antique shop in St. Augustine and asked me to evaluate the store's inventory. Keep me company."

After the row with Ray, I disliked myself more than ever. Charles' offer was inviting. His voice soothed me, like Mr. Roger's jingle, *I like you just the way you are.*

"Come see the place. It's late, but tomorrow ... for lunch. You'll need to show a photo ID at the gate. Is it Ms. Webb or Mrs. Garner? They'll want to know."

Another lunch with him alone would imply something I was not ready for.

"My license says Joy Garner, but only if I can bring my friend, Carrie."

After I hung up, Carrie said, "You didn't ask me if I wanted to go."

"You must meet Charles. I could be happy with him. A life with Ray will always be marked by the past and his inability to forgive me."

In the morning, I thought of Ray, and hoped he had sobered up, and relieved he hadn't phoned. Carrie checked out the Hammock Beach Resort website and decided we needed to bring swimsuits.

In Flagler Beach kites flew on the beach. People appeared to be having fun. The scenery went from drab to affluent during the drive. In Hammock, flowers were everywhere. The yards were not only mowed but edged.

At the entrance, there was a wait. Until a guard missing his smile said, "Your identification, please."

He studied me and the license as though his eyes were magical, and could uncover something more than what appeared on the card. Then, glaring back and forth at me and Carrie several times to prove some sort of point before saying in a baritone voice, "Follow the driveway and the valet will assist you."

I pulled in front of the hotel. A valet opened my car door and offered me his hand.

"Mrs. Garner, welcome to Hammock Beach Resort." Carrie got out of the vehicle on her own much to the chagrin of the doorman.

The foyer, decorated in tasteful aqua and brown, complimented the heavy wood and gold furniture. A housekeeper cleaned a Persian rug with a silent butler. Fresh flowers filled a large vase on the baby grand piano.

Charles appeared out of nowhere.

"Welcome, I'm glad you came. You must be Carrie."

There were smiles all around.

"Come upstairs ladies. We can relax and enjoy the view. I'm in the North Tower."

The all-glass elevator offered an ocean view. The ride to the top floor left us speechless. Charles broke the silence.

"It's quite lovely, isn't it?"

When the elevator stopped Charles swiped a card to open the door. Inside the penthouse, the view was more spectacular.

An open floor design with windows on all sides. Grey walls complemented white furniture. A long mural in shades of red, yellow, and blue added color to the space. The smell of sea air everywhere.

Carrie's expression varied in astonishment with oohs and aahs like she was Charlie in the Chocolate Factory until she exclaimed…

"Holy crap, Charles! You have a Highwaymen collection!!"

"You are acquainted with their works?"

"Yes. But I've never seen the originals. I have Bob Beatty's book though."

"Marvelous. Beatty's an exceptional photographer. Come, have a better look. I brought them home to Florida, where they belonged."

I watched Charles finesse Carrie with words, sometimes putting his hand across her shoulder, and wondered what it would be like to kiss the man.

We studied the oil paintings, some intense in color, others less. They were all Florida landscapes similar in style, but signed by different artists."

"Who were the Highwaymen?" I asked.

Carrie and Charles talked simultaneously, "African American artists, from the Fort Pierce area of Florida."

They were stepping on each other's words and laughed together. Carrie deferred to Charles and he continued.

"In the 1950s and 60s, Negros living in the south, were lucky to have a job in the citrus groves and escape the wrath of the Ku Klux Klan. The Highwaymen lived in Blacktown, about one hundred miles north of Miami. To break the cycle of poverty, they learned, with the help of A.E. Bean Bachus, oil painting, and sold their art from the trunk of cars."

Carrie stood close to a painting, studying the brush strokes, her arms behind her back, in an effort not to touch the canvas.

"The work is incredible." I injected, wanting to be part of the conversation. "Carrie's an artist."

Charles cleared his throat.

"Well then, we could converse all day about art, and the Highwaymen. But certainly, you must be hungry."

He swept his arms like a musical conductor to go with his invitation.

"Mademoiselles, come this way."

He showed us to an outdoor patio that resembled a fancy backyard, trees and all. We sat in the shade and he handed us fancy glasses.

"What's this?" said Carrie.

"A Pink Lady." Charles raised his glass. "To us." And gazed into my eyes and then Carrie's.

He was taken with Carrie, although I'd never have guessed she was his type. I was surprised by my jealousy.

"You've got some place here," said Carrie. "When do we eat and what's for lunch?"

"Grilled scallops on a bed of fennel and orange salad."

* * * * *

After lunch, Carrie said, "Anyone for a swim?" We could see a large pool on the lower level.

"You go ahead. Joy and I can join you later. If you take the elevator down to the pool level and follow the signs, you'll see the lap pool."

How will I get back in? Don't I need the card you swiped?"

"No, ring the bell."

Carrie looked perplexed but changed into her suit and said, "See you later," as she left.

She wasn't gone for one minute. Charles looked at me with empathetic eyes.

"When you're ready, we need to talk about Ray."

I walked to the rooftop wall for a closer view of the ocean.

Charles joined me.

"We're not children, Joy."

"I care for you, Charles. I like myself when you're around, although we hardly know each other. Returning to Daytona has brought up many issues ... I don't know who I am."

"I do. You're Joy Webb Garner. You left home pregnant and suspicious of your father. Once in New York City, you married. You've returned to Daytona Beach ... Let's say to ... make peace with your past. So, tell me about Joy Garner's life. Did you love Benjamin Garner?"

Tired of dealing with my past and the lingering issues, I contemplated his question and decided to turn the tables. After all, I didn't know Charles's history or his infatuations.

"You know more about me than I know about you. Why not tell me who Charles Dunmore is and why you never married? You said you grew up in the South. The Mason-Dixon Line cuts across Cape May, New Jersey. That's more than a few states."

"Mostly Georgia and the Carolinas. Joy, my life is a bore. I insist, ladies before gentlemen."

"I told you in New York, Ray is the father of my child. I didn't have an abortion. I gave my son, Jason, up for adoption."

The pain of visiting that time, again, felt like being caught in a tidal wave. I knew how to get out, but lacked the strength.

"Did I love Ben? Initially, it was more like, than love. I grew to love him, our marriage, and his kids. He never knew about Ray or Jason. Ben loved the person I pretended to be. Only, I didn't know I was pretending, until he died."

Charles pulled me close to him, and I experienced our first kiss. A flood of pleasure traveled through me. I closed my eyes, lost in the moment. When we came to our senses, Charles asked. "Do you love Ray?"

The windy sea air and roar of the ocean hinted at romance. I froze. Reluctant to say Ray was the one. Will always be the one. A burden of honesty was hidden in the question, but should I be brutally honest?

"I still love Ray. However, I've inflicted so much hurt. I cannot envision us together. It's a relationship that was never meant to be."

I composed myself, hoping Carrie would return soon.

"It's your turn. Who do you love?"

Charles caressed my hand. "No one, except you, Joy"

I pulled my hand away. "Be serious, Charles!"

He looked like a scolded schoolboy but recovered quickly.

"Please don't be offended. I didn't mean to frighten you, Joy." He paused, then continued.

"I have relatives from the past. Occasionally I hear from them requesting funds for this emergency or that."

His smirk was followed by a laugh.

"It's hush money and I thank them." He paused to gather his words. "I wouldn't be who I am today if it weren't for them."

It was an odd comment. I assumed his childhood had been troubled but didn't respond. I listened.

"Early on I knew who I didn't want to be."

Thankfully, Carrie rang the bell and we were both ready to leave.

On the drive back Carrie chatted endlessly about Charles's penthouse, the Highwaymen collection, and the amenities – tennis, golf, gym, spa services, and the designer gift shop she had discovered downstairs.

"I liked Charles. If you're looking to get married, he'd be my choice," she said.

"Go ahead, he's all yours."

"What got up your tush? Did something happen while I was gone?"

It was Charles. His words, 'I knew who I didn't want to be,' had me thinking. I knew I didn't want to be a lonely bitter widow. More importantly, I didn't want to be single and alone.

"Charles kissed me and said he loved me."

"Get out! Isn't that what you wanted?"

"Yes, but no. Ray has always been the one."

"And if you can't have him, you'll settle? Didn't you already settle when you married Ben?"

"I don't want to be alone."

"Why?"

"The past is my only company."

Carrie pulled to the side of the road and put the car in park.

"You're killing me with this crap! Stop with *he's the one, and the past is your only company.*"

She shook her head and sighed as she watched me cry.

"You're wallowing, and not the only one with heartache. Most people are sitting on a bucketload of shit. You and Ray are lucky. You're both alive, healthy, and know where your son is! Grow up!"

Her harsh words brought me to my senses. I'd always thought of myself as strong and in control. I had confused strength with wearing a bullet-proof vest.

"Carrie, what am I going to do?"

"Try marriage counseling, although improbable, it's not impossible to resolve the past."

She put the car in drive and drove home.

* * * * *

Her name was Mariposa. Carrie knew her as a regular at the Maverick. I spoke with her on the phone and had the impression she wore buttoned-up clothes and comfortable shoes.

We met at the Maverick for coffee and boy, was I surprised. She was attired in a Bruce Springsteen t-shirt, shorts, and flip-flops. Her wild, silver-gray hair was plopped on the top of her head and about to topple.

We walked on the beach, talking like girlfriends for several sessions. When I inquired about her credentials, she used her phone to access a New York Times article about herself. She was an expert in her field.

I came to realize keeping Jason's pregnancy a secret was about my feeling unlovable and not ready to be a mother.

She suggested Ray join me for a session at her beachside cottage. I was curious about the location change, but wanted to see where she lived. Then again, a public couple's session might get heated.

Once more, I was surprised. The appliances were from 1960, but new. Pastel Melmax dishes decorated open shelves. A scented diffuser lobbied for calmness and mystical music tingled our ears.

I introduced them.

"Ray, this is Mariposa." They shook hands.

Mariposa lingered to study his eyes and eventually said, "Ray. I'm happy you came."

She wore a white sundress and her piled-high hair glowed in the morning light like a halo.

He liked her instantly.

At the end of the session, she said. "Joy, would you mind if I met with Ray, alone?"

"No, not at all," I said, taken back by her question.

"Good. Ray, what is best for you mornings or afternoons?"

Over the next month, I refrained from questioning him about his sessions and if he was going. I figured it was real personal growth on my part. My need to know was balanced by confidence.

Now, we sat side by side on her couch. Mariposa asked, "How are you both getting along?"

Ray reached for my hand as we said, "Good," at the same time.

"We've talked about the past."

"You obviously love each other, but are you ready to let go of the past and grow together in the future?"

Ray crossed his arms and held them close to his chest.

"Well Mariposa, I've come to realize that Ray has, or had, the bigger boo-boo."

Ray leaned back on the couch but didn't uncross his arms. I kept my eyes downcast.

"The decisions I made thirty years ago were those of an immature, scared, insecure girl, who thought she was choosing a better life for her unborn child. So scared I suspected my father of murder. I'm not that person anymore. I don't even like her much, and almost don't need her statement car."

Ray laughed.

"I lacked the courage to deal with things and just wanted to disappear. So I did."

Ray wore a half smile when I paused. I wanted to yell, *please use words to tell me what you are thinking*, but didn't. Instead, I sat quietly.

"Joy, it sounds like you want to tell Ray you're sorry," said Mariposa.

"I just did, and have many times before."

"Perhaps Ray's emotions wouldn't let him take it in as your emotions kept you from feeling his deep love for you."

Ray and I looked at each other, but didn't know what to say.

"I believe you can have a wonderful life together. Can you both stand, face each other, and share how you feel in this moment?"

We did.

"Ray, I am sorry. Please forgive me. I should have told you I was pregnant. I love you."

"Joy, I forgive you ... if you forgive me."

Mariposa nodded in approval. Ray continued.

"I was caught up in the job and took your love for granted. Your disappearance almost destroyed me. I have always loved you."

I felt the years of hurt and isolation melt from my body like I'd been a frozen creamsicle, too hard to enjoy. I fell into Ray's arms.

We kissed and left Mariposa's office feeling like a married couple. And, drove to Cedar Key, where we had first fallen in love.

Aunt May's cottage was still old and quaint, but several bungalows on the street had been renovated. I could feel a change coming. Expensive cars were parked in the driveways of homes in need of serious repair. Letters to the editor in the local newspaper debated the attempt to pass an ordinance banning the replacement of old house trailers with new ones. Permanent hurricane-proof housing would be mandatory.

But, we could still fish at the edge of Aunt May's property and watch the sunset as we rocked on her back porch.

It was that time of day, when the wind held its breath, and the surrounding noise came to rest, when I said, "I've been uninvited to the gender reveal party."

"So what?" he laughed. "We're going anyway." He stood and stretched his neck from side to side. "Let's go fishing."

I was surprised that he'd be okay with just showing up, and a little concerned the honeymoon might be over, but I let go of those concerns.

I contacted Carrie, thanked her for her tough-love, and told her I wouldn't be staying with her any longer, she asked, "Can I accept Charles's lunch dates? He's been bugging me."

Chapter 30

Long Island

July 4, 2014

Saturday, the Long Island Expressway was bumper to bumper through Nassau County. It was noon when we exited onto Sunrise Highway.

A flood of memories dominated my thoughts as Ray changed lanes and drove to Marigold's beach house. Marigold insisted we use the house to attend the Gender Reveal Party. Rumors about Jason, the Dolans, and me were flying around since everyone had attended the same private school.

Ray stepped out of the car and stretched. "That's Long Island Sound?" He pointed toward the beach.

"No, this is the Atlantic Ocean. The Dolans are on the Sound."

"The air smells different. Saltier than Florida." He bent over and touched his toes.

The distinct scent of musty clams and seagrass played havoc with my senses. I had walked this beach, believing Ray did not love me, debating whether to give Jason up. A sadness came over me, but I snapped out of it when Ray popped the trunk and removed our luggage. With Mariposa's help, we had a commitment, and things were going well.

Renovation had transformed a summer cottage into a quaint

beachfront home. Marigold's style dominated the appeal. French doors lead to the outside pool, and rock piles that appeared to have tumbled served as wave breakers. A circular fire pit, decorated with sand chairs and hippy pillows, was nearby.

"This is spectacular," said Ray. He put his arm around me.

"Soothing. Isn't it?"

Ray answered with a sigh. The memories were like a hand grenade threatening to go off.

"We'll need to be at the Dolans before 3 p.m."

"You explained, it's a short drive and ... not everyone will be happy to see us." He opened the refrigerator. "Can I help myself?"

"I'll be upstairs."

"We could skinny dip in the pool instead," he smiled.

"Only if you want to be late for the party."

We arrived last minute, and valets were hustling to park cars. The memories of this house, the house where a midwife had delivered Jason, made me dizzy. Money had descended on this rural part of the island. The Cape Cod bungalow now appeared to be an estate. With Ray at my side, I gathered the strength to go in. Large white sectionals, stone fireplaces, wood mantels, and crown molding were classic old money. An all-glass wall revealed a tiered patio and ocean view. A musician dressed in a white dinner jacket and black t-shirt played piano, his smile may have been painted on. Light jazz filled the room.

We were greeted by Ben's ex-wife, Jackie.

"Joy, the kids said you were in town," she said and air-kissed me. Her flowing dress revealed too much.

"Are they here?"

"Yes, somewhere. But, tell me ... who's this handsome guy?"

"Jacqueline, this is Ray. Ray, this is Jacqueline."

"I was Jacqueline to Ben. Call me Jackie, Ray ... Daytona Beach must be hot if you live there."

She sucked in her stomach, pushed up her chest, and moved closer to Ray.

"Don't you need a drink? Let me show you where the bar is."

She slipped her arm under his and led the way.

Left alone, I gravitated to the wait staff offering champagne as Connie, Dolan's receptionist, waved and strolled toward me. I chugged the bubbling wine and swapped the empty fluted glass for another, by the time she stood at my side.

We exchanged a standard fake kiss as she whispered, "Why are you here? You were told not to come."

She stepped back and spoke louder.

"Congratulations on your longstanding performance... all the years ... pretending not to be Jason's mother. It was an Oscar-worthy performance. I can hear the applause."

She clapped her hands with approval.

I ignored her attempt to confirm the insider information and reminded her, the Dolans had pretended too. Instead, I said, "The weather is perfect." I felt the sun's heat on my back. "The renovations to the house are spectacular. I haven't been here in years. When will they make the announcement?"

"Any moment now. Pink balloons or blue balloons will flood the pool area. You should leave now, Joy."

I saw Jackie with Ray over by the bar and hoped they would stay put. Matthew and Sara Dolan joined Jason and his wife, Alison, by the piano. The pianist struck a chord to signal the announcement. Alison patted her baby bump as the music crescendoed and both pink and blue balloons filled the pool.

Jason yelled. "We're having twins, a boy, and a girl."

Screams of glee enveloped the crowd and Connie raced across the patio to join the Dolan family. The excitement blanketed Ray's and my presence. I found him at the buffet table.

"Well, damn, this is exciting," he said, holding a plate. "I'm glad we were able to sneak in." He handed me the plate and grabbed another one for himself.

We were about finished eating when Matthew and Sara Dolan approached us.

"This must be Ray Atwood," said Matthew. He thrust a hand out for Ray to shake.

"Yes, sir," said Ray. He wiped his hands on his slacks before grasping Matthew's.

"And you'll be leaving shortly. We don't want any drama today," said Sara. She stood alongside Matthew, her hands clasped, portraying her matronly status.

"Of course, if that's what Jason wants," said Ray.

"No Dad, I'd like him to stay," said Jason. He and Alison appeared out of nowhere.

"Twins, congratulations!" Ray stood and hugged Jason.

Jason glanced at Matthew Dolan. "Ray and I have been texting and yes, I've reconsidered. If that's okay with you and Mom." Jason studied Sara Dolan.

"Your mother and I will support any decisions you've made. We wanted an open adoption from the start, but Joy – thought differently," said Matthew.

"Joy, the woman who pretended not to be my mother?" He scowled at me.

Many of the people attending the party knew me and would be shocked, as Jason had been, to learn I was his biological mother. Not wanting to create a scene, I walked away, quietly.

The house looked out at the bay. The sun, low in the west, glowed. The rumble from the waves was background music for that twenty-year-old dancing on the navy water. It was a happy time, free from the stress of my parent's marriage, dad's drinking, mom's depression, and my attending college to make them proud. My parents pushed education and teaching. I wanted to be a lawyer, which my father labeled them as fancy thieves.

This was the first time I thought of the Dolans as *fancy thieves*. They stole Jason from me with a clever agreement; if he asked they would tell him who his mother was. Now, they stood and watched me accused of pretending, when they pretended for thirty years, too! Connie doesn't think they deserve an Academy Award, but I do!

Ray found me outside.

"Why didn't you tell me you and Jason were texting or talking?"

"Why didn't you tell me I had a son?" Sarcasm punctuated each word.

"You know why I didn't tell you I was pregnant."

"Right, you didn't think I loved you. Anyway, Jason asked me not to. He wants nothing to do with you. We're going for breakfast in the morning and … unfortunately, Joy, you're not invited."

He was clearly under the influence.

Silence came with us on the drive back to Marigold's beach bungalow. I had asked Jason to give Ray a chance, and he had. I was in the doghouse now, and it hurt, but oddly felt good, because I deserved it.

The moon bleached the dunes protecting the house from sea erosion. I stayed outside to stargaze. Ray brought me a glass of wine, but we still weren't speaking. The stillness was somehow cathartic.

He gathered kindling and watched the fire ignite, then re-filled my glass and said, "I'm sorry, Joy. That was mean of me."

"It was mean." I held tight to Mariposa's advice and continued. "I forgive you, Ray. I love you and want you in my life."

He kissed me in all the right places, as the fire danced dangerously into the night.

* * * * *

When I woke the next morning to the sound of the ocean brushing the shore, Ray was gone. There was a note saying, he'd phone after breakfast. Last night was perfect. Selfishly, I had envisioned the remaining days we planned to stay on Long Island, with Jason and Alison. However, Ray deserved time with our son, alone.

I texted Ray, I would take a car service back to the city. He'd return the rental car at the airport and we'd reunite on the plane back to Florida. I included several smiley faces.

He replied, "Sounds like a plan."

* * * * *

Back in the city, Bryce and Scarlet greeted me in the apartment lobby.

"What a pleasant surprise."

I guessed Jason told them I had returned to New York, and hugged them, but they pulled away.

"Let's go upstairs where we can talk."

"How could you just show up at the party and pretend nothing happened?!" Bryce said once inside the apartment.

"Everything our mother said about you is true. You're a liar and a gold-digger." Scarlet yelled. Her eyes glared.

Jackie was probably fueling their rage and I thought it best to let them explode.

"What the fuck! You're my best friend's mother. How could you? Do you have ice in your veins?" Bryce clenched his fists, punched a wall, and yelled, "Did Dad know?" grimacing in pain.

"We want the apartment, if Dad hadn't married you, we'd have inherited all of this," said Scarlet. She circled her arms above her head as though she'd tossed a baton.

In the short time she'd been living with her mother, Jackie's greed had seeped into her pores, and spilled out like pus from an open wound. Ben never knew my past and unfortunately for them, there was no inheriting the apartment. The property had been and was in my name, not Ben's. However, this was not the time to address either issue.

"How was I to know that you and Jason would become good friends?" I directed the question at Bryce. "Would you have preferred I'd announced it at a sleepover?"

He looked deflated, sat on the living room couch, and rubbed his bruised hand.

"The Dolans knew, and never said a word either. Are you angry at them?"

The comment put salt in this wound.

"When your father died ... so suddenly ... I fell apart and went home to Daytona Beach to sort things out."

"What the heck? Like spring break Daytona Beach?" said Scarlet.

"Yes. I grew up there, got pregnant accidentally, read a newspaper advertisement for a private adoption, and met the Dolans. I stayed in New York City after the adoption and began working as a nanny, and met your father."

My stepchildren didn't need to know everything, but they did deserve some explanation.

"An accident? Nobody gets pregnant accidentally today." Scarlet's face turned red. "Bullshit, your affair with my father broke up his marriage."

"Scarlet, that's not what happened. You were too young to understand. Mom and Dad were divorced before Joy was our nanny," said Bryson.

Scarlet's strawberry-curly hair framed her face but the chubby cheeks were gone. She was five years old when Ben and Jackie divorced and was protected from their screaming matches. I played Nerf ball in the lobby while waiting for Jackie, who always arrived late and usually under the influence, for her scheduled visit. Ben stayed upstairs.

"Calm down, Scarlet," said Bryson. Scarlet looked at her brother then sat on a nearby sofa.

"I understand you're both upset and rightfully so. I'm sorry you found out this way."

"We relied on you – trusted you. Scarlet thinks we can't do that anymore."

"That's plain silly," I said. "There were no lies. I withheld the truth in the best interest of others. Did Jason ever talk about finding his biological parents?"

"Not to us," said Bryce and Scarlet simultaneously.

"If he had, or asked his parents – there was a letter I'd written." I hesitated to wonder how much of his life Jason wanted to be shared. "When Ray Atwood learned he had a son, he was determined to find him."

This was more difficult than I expected, and I began to cry.

"Once Jason knew who his biological father was, he asked about his mother ... and Matthew Dolan gave him the letter."

I wiped the tears rolling down my face.

"Jason is not talking to me and that's fine, but please, don't let this be a wedge between us. You guys are my life, remember the holidays, ski trips, and summers at the beach?"

I was on the verge of tears again. Bryce stood and put his arms around me.

"Mom, don't cry. It will be all right," he said.

"I know it will be. We all need time." I said in between sobs. I wiped my tears and forced a smile. "I have crumb cake. I'll make coffee?"

Our conversation was civil at best, although the kids enjoyed the crumb cake. I spent the next few days, sorting through papers, reviewing finances, and thinking about life.

Why couldn't I go to law school or study forensic science? Perhaps, something in fashion. I had to be prepared for the worst. Ray and I might not last ... forever.

* * * * *

When I boarded at JFK, Ray was on the plane.

"Well fancy seeing you here," he said.

"Hey stranger," I answered.

We were going home together, but turbulence ruled the skies, teasing a crash. I knew it was going to be a bumpy ride.

"How was your time with Jason?"

"Great! It was like we'd always known each other. We have the same interests. He loves racing, horse racing... Not cars but it's the same."

Ray looked out the window.

"I've never felt like this – so grounded – a missing part has been found. And I'm not willing to risk losing it."

I knew what he was going to say and asked for another drink.

"Joy, I have feelings for you ... but Jason is angry. Hopefully, he'll keep in touch with me, and if he does ... You can't be in the picture, for now."

I decided to buy Morningside Drive by the time we landed. The dream of a family, well, the best scenario would be that Roxanne and my father would include me in their future. At the very least I wouldn't be staying at the Maverick when on the outs with Ray or Carrie.

Chapter 31

More Upheaval

'Great news! The house sold! We got a cash buyer and get this – they wanted it for ABOVE asking price," said Dad.

I phoned Roxanne and made the offer, shortly after landing. She agreed to present it anonymously. Now I had the task of telling him I was the buyer.

He was in the kitchen brewing coffee, and I put a crumb cake on the table. He turned and hugged me with a big smile.

"This is perfect. Now to charm Roxanne into marrying me."

"Would it still be perfect if I told you I was the buyer?" I said and reached into a cupboard for cups.

I surveyed the kitchen and imagined demolishing it, installing granite countertops and white cabinets. The open floor design would include doors out to a pool, a master bedroom suite, and a two-car garage.

"You bought the house! You're moving to Florida? That's fantastic, Joy."

He wore a big smile and made a belly laugh.

It was fantastic and solved a few family problems if we ever became one. I planned to leave Morningside Drive to Carrie, and now, Dad had cash to invest or pay for the new house. It was probably not smart to mention my plans to renovate.

"What a hoot, put your mother's fancy stuff back in the hutch. It's party time."

"Dad those are your memories. They need to go with you."

"Dust collectors? No, thank you. We're getting a pool table. Maybe put a keyboard or jute box in a corner. Roxanne thought a music motif would work. She was shopping online for a poodle skirt."

"You're not taking the furniture?"

"Furnished house for sale, move-in condition. You read the fine print, didn't you? Closing day will be your lucky day."

"Lucky?"

"Yes, lucky." He studied my disbelief, paused, and said, "Oh ... I get it. This stuff is not good enough for Miss Fancy Pants." He put down the glass of beer he'd been drinking. "You think you're better than everyone, don't you?"

"No, I don't!"

"Yes, you do. Check yourself in a mirror. You have a turned-up nose. I see the way you study Roxanne's clothes and my flip-flops."

"That's what you think of me?"

He eyeballed me. My confidence was at an all-time low. Everywhere I turned people were angry with me. Ray was keeping his distance to establish a relationship with our son. He loved me, so long as Jason didn't find out.

The walls were closing in, and I wanted to run and hide. But where? I was equally unpopular in New York City. Bryce and Scarlet continued to wallow in disbelief that I am Jason's biological mother.

Dad got quiet, shook his head, and said, "Come here, I'm sorry."

I let him hug me.

"Forget about the old worn-out furniture. Do whatever you want with the place. You're the new owner."

He broke our embrace and did the cha-cha-cha around the kitchen.

Roxanne and Carrie arrived.

"What's got him going?" said Roxanne.

"We've got something to dance about! Try to guess who bought the house ..."

He had forgotten she was the realtor.

They giggled like two school girls, and I watched like a cheerleader coach from the sidelines; encouraging Dad as he cha-cha'd into the living room.

"Replace the kitchen window with French doors and move the sink," said Carrie, after she caught her breath. "These ugly brown cabinets will be replaced." She opened and closed the cabinet doors as she spoke.

"I agree," said Roxanne. "Nobody wants to wash dishes facing a wall."

"Plus ... four stools will fit under the island and max out the living space."

"And everyone will have a view of the pool," I added. "Mom's sewing room will stay. I might start quilting."

We all stopped talking, when Carrie said, "You might want to save this." Mom's crumb cake recipe, yellow with age and grease marks, was taped inside a cabinet. As a young girl, I watched her whip up the batter, and crumble the cinnamon-sugar-butter on top. I found myself crying with Roxanne's soft loving arms around me, like a bear hug, I did not think I needed.

"It's Mom's friend, Barbara's, recipe. It's better than any store-bought or bakery," I said in between sobs.

"Well … since it's a favorite, we'll just have to bake it. How about tomorrow?" Roxanne said.

It had been months since I'd returned to Morningside Drive, with apprehension and accusations, things appeared to be falling into place, and I relaxed my shoulders.

I would focus on transforming the house into a winter get-away, keep my anger and jealousy in check, and maybe, just maybe, Jason would speak to me.

I was no longer dead to my father, or Carrie, and Ray and I had a comfortable loving relationship. Life was good.

And then my phone rang.

* * * * *

It was Jason.

I knew by the sound of his voice that something tragic had happened.

"Mom! There was a car crash and both Sara and Matthew are in intensive care."

"What hospital?" I was moved by the way he called me mom. It was different than all the other times he'd called me mom.

The first time Bryce brought Jason home after school I was stunned and had to act like any parent whose child had brought someone home. The time between classes ending and the start of lacrosse practice for the boys was such that Jason spent the time in our apartment. They became good friends and shortly after on a Friday, pizza night, Bryce asked if Jason could spend the night. Waking up to my son was a real pleasure. He started calling me Mom, rather than Miss Joy or Mrs. Garner, and so did the other teenagers.

"Stonybrook Southampton."

"Ray and I are on our way."

It was an automatic response. If Matthew and Sara Dolan were to die, not that I wished that would happen, we would naturally fill the void.

"Wait there's more! Alison is in labor."

* * * * *

Ray arranged a police escort to Jacksonville airport and we boarded a small private plane to McArthur airport in South Hampton and rented a car.

Jason met us at the hospital emergency entrance.

"Matthew is on a respirator. His MRI revealed a head concussion and spine damage. They stopped the internal bleeding and set his leg. It's too early to tell if he will be paralyzed."

The doctor joined us in the waiting room, and put his hand on Jason's shoulder.

"We're more optimistic about his recovery than your mother's. You'll need to make some decisions. We could transport her to the trauma center at New York University Hospital." He studied the floor as he told Jason. "She wasn't wearing a seatbelt. I'm sorry."

"That can't be true, she always wore a seat belt and would pull to the side of the road, if someone else wasn't."

I watched Jason react in despair and wanted to comfort him.

"Did she have a living will?"

"We're lawyers, of course, she had a living will." Jason laughed nervously.

"Did she want to be on life support?" He glanced at his pager.

"What are you talking about?"

"The charge nurse, Nurse Wilson, will help you. I know you have your hands full, with your wife in delivery and all."

Jason stood in shock as he watched the doctor leave the room.

"They can't die. They can't. I dreamt about being a parent, my whole life, now it's a nightmare." He sank to his knees and held his head with both hands.

Nurse Wilson interrupted. "Mr. Dolan, you're wanted in delivery."

Chapter 32

Goodbye Sara

August 30, 2014

Jason pressed his nose against the glass of the infant room. The twins were a cesarean delivery, and Alison was doing well. He had been allowed to go inside but not hold them yet. Both twins were hooked up to a variety of machines and monitors.

"Did you hold me?"

I froze listening to his question and the sound of incubators like backup singers at a revival meeting, unable to respond.

He put his hands on my shoulders.

"Did you hold me? Want to hold me? I'm desperate to hold my babies."

I closed my eyes. His birth was a blur, and I knew if I held him I would change my mind. The memory of Sara Dolan holding Jason was vivid.

He shook me and shouted, "Answer me," forcing me back to the present

"Of course, I held you and wanted to keep you!"

I recalled writing and rewriting the letter and memorizing each word.

Close your eyes and feel my arms surround you with a love that will never let go. I hold you and pray I'm making the right decision. The Dolan's are good people. When I put you in their arms, they checked for my hesitation, but I could not weaver, as I believe my certainty is a gift, I can give you both. My heart is breaking. If circumstances were different, I would raise you on my own. I hope someday you'll want to meet. Ask your parents where to find me.

Your loving mother,

Joy Webb

I burst into tears, sobbing, and shaking from head to toe. Ray put his arms around me protectively and looked at Jason.

"Son, this is not the time for this. We're here now." Ray pulled us into a hug.

Jason broke free. "I hate you! You should be the one on life support."

Why hadn't I let sleeping dogs lie? Never returned to Daytona. Never questioned my dad about the Martins. Never told Ray about Jason. There was no way to defend myself, so I lashed out at my son.

"That door swings both ways, Jason." I wiped the tears from my face. "You never questioned who your biological mother was. Matthew would have given you my letter if you had. Think of your life, with me, a single mom, working for minimum wage."

"That's just bullshit!"

We were interrupted by a nurse. "Your father is asking for you."

"Tell him, I will be right there." He turned toward Ray. "I'd like you to come too... We'll leave her behind."

Jason's reference to me as her was like a bee sting and as the hurt circulated through my mind and body, anger seeped from my pores. Why was I the target of his betrayal? The Dolans were complicit in keeping my identity secret. Furthermore, they never asked or had an interest in who was Jason's biological father.

When they had left the room, I broke down and cried.

* * * * *

"Jason," his father mumbled.

Jason stood by the bed and grabbed Mtthew's hand, then leaned down to hear what he hoped was not his dying words.

"Your mother is not doing well. She's in a coma. It's time … we need to decide."

"Don't worry, Dad, I'll take care of things. You just rest. Everything will be okay. You are a grandpa! Healthy twins and Alison are doing great. We haven't named them yet."

"Think about naming your daughter after Mom … she'd like that, or would have."

Matthew drifted off. Ray moved to Jason's side and put his hand on his shoulder. "It could be the medication. I'm sure he's heavily sedated for pain."

Sara Dolan lay unconscious in the next ICU room. Jason studied her from the doorway with Ray at his side. The constant repetitive sound of life support machines did the work of keeping her alive. Her eyes were shut. Her auburn hair framed her face. She lay peacefully as if nothing was wrong. The vehicle had been hit on the passenger side and Sara's injuries were massive internal bleeding and head trauma.

Jason stood bedside and whispered, "Mom."

There was no response. He pulled a chair alongside the bed and sat thinking.

Sara Dolan was never a stay-at-home mom. As a psychiatrist, the demands on her time were huge and Matthew was home more than she was. She was a great parent, but not the snuggle and cuddle type.

Jason always knew he was adopted. Sara read him stories about adopted children. In kindergarten when asked to draw a family picture he highlighted his dark hair, and tan skin and gave his parents yellow hair and sunburns.

The thought of Sara not being in his life was overwhelming. He had assumed there would be summers at the beach house with grandma and grandpa. They would watch the twins when he and Alison could get away for a weekend. The reality of things hit him hard.

He stood and kissed her forehead; it was ice cold. Ray put his arm around Jason when the doctor entered the room. He turned on a penlight and raised Sara's eyelids. The clicking sound echoed through the room with doom and gloom. The doctor looked at Jason.

"There's no brain activity. I'm sorry." He sighed compassionately.

"What if we wait a few days?" Jason asked.

"She'd have to be put on kidney dialysis. Miracles can happen ... but, in my professional opinion, unlikely."

"Let me discuss it with my dad."

"Jason, your dad is in an induced coma, to reduce brain swelling. It was a medical decision made after you left the room. There was no time to inform you, unfortunately."

"No, Ray ... my biological father."

* * * * *

In the hospital chapel, Ray knelt beside Jason. He knew he'd have raised his son without religion, but was happy Jason had a religious background. Bad things happen to good people, the lucky dance through life free of loss and tragedy. Saying everything happens for a reason, annoyed the hell out of him. What reason did God have for killing Sara, the day her grandchildren were born?

Praying seemed to help.

Jason said, "Mom put it in writing. I'm going to respect that."

He hung his head, wiped his eyes, and then regained composure repeatedly while lamenting.

"She never hung out with us kids. Joy did … was the fun mom. Today has been like running through a minefield while dodging bullets to get to Alison … like playing a twisted game of who do I love, and Joy's watching from the sideline."

"Jason, you can do this. I'm right by your side, son."

Neither let go of their embrace for a long time before informing the doctor.

Chapter 33

Call Me Pop

September 2014

❧

"D amn," said Frank as he exited the limousine under a portico. He turned and helped Roxanne from the car.

"Welcome, Mr. Webb," said the housekeeper. "Jason told me you were coming."

Inside the home, a large buffet was pressed against the foyer wall, cluttered with car keys, newspapers, and mail. A scent from a bouquet of lilacs dominated the foyer. Frank and Roxanne stood quietly absorbing the elaborate woodwork and polished floors.

"This was originally the summer home for The Cornell Family. It's an easy commute into Manhattan," said the housekeeper. She ushered them into the main hall.

"There are seventeen rooms in the house," she said. "All seven bedrooms are upstairs."

"Holy crap," said Frank as he studied the high ceiling and stairs leading to separate wings.

"Mr. Webb," she smiled insincerely, "let me show you around."

"Call me Frank ... miss?"

"Ms. Manners."

"That's a joke? Right?"

"No, that's what I prefer to be called."

"Well, Ms. Manners. How about you show Roxanne how to work the stove and I'll show myself around?"

After the woman left, Frank said, "I didn't see a recliner anywhere... nor a television."

"I'm sure a TV is tucked inside a wall or armoire somewhere," Roxanne said.

"Do you think there's any beer in the fridge?"

It made sense for Frank and Roxanne to come from Florida to help the new parents. Roxanne was the mother of six children. Jason was still furious that Sara was dead and I was alive. I deserved nothing less.

Only Ray had been asked to attend the Mass and private burial held ten days after Sara's death. Matthew was still hospitalized with months of rehabilitation ahead and unable to attend. We stayed hoping to be helpful, until Roxanne coaxed us home, and suggested she and Dad take our place.

Roxanne cooked breakfast and Frank scoured the New York Times, trying to find the sports section. The kitchen did have a breakfast nook and a television anchored to the wall. Frank had to slide down in the bench seat and tilt his head back uncomfortably to view it.

Ms. Manners arrived shortly after and insisted she make lunch. Now, they sat in a glider under the covered porch. The porch stretched across the back of the house and viewed an in-ground pool. The afternoon sun reflected on the water.

"You know, Roxanne, the stairs are good for me. It's like a gym workout. I have to rest and recover halfway up and once or twice on the way to our bedroom."

He drank a beer he'd discovered in the outdoor refrigerator.

"Did you bring a swimsuit?" Roxanne asked.

"No, I thought we'd skinny dip." He winked.

Roxanne shook her head and, smiled.

"They must be here. I heard car doors slam."

* * * * *

A month had passed since Sara Dolan had died. Jason and Alison had stayed in Manhattan to be near the twins as they gained weight. Today, the family was coming home to their life, without Sara.

The driver helped them from the car. Ms. Manners reached for one of the twins. People shifted babies and diaper bags trying to greet the exhausted couple.

"Come here young man, I'm your granddad! No shit! We finally get to meet."

Frank embraced Jason in a bear hug.

"How the hell are you holding up after all the crap you guys have been through."

Frank turned to Alison. "And this beautiful lady has got to be my new granddaughter-in-law."

He lifted one of the twins from her arms as he kissed her.

"Roxanne, come here and meet my grandson and great-grandkids. This has got to be the happiest day of my life – unless you marry me."

Both twins started crying, a feed-me change-me scream.

"Let's get everyone inside and upstairs," said Roxanne.

Alison insisted the twins were brought upstairs and Roxanne knew changes would have to be made. Running up and down the stairs to get a bottle was unrealistic.

In the morning, Roxanne suggested Jason buy a college dorm refrigerator and microwave to be put in the huge master suite bathroom. It turned the suite into a small apartment, and Alison didn't have to manage the stairs unnecessarily.

With Roxanne and Frank there, something close to normal was achieved. They sat on the porch rocking and cooing the grandbabies as they had their 10 a.m. feeding.

The babies were easy, thank God, after all the trauma everyone had been through. Ms. Manners circulated from 8 a.m. to 4 p.m. weekdays. She ordered groceries that were delivered, supervised cleaning, doing more cleaning than cooking.

"I don't know what to call you, Frank," said Jason one morning. "Nor Ray ... I don't know what to call him either."

Jason's father, Matthew had been transferred to rehab for extensive physical therapy, but ... there was no guarantee he would fully recover and assume his role as dad and granddad. Sara was gone.

"Well, you could keep calling me Frank." He studied Jason. "My father died when I was young and I never knew his father or my grandfather, and I never had a son, lost my daughter, or thought I lost my daughter ... you know your mother, Joy?"

"You thought my mother ... Joy ... was dead?"

"Yeah, you know because she went missing."

"Went missing? I don't know what you're talking about. She married Ben, and Bryce and Scarlet are her stepkids. We went to prep school together."

"I guess there's a lot you don't know." Frank handed the baby to Jason. "Why don't you call me Pop?"

"Okay, Pop," said Jason, trying it on.

"I'd like to see my old neighborhood. Why don't we take a ride?"

* * * * *

They left New Jersey, crossed the George Washington Bridge, and exited onto the Bronx River Parkway. Little had changed since Frank left the area, although no one was playing basketball at the court on Metcalf and Morrison Avenue, and there was a ton of garbage spewed about.

The Bronx River was visible from the parkway and when they passed Fordham Road, the Bronx Zoo, and the Botanical Gardens, Frank knew he was home. Arthur Avenue was a stone's throw away.

"Stay to the right and take the next exit, Gun Hill Road," Frank instructed Jason.

They drove down Bainbridge Avenue and Frank pointed out the apartment building he lived in, Public School 72, and other landmarks from his childhood.

"Let's go down the Grand Concourse to Yankee Stadium. I loved sitting in the leftfield hoping I'd catch a ball," said Frank.

When they passed the Catholic church, he said, "That's where your grandmother, Mary Elizabeth, and I were married."

"Mary Elizabeth?" Jason questioned.

"Yup, Mary Elizabeth, your grandmother. Joy's mother. She died from cancer and worried about your mother."

Jason kept his eyes on the road while Frank lamented about The Grand Concourse.

"Holy crap! This area used to be majestic. We called it the

Park Avenue of the Bronx. It was designed after the Champs-Elysees in Paris. Now it's a four-lane garbage dump. Mary Elizabeth must be rolling over in her grave. Look at the gargoyles decorating the buildings, they're falling apart, and those empty planters adorning the stairs … would overflow with flowers … in the day."

"Why did Joy … my birth mother … run away or go missing?" asked Jason.

"I lied," said Frank.

"You lied? Your daughter disappeared for thirty years because you told a lie? It must have been a big one!"

Frank considered his grandson's comment before responding.

"It was a little lie … but attached to a big incident made me a murderer in your mother's eyes."

They stopped at a red light on Fordham Road, the light changed to green, but Jason didn't accelerate and car horns honked and continued to honk as he stared at his grandfather in disbelief. Because he hesitated, pedestrians jaywalked and clogged the intersection. Then the light turned red again.

"Did you?" asked Jason with both hands on the steering wheel, staring ahead.

"Of course not. Drive the car, Jason." Frank gave the finger to a pedestrian. "Turn right at 161st and pull over when you see Yankee Stadium."

The new stadium resembled the old iconic structure, but there was no easy way to walk down the street from the D train subway station, buy your ticket, and go inside. Frank sighed.

"It was 1984, early summer. Not too hot in Florida yet. Your mom and grandmother had gone to bed, I was watching TV. The doorbell rang. A former student I'd been in love with and her ten-year-old daughter were at the door. She came to tell me I was the girl's father and needed money. I gave them a few hundred bucks and drove them home. They were never seen again. You look a little pale, Jason. You feeling all right?"

"Well, you tell me Pop, how I should feel. It's kind of like being hit below the belt. I find out my best friend's stepmother is my mother ... and now add you had an affair and your daughter believed you killed the woman and her daughter. Why? ... to keep them quiet?" The lawyer in him came to life. "Were you the last person to see them alive?"

"You know I could use a beer. If memory serves me right, there's an Irish pub down the street."

"Pop ... Did you lie?"

"Geeze ... It was a white lie. You want the whole shebang?"

Jason nodded yes.

"Joy asked me who came to the door that night. She'd been watching from her upstairs bedroom window ... the BIG LIE ... I made up a story about a missing dog. I had nothing to do with their disappearance and was NOT about to become a person of interest. It would have killed your grandmother to learn I had an illegitimate child. Diane walked her daughter to school in the morning and then went to work."

The Irish pub was no longer there. Frank fell asleep crossing the George Washington Bridge back to New Jersey. He woke up as they pulled in the driveway.

"You know son, you should rethink this not talking to Joy. She is your mother and for better or worse she thought adoption was best."

"Okay, old man ... I'll think about it."

"Old Man! Don't be a wise ass."

Cars were parked everywhere, even on the lawn. Laughter,

hoots, and hollers, as Frank described them, could be heard out back.

"Sounds like a pool party, Jason. I'll need to borrow a suit."

"My kids surprised us," said Roxanne once Frank joined her on the veranda.

"All six of them?" asked Jason."

"Yes, and all their kids!"

There were at least ten people in the pool, playing Marco Polo.

"Where's Alison and the twins?"

"Upstairs with all the daughters-in-law."

Feeling proud, Roxanne criss-crossed her arms, put her hands on her shoulders, and gave herself a hug.

"What's Marco Polo?"

Roxanne introduced Frank to her boys; Thomas, Timothy, Terrence, Troy, Travis, and Michael.

Then said, "We kept trying for a girl, which would have been named Michelle. Michael was our Michelle."

The boys laughed, even Michael, or Michelle as he was regularly called. A free-for-all ensued. They were all New York City firefighters, lived in Queens, and were on duty September 11, 2001. They all ran toward the towers, only to see the towers collapse. Grateful to be alive, their only fear was the aftereffect of toxins. Consequently, each day was a gift they knew to enjoy.

When Jason was introduced, the boys threw him in the water and played Marco Polo.

He waded around the pool with his eyes shut saying, Marco Polo, listening for a response. It was a swimmer's version of hide and seek. Jason caught on quickly and taunted the brothers, especially Michael, calling them wimps and sissies and threatening, "You're on my turf, I can throw you out!"

The boys had brought all the fixings for a barbecue and a good time was had by all, way after Jason and Alison retired with the twins.

Snuggled in a king-sized bed, neither of them was used to, Frank said, "What a day! Praise the Lord, Roxanne. I have the sons, daughters, and grandchildren I've always wanted."

"Say goodnight, Frank," said Roxanne.

"Goodnight, Frank."

Chapter 34

Morningside Anew

❦

Carrie was general contractor for the renovation of Morningside Drive and she had outdone herself! Her artistic flare and her eye for interior design transformed the house on par with a television makeover.

She complained I overpaid her. It was my attempt to make amends. The extra money might help pay for college. She'd have salary, benefits, and time to complete her projects, as an art teacher.

While the coffee perked, I went outside to get the newspaper. It rained during the night. The paper was covered in plastic and dripped water. A sense of déjà vu overcame me. The memory of Dad picking up the newspaper, last January, flashed in my mind as a woman across the street had stopped to study the house. It wasn't a surprise, the pale yellow and soft blue outside had curb appeal. I recognized the dog … before I recognized Carrie.

She yelled. "You're back!"

Lucky, unleashed, ran across the street wagging his tail.

I was thrilled to see her. "Come have coffee. I just made a pot."

"When did you get in?" She walked across the street and

hugged me.

"Late last night. Oh my God! You look great!"

"I've lost a few pounds and been working out." She flexed her arm muscles.

"I love the renovation. I could not be happier about what you've done."

"I can't take all the credit ..." She became surprisingly coy. "Charles and I have become ... friends."

"Just friends, or friends with benefits?" I raised my eyebrows and poured the coffee.

"OH... benefits ... lots of benefits," she giggled. "Charles has offered me a scholarship and stipend to complete my art degree. He suggested I apply to Persons' undergraduate program."

"Persons School of Design in the Village?"

"The one and only. He knows people and believes my portfolio will get me in."

I was thrilled for her and gave her a big hug.

"Are you moving to New York City?"

"Well? Charles said I could use his New York apartment. I might sell the house here, or have one of the boys move in. I already told Lucky he can't come."

"You know his apartment is in THE PLAZA HOTEL!"

"Well, he mentioned a hotel ... The Plaza? Must be special if you're yelling about the place."

"I'm just concerned ... you know what you're getting into?"

"I think I'm in love. He bought the boys a fishing boat. Out of the blue, Joe's pal at the marina phoned him and said 'Dude, there's an abandoned boat down here, and your name is on the title.'"

Charles always was a too-good-to-be-true catch. We still

didn't know much about his past life. I had to be blunt.

"Are you in love with him, or his money?"

"What's the difference? I'm having the time of my life. Didn't you marry Ben for his money?"

"That's a low blow, and everyone's impression, but far from the truth. What if he's a serial killer or sex pervert? Be careful, the only income you have is from waitressing. Don't let Charles take advantage of you."

"I'm single. Almost fifty years old. Have a mortgage I struggle every month to pay. I quit the Maverick. How could Charles take advantage of me financially?"

"How about emotionally? What does anyone know about him?"

"You were the one about to jump the broom with him, Joy. You tell me."

"He sounded too good to be true then, and more so now. I asked about his family. He clammed up. Didn't want to talk about anything personal."

"Joy! Relax. I've got my big girl panties on ... Although, I could Google him or find him on Facebook."

Our conversation was interrupted by a cell call. I laughed and answered the phone.

"Jason," I said and my heart braced for another disaster. Carrie studied my face for clues. Jason was still angry with me and grieving the loss of Sara.

"We'd be thrilled," I said. "How's Matthew ... your father doing?"

I did not want to sound insensitive or forget Matthew was still in recovery.

"I'm glad to hear that. Like you said, hopefully he and Connie will be at the christening."

"What was that about?" Carrie asked as soon as I hung up.

"Jason wants Ray and me to be godparents for the twins."

"You and Ray?" She clapped her hands. "Last I knew Jason wasn't talking to you."

"Evidently, Dad straightened him out. Jason said Dad told him the whole 'shebang' and ranted about the twins having grandparents and great-grandparents. I can hear Dad saying 'Children never have enough people to love them.'"

"Holy crap! Shebang rant … your dad and he must like each other," said Carrie laughing.

"No malarkey, the baptism will be on Sunday, the 19th of October, followed by brunch at their country club."

"And Ray?"

"We have our ups and downs. Mariposa thinks it's normal. But get a load of this! Connie moved in with Matthew."

"Connie, the receptionist at Dolan & Dolan?"

"And family friend … their excuse? Matthew can work from the apartment, and Connie, doesn't have the long commute from Brooklyn."

Carrie and I reeled with laughter.

Although the Dolans appeared to be the perfect couple, I rarely saw them together. Connie attended Jason's school events, frequently, in place of them. No one could have accused Sara of being unloving, but looking back, she was more perfect than loving. Perhaps, in retrospect, Matthew wanted a son and Sara went along, probably because she was of the you-can-have-it-all-generation.

"The christening is on the 19th. That doesn't leave much time ... to make two christening dresses."

Carrie removed her phone from her back pocket.

"Remember fighting over your mother's wedding dress? Roxanne saying the gown was in perfect condition and could be made into christening dresses?"

"How could I forget? It was not one of my finest moments."

"I'll find out if she still has the dress. They're usually sitting on the veranda, as Dad likes to call it, and one of them answers their phone."

"You talk to them every day?" My anger was like a bolt of lightning.

"Don't start that again, Joy."

She walked out the patio doors, and I retreated to the bathroom, silently counting to ten, as Mariposa suggested. I overheard her say, "Roxanne, this is Carrie. Are you busy?"

The ease of her conversation teased my sense of well-being. Intimate, yet casual, and carefree. I dripped with jealousy, and anger ... for letting my emotions creep up on me.

Carrie returned to the kitchen, and I came out of the bathroom.

"She has the dress. Your father and her are returning to Florida in a few days and she'll make the dresses." She was curt and to the point. Then called Lucky.

"Come on boy, it's time to go."

"I'll walk with you."

* * * * *

I met regularly with Mariposa and was beginning to understand why I was angry and jealous.

248

It was a shield from being hurt again. If I loved someone, they were going to hurt me. I'd been super-sensitized to hurt. The tiniest hurts, felt big. Her advice, "Count to ten, even hide in a bathroom, if you must. Something to gain perspective." It sounded simple, but was not.

* * * * *

"Glory be ... Doug Dillon's outside," said Carrie as she opened the door.

The last time we bumped into each other we were both miserable and angry. The haggard look he had worn so well was gone.

"Carrie! I was hoping to see you."

"Me? We don't know each other." She wore a puzzled face. Lucky pulled Carrie ahead.

"What DO we have the pleasure of, Doug?" I counted to ten, and wanted to say what the hell happened to you, instead, said, "You look well."

"I had a stroke and almost died."

"I'm sorry." Carrie turned around. I stopped walking.

He bent down to scratch Lucky behind the ears. His hands appeared longer and less pudgy. His face wasn't beet red and even his ear lobes did not hang down as low. I could see he had been handsome in his youth.

"I need a favor, Joy."

"What can I do for you?"

"I need a follow-up story. Aren't you and Ray back together? Talking about babies."

"You want me to spill my guts about the past thirty years and talk about my love life."

I was not about to tell him the babies were grandbabies or that Ray never knew he had a son.

"Something we can expand into a book. Your memoir and the emotional trauma of thinking your father was a killer, the courage required to come back and help solve the cold cases."

I had been on my best behavior but the creep was pushing the envelope. I bit my tongue in an attempt not to chew him out, closed my eyes, and counted to ten.

"Here's another idea; write a story about a reporter who had no life and almost died chasing stories. I can see the headline, Overweight, out of shape reporter recovers. The before and after pictures would be terrific."

"Not bad." He paused and reflected on the plausibility." My doc said 'considering my lifestyle, my chances were slim to none.' I could interview him! That might fly with my boss, especially if romance was involved. So that's a no. How about this …"

"How about what?"

"Carrie, I've always been attracted to you … You're the best waitress in the world … Would you like to go for coffee? Not at the Maverick!"

It was the straw that broke the camel's back. I glanced over my shoulder at Morningside Drive.

"Doug, your car door is open."

"I left the car door open so you wouldn't lock me in again. I wasn't sure how you'd react to seeing me."

"I locked you in MY car because you … wouldn't leave me alone."

"I needed a headline."

"Is your car running? Where are your car keys?"

Doug Dillon patted his clothes, yanked his keys from his pants pocket, and hit the lock button. The alarm went off, Lucky barked and Doug Dillon took off running toward his car.

"Thank you, Joy," said Carrie.

It had been a good day.

Best of all ... Mom's crumb cake recipe was waiting to be used.

Chapter 35

The Christening

October 19, 2014

The morning of the christening, the air was crisp. Bright yellow and red colors decorated the fall sky, and the leaves rustled. I was relieved not to find Doug Dillon and camera crew, parked outside Jason's home in New Jersey, lurking for a follow-up story.

Roxanne transformed Mom's wedding dress into gowns for the twins, who now had names, Sara Elizabeth and Matthew Francis for their grandparents and great-grandparents. Ray and I had been included – we were the godparents.

More than one hundred people attended. Those who were unable to make the christening, like Roxanne's sons, and Matthew and Connie, planned to attend the luncheon at the country club.

Ray embraced me outside the church.

"This is the happiest day of my life. My dreams of having a family, a son, and grandchildren have come true."

He wiped the tears sliding down his face.

"When you came back, I was angry with you, Joy ... and heartbroken."

"And now?"

"Now, I'm in love with you. I never stopped loving you, even when you were dead."

"I was not dead. I didn't want to be found."

"I can't believe you thought I didn't love you. That I would walk away from our son. Thank God you didn't abort Jason."

I was Alice in Wonderland entering a world of unknowns. I'd been on the outside, now I am inside, a part of things and for the first time not pretending to be someone else.

I hoped not to screw things up. I wanted to say, *If only you had phoned me, one phone call would have changed our lives. You never missed me.* I kept those thoughts to myself, but started to cry.

"Are those happy tears?" Ray asked.

"Yes. This is the happiest day of my life, too."

"Looks like you could use one of these," said Jacqueline as she held out a tissue.

I was shocked to see her, Scarlet, and Bryce. All wore scowls.

"You came!"

"Wouldn't miss it." Jackie exhaled cigarette smoke, tossed the butt on the grass, and ground the filter into the soil with a designer shoe. The smoke circled her head like a warrior signal.

"You remember Ray," I said.

"Who could forget this good-looking guy," she said. "Why don't you show me where to get a drink, while Joy apologizes."

"You're in church, Jackie, there is no alcohol," I said.

"But, inside, they pass the chalice at communion. Let's go light a candle, Ray."

As they walked away, I wondered how Ben would handle the situation if he were alive. Jackie was all about drama and being the center of attention. I was not going to take part, not today.

"Mom's right. Apologize ... Not that it will make up for all your lies," said Scarlet.

She started to walk away as well but stopped.

"I thought you were cool, but it was all an act – an award-winning performance. You conveniently hooked up with my dad, who conveniently knew your son's adoptive parents. And – surprise, conveniently ... marry him and then he dies – conveniently of a sudden heart attack, conveniently leaving you, my inheritance."

She waved her hand as if holding a baton and conducting a symphony. "Conveniently" was the high note.

"You planned it, a cold calculated plan that gives you everything. We want the apartment. Mom has got her lawyer working on it." She gasped for breath.

Jackie would never get the apartment. I was and had always been the sole owner of the property. The luxury condo was bought after selling my agency to minimize capital gains. But I remembered being her age, afraid and alone. I had drawn the wrong conclusions about Ray and did not want her to make similar mistakes.

"Scarlet," I said. "Please let me apologize. It was wrong to keep secrets from your father and you. I have hurt many people. An abortion would have humiliated my family and was against our faith. I believed what my dad told me, that Ray was using me for sex. I hope you can forgive me if not today someday.

"Your father and I loved each other, it wasn't you're-the-only-one love, but we were friends, we liked each other and I think we did a good job of being kind, loving parents for you and your brother."

"Right, friends? Don't make me laugh, Joy."

"Stop this right now, Scarlet," said Bryce. "Dad taught you, us better. There is no reason for you to be unkind. You sound

254

like Mom, and we both know the happy life she has."

From the church steps Jason called, "Mom! We need you for pictures."

"Great! Now you are MOM to Jason!" Scarlet said.

My head swung from side to side as though I was at a tennis match. I was thrilled Jason called me Mom and shocked at my stepdaughter's response.

"All right … All right … All right, Scarlet," said Bryce, coming to my defense.

"Jason's real mom is dead," she mumbled loud enough for me to hear.

* * * * *

Frank promised Roxanne not to smoke, but later said, "Just to be near nicotine will give me a jolt." So it wasn't a surprise that he found his way outdoors at the country club to be near Jackie and Scarlet while they smoked.

"Can you believe Jason's calling Joy, Mom?" said Scarlet.

"I'd believe anything. But now you know what's been going on for the past 20 years. Your father vilified me, and took up with that woman."

"Hey, that's my daughter you're yapping about," said Frank as he moved toward them to experience a nicotine high.

"Frank, you want a cigarette?" Jackie asked. She posed like a model in a magazine ad.

"No thanks, I promised Roxanne."

"You're not the type who'd let a woman boss you," she smirked.

"Right, but I'm changing my ways and no longer a grump."

"Rumor has it you were more than a grump, Frank. Didn't your daughter accuse you of murder and weren't you arrested for assault? You've got to be angry about that. Joy's a liar. I know firsthand because she told lies about me and destroyed my marriage. I'd still be married to Ben if it weren't for her and now, she collects his money."

"Oh ... I see where this is going. You know, you people frost me."

A waiter brought Frank a high ball and said, "The bar will be closing soon, sir."

Frank continued, "You got high falutin expectations."

"High falutin expectations?" Jackie tossed her head back and laughed.

"Yep. Nose in the air, better than anyone else. You wear disagreeableness like a designer's dress, hoping to be noticed, but you're miserable!"

"What makes you think I'm miserable? I do not have my nose in the air. I am happy!"

"Okay, define happy," he said.

"Well happy ... it's designer shoes and an expensive bottle of Chardonnay."

"That's what I'm talking about. Once upon a time I was happy staying up late drinking beer and watching David Letterman, alone. There was pleasure in being acerbic when people knocked on my door. Yep, exactly like you, angry and bitter because life let them down. My boo-boo was the biggest boo-boo in the world, and I blamed others."

"Now, I'm acerbic!!!!!!!!!!! What the fuck does that even mean?"

Heads turned in the dining room and Jason and Roxanne appeared in the doorway.

"Is there a problem?" Jason asked.

"My apologies," said Frank. "Jackie's woeful life is none of my business. My daughter didn't believe I loved her, because I chose alcohol over her. I felt sorry for myself and drowned my sorrows in booze. Eventually, people got fed up with my crap. Don't let that happen to you, Jackie."

Frank stood alongside Roxanne.

"Fortunately, I met someone who looked past my flaws and taught me to love."

"Pop, don't forget about Jason, me, and your grandkids," said Alison. She had been making the rounds, saying goodnight to the remaining guests. Jason put his arm around her.

"That's why I'm giving Jason the Cadillac Eldorado, Alison."

Roxanne found the picture of the car on her cell phone and showed Jason.

Frank puffed his chest out.

"Joy wants to add a garage, and who knows what else. I can imagine you, Alison, and the twins driving up the Bronx River Parkway with the top down, for a Sunday drive."

He was short of breath.

"After it's restored, of course. You'll probably, want to change the color. Mary Elizabeth never liked Crown Beige, although when all shined up ... it looked good."

Alison whispered in Jason's ear.

"Why would you want that old thing? And the Bronx River is polluted and surrounded by slums."

Jason hugged Frank. "Thank you so much. The twins will love riding in a convertible. I think I'll have it painted red."

Well, your great-grandmom, Mary Elizabeth, God rest her soul, nagged about yellow. It's got a few miles on it. We paid twelve grand for the car, the year I retired and drove cross country and back. It was a trip of a lifetime."

Alison gave her husband that don't you dare look.

"Jason, that vehicle is unsafe. I would never let the twins get in that car, let alone have it taking up space in our garage."

Jackie identified with the young wife, stepped forward and said, "Frank does that piece of junk even … start?"

"Jezebel turns over every time I get in the driver's seat."

There were a few oohs, in response to his spunky comeback.

"I'll buy Jezebel from you Frank, for the twelve grand," Ray said. "I'll have it restored and painted firecracker yellow. On Sundays, you, me, Roxanne, and Joy will go for rides."

"Fourteen thousand, hot yellow, and drives to Rye Beach," said Bryce.

Then Roxanne's sons joined in, out-bidding each other.

"It has a two hundred and seventy-five horsepower engine. Sixteen."

"Eighteen, and goes from zero to sixty in seven point four seconds."

Finally, Thomas doubled the last offer. Expecting Frank to say, "SOLD TO THE HIGHEST BIDDER!"

But, Frank didn't. He said, "Sold to Ray Atwood for twelve hundred dollars."

People slapped five with each other. Joy and Ray kissed. Alison was relieved. Jason was brokenhearted.

Frank got between them. "I apologize." He kissed Alison on the cheek. "Jason, it will stay in the family and the adults will drive around when you visit. You are going to visit?"

Alison smiled. "Of course, Pop."

The twins' christening was one to be remembered.

Chapter 36

Thanksgiving

The humidity lifted, finally. November was the month the snowbirds returned, and for the next five months enjoyed Florida without sweating. Ray was working on the Eldorado, aka, Jezebel, when he wasn't busy solving other cold cases.

Carrie attended the University of Central Florida and studied nights. Roxanne and Dad lived at Crane Lakes, although I had no idea in whose house. They were happy. We all reconnected on Sundays, somewhere.

This Sunday, was the anniversary of Ben's death.

Ray offered to grill steaks if we brought the sides. I didn't know how to tell him, the timing felt like a commuter train had reached the end of the line, not stopped, and was going to hit a wall.

Last Thanksgiving, I refused dinner invitations and spent the day alone. This Thanksgiving … I didn't want to be alone. I phoned Carrie.

"What are you doing for Thanksgiving?"

"I'm thinking more about Renaissance artists, than Pilgrims. I know, I won't be cooking venison. What do you have in mind?"

"Nothing yet. I just don't want to eat alone."

"In the past, I worked. The boys and I ate turkey, the Sunday before, or after. Listen, I'm working on a paper. Call Roxanne and see what she has in mind."

Roxanne said, "Your dad and I might take a road trip north and surprise my boys. On the way back we'll stop in DC, the White House will be decorated for Christmas."

"Can I come?"

* * * * *

That Sunday, as Ray grilled steaks, we did not talk about Ben. We talked about Thanksgiving. Everyone was excited, we'd have dinner with Jason and Alison, see the parade, and tour the White House decorated for Christmas.

Later that night, I phoned Jackie to find out how Ben's anniversary service had gone.

Bryce answered and said, "I'm sorry, Joy. Neither Scarlet or Jackie can come to the phone."

Jackie was playing the martyr, seeking attention for all she had sacrificed. Ben would not be happy about being the sacrificial lamb.

"It is her version of love. A bucket load of grief means she loved your father, and maybe she did." I explained.

"After their divorce, she hated him," Bryce said.

"You can't hate someone you don't love; you'd be indifferent."

I sensed Bryce's confusion and quickly changed the subject.

"Ray and I will be in the city for Thanksgiving." I purposely left out going to Jason's after the parade. "How about we all go to a play and Carmine's on Friday?"

"Sounds great. Scarlet is still angry and probably won't come."

"I'll find something she will enjoy. If she decides not to come, the three of us will still have a good time."

Scarlet and Bryce were important to me, I loved them. Bryce had taken a liking to Ray and I hoped Scarlet would come around.

"Aladdin is her favorite."

* * * * *

It snowed Thanksgiving eve, flights were delayed, and people slept in airports. Ray and I never made it to the parade or Montclair for dinner. We couldn't get a cab, and walked the ten blocks, in freezing temperatures, to have Thanksgiving dinner with Charles and Carrie, at The Plaza.

I told Carrie to bring heavy winter clothing and hoped she had. Ray had not. He borrowed one of Ben's coats for the trek. I was embarrassed when I opened the closet, and his clothes were still there.

"You've got a lot of expensive suits, to get rid of," Ray said as he picked out a down parker.

"Bryce might want some of these designer ties."

On the walk back, the city was its finest. Snow flurries tickled my face. The streets glittered with red and green, and the quiet hugged me like a bunny rabbit prom cape.

Ray asked, "What was Ben like?"

"Ben?" I stopped walking. "He was easy-going and made me

laugh." I smiled as the words flowed out into the night.

"Just like me, right?"

My answer was not important. Ray's acknowledgment of my past was. Since there was no bathroom to hide and cry in, I challenged him.

"I'll race you to the next block."

"On your mark, get ready, get set … go," he said.

The next day, the snow had either turned to ice or been cleared. Scarlet arrived at the theater, looking pale and minus the attitude. I assumed it was the cold weather. When the curtain went up, the color returned to her face.

After the applause, we walked to Carmine's on Broadway. Ray ran ahead, saying he would get in line for a table, his excuse for not wearing Ben's heavy jacket. He thought the kids would recognize their father's coat. He was right.

Carmine's southern Italian menu never changed, and was reasonably priced. The restaurant was known for its New York vibe. Heavy burgundy drapes trimmed with gold fringe, framed the windows. Long tables, covered with white linen cloths and napkins, confirmed it was family style. Bottles of Chianti surrounded by candles decorated the table tops. It hinted at mafia ownership and, although false, made for interesting table conversations.

Ray loved the place and Bryce filled him in on the mobster, Carmine Romano, emphasizing that Carmine was never the owner and long dead.

We ordered. Scarlet, who hadn't touched her wine yet, asked me to join her in the ladies' room. The noise of hand blowers and chatter didn't prevent me from hearing her whisper, "Joy, I need your help. I think I'm pregnant."

We were next in line. I squeezed her hand and said, "Let's

have lunch tomorrow." She nodded, yes. "I'll have Carrie join us."

* * * * *

The next day, Carrie met us downstairs at Palm Court. I was glad she had come to the city. Her sons were so accustomed to having turkey with her on an alternate day that they did not mind.

Ray and Bryce were happy to skip the Tea Room experience and planned to meet us at Rockefeller Center to see the tree after dark and possibly ice skate.

"Love the jacket! Where did you get it?"

She wore a lamb's wool jacket over jeans and leather boots. Lamb's wool coats were fashionable in the nineteen fifties and sixties, just as warm as mink, and a lot cheaper.

"A consignment store, a couple of blocks from here. Charles offered to buy me a coat he saw in the hotel lobby store. But I said no. I can still pay for some things. It was like fifty bucks."

"How is Prince Charles? Did you Google him?"

"No. I'm starting to think he is too good to be true ... and I'm not ready to blow up my world."

"You could start with Facebook. People tell lies that are easy to get away with on that site."

Scarlet arrived and Carrie embraced her.

"Joy told me what you're going through."

After we ordered, I let Carrie do the talking.

"Scarlet, I had an abortion, at your age. But I think of that baby, more than just from time to time."

"I'm on the pill or was. Do you regret it?"

"No. Do you love the guy?" Carrie inquired.

"I hardly know him."

"Do you know if you want to get to know him?"

"I don't think so! Isn't abortion murder?"

"Depends on who you talk to. And the debate is endless. You're struggling with a decision that will affect you – no matter what you decide – for the rest of your life."

Scarlet was in tears and I clasped her hand by the side of our chairs.

"My situation was like yours. Joy's was entirely different."

"I want to have the abortion, but I'm scared and embarrassed. I was on the pill!"

"Everything's going to be okay," I said. She was going through what I had gone through years ago. "You can stay with me in the apartment."

"No! Ray and Bryce will know. I don't want anyone to know. Not even my mom."

"You can stay with me, here at The Plaza. Charles will understand and be sympathetic. Do you have a doctor?"

"No! You can't call my doctor." She left the table. I assumed to cry in the powder room.

"I'll phone Marigold. She knows the medical community."

I told Scarlet when she returned.

She apologized for being emotional and angry at me.

"Now I know what you went through, pregnant with Jason. I'm so ... so ... sorry. Please forgive me."

Chapter 37

What Do You Want for Christmas?

D ad missed his morning routine and new recliner. Disenchanted with crowded streets and bumping into pedestrians, Ray flew back to Florida with Dad.

Roxanne and I drove and stopped in Washington D.C. for the White House Christmas tour. The theme this year was "A Children's Winter Wonderland."

Huge red Christmas ornaments trimmed the outside doors, inviting us in. Inside technology supplied movement for the Obama's family pets. Bo, wagged his tail, as he stood alongside Sunny. There were trees decorated in red, white and blue to pay tribute to military families. Gold stars signified fallen soldiers.

We wandered from room to room amazed at the beauty and detail, a team of one hundred and six Santa's Elves transformed the White House into a Winter Wonderland, Thanksgiving weekend.

It was memorable. Ben and I had taken his kids to visit the nation's capital but had never been inside the White House; neither had Roxanne.

Portraits of the first ladies and past presidents hung through the historic residence. I stood teary-eyed viewing John Fitzpatrick Kennedy's portrait by Elaine Kooning. His arms folded and chin turned down, absorbed in prayer. The artist had captured the poignancy my parents spoke about, often.

Roxanne and I scheduled a night bus tour, and saw the Jefferson and Lincoln memorials lit up. We were becoming friends ... comfortable enough for me to confide in her.

"Scarlet was never pregnant. She was late."

"It was the young girl's first grown-up decision," said Roxanne.

I did not understand at first.

"When Ben died, she joined her mother's pity party for a celebration of self. This time she examined her feelings as well as yours. She now understands your decision to give Jason up."

Roxanne was right. Scarlet had sent me a lengthy text thanking me and Carrie.

On the last day in D.C., we visited Arlington Cemetery and then checked into a motel. The following morning, we were up early and drove ten hours to get back to Daytona Beach. Life was good.

* * * * *

The Eldorado was in better condition than we thought, although it needed a new radiator, brakes, and exhaust system – the parts that rusted normally in Florida's salt air.

Painted metallic yellow, as Ray promised; we went for Sunday drives, with the top down, and then ate together. The weather was perfect.

The conversation turned serious, when Dad commented,

"We have too many houses."

I knew what he was hinting at. He wanted Roxanne to move in with him and get married.

"Count them. Roxanne and I own two, Joy and Ray three, and Carrie at least one, unless you count Prince Charles. It's a mystery as to how many castles are in his kingdom. Right, Carrie?"

Prince Charles was the nickname Dad knighted Charles with. Carrie was squeezed between me and Roxanne in the back seat.

"I'm not living with a pool table and jukebox in my living room."

"You were all for it when I bought the place. You measured the room."

"Oh, Frank," she giggled. "It's perfect for you, and I love coming over, dancing and fixing food for the crowd. But Laptop and I need our own space."

I imagined him, like an out-of-control steam locomotive barreling down a mountain, with steam blowing out of its stack and thought, those happy pills must be working, because he said, "And Carrie is going to leave Lucky with me when she goes to school in New York."

He turned and winked at Carrie.

"Besides, I checked something off my bucket list."

He threw the ball back to me.

"How about you, Joy? Are you ready to sell Morningside Drive?"

"Hell no! I just renovated, and not interested in manly man sounds and smells every morning for the rest of my life."

We picked up pizza, went to Dad's and played pool. Ray was

chewing on a slice, but answered quickly, when Dad asked, "What's on your bucket list?"

"Skiing!"

"Skiing?!" several of us responded.

"Yes, I haven't skied since I was a kid. I've dreamed of skiing in Stowe at Christmas."

"Well, that settles that … we're all going to Stowe, Vermont for Christmas," said Dad.

* * * * *

It was easier said than done. Everything was owner-occupied, or rented for the holiday. Dad said, "What about Prince Charles, he has a castle on every mountain. Probably owns something near the Von Trapp family."

"Charles mentioned skiing in Vermont … The Von Trapp family? Who are they?" asked Carrie.

"The movie, The Sound of Music, starring Julie Andrews?" Roxanne reminded her.

Sure enough, Charles owned a twelve-bedroom ski house that would accommodate all of us, including him. He would join us for a few days. Some of us would fly in early, and others later in the week.

I decided to perfect Mom's crumb cake recipe and planned to have the breakfast treat on hand at the ski house. There would be many mouths to feed, although Charles offered to hire a chef, who would shop for food and cook.

We were sampling a piece with coffee when Carrie said, "Charles's picture on Facebook doesn't match his picture on

LinkedIn."

I almost spit out my coffee. "YOU'RE joking!"

"No ... wish I were."

"No way. Where's your computer?"

Sure enough, she was right. There was no slamming Pandora's Box shut, but how could we cancel Christmas?

"I'll ask Ray to check up on him. Do you know his date of birth, driver's license number, social? Anything?"

"I have a $500 money card he gave me for college expenses, but it's in my name."

"Let me take a picture and send a text to Ray. Meanwhile, we'll pretend nothing's wrong. Okay?"

"Are you forgetting I plan to move in with him? My courses in Florida are finished. He pulled weight to get me into Parson's."

In the movie Apollo 13, Tom Hanks says, "Uh, Houston, we have a problem here." I imagined Carrie and I in spacesuits, prepared for a crash landing.

* * * * *

Some family members had holiday plans already. Jason and Alison were spending the holiday in Fort Collins, Colorado. Her family would finally meet the twins. Bryce and Scarlet would spend Christmas Day with Jackie and then join us in Stowe. It was understandable but disappointing. We would not be alone; however, Roxanne and Dad had traveled with us.

Last Christmas, I felt like a bandage had been ripped off my heart. This year I took the disappointment in stride and even cried. Dad and I had a relationship, and Roxanne was like a friendly mother or sister. I was grateful.

This Christmas, Ray and I would sleep in the same bed, and open presents in the morning, together. I was not going to let anything spoil the occasion. Skiing in Stowe on Christmas was going to get a check mark on his bucket list. Having fun was my New Year's 2015 resolution.

The weather was perfect. The temperature hovered in the twenties. Light snow, great for skiing, painted a picture, Norman Rockwell style. I took a ski lesson and practiced snow plowing. Ray flew by me, often, rushing for the chair lift.

It felt like Christmas, and I kept squinting at the sky, convinced I'd see Rudolph's red nose. We watched Miracle on 34th Street, drank eggnog feeling the warmth of a log fire, and then retired to kiss and cuddle in a king-sized bed.

On Christmas Day, we buckled on snowshoes and went exploring.

Finally, I found the right time to ask about Charles. He and Carrie would arrive in a few days.

We were having coffee in front of a morning fire.

"What did you find out about Prince Charles?" The nickname seemed to suit him better than ever.

Ray put his cup down, stretched his arms overhead, and twisted his neck from side to side. "Yep … there's a problem. A Calvin Dunmore, about the same height and weight; served time in North Carolina. But … the pictures don't match."

"Thank God!"

"Don't jump to conclusions. The dudes look alike! There could be a family connection. What did Charles say about family?"

"He said he didn't want to talk about it."

"Calvin served time for drugs and money laundering. I wouldn't want to talk about it either."

"Charles isn't the type to be involved in anything like that."

"Don't be naive, Joy! Some people are good liars. The best way to find out is to ask him. He'll either dig a deeper hole for himself and lie or have a plausible explanation. He must know, the Facebook picture isn't him."

"Do you think he's dangerous?"

"We're going to find out."

I knew that Ray carried a gun and wondered if Charles did. The song from Mr. Roger's television show, *It's a Beautiful Day in the Neighborhood*, refused to stop playing in my head, but I did not hum along.

The next day Roxanne's boys arrived, each with their oldest child, to ski. I graduated to the T-bar, and from time to time, saw their smiling faces as they horsed around on the chairlift overhead. Ray seemed to be having the time of his life.

In the evening, we went to the Von Trapp restaurant and brewery, where they continued to razz him about the Eldorado that was now painted yellow – a sissy color, they told him.

When they said farewell, Dad was included in the backslapping and bear hugs. All six kissed me and Roxanne, with promises to visit Florida.

The next day, Scarlet and Bryce arrived and quickly connected with a younger college crowd.

"Don't worry if we don't come back tonight," Bryce yelled as he and Scarlet went out the door, late that evening.

I prayed Scarlet had learned her lesson about partying and casual sex.

Now I waited for Carrie and Charles to arrive. A driver would pick them up at Knapp State Airport. When they did, I pulled Carrie aside; with the excuse of showing her the unbelievable ski lodge Charles owned.

"Did you confront Charles about the mismatched pictures," I asked in hush tones.

"I was afraid to. What did Ray find out?" she whispered.

Roxanne burst into the room interrupting our private moment.

"Carrie! I'm so glad you're here," she said.

Carrie was the fun one and probably her favorite. I counted to ten and controlled my jealousy, without hiding in the bathroom.

Roxanne stepped back, rather than hug Carrie as her outstretched arms suggested.

"What's going on? Did I interrupt something?"

"No, not at all." Carrie hugged Roxanne.

"Joy's been teaching me how to bake crumb cake," said Roxanne.

"Actually, Carrie," I said, glad to change the subject, "Roxanne showed me a short cut; make the crumb mixture the night before. The first one up turns on the oven."

"The whole house wakes up to a cinnamon winter wonderland."

"I can still smell it. I thought it was a candle," Carrie said.

Downstairs Charles, Ray and Dad were having afternoon cake and coffee, and we joined them. I knew Ray planned to confront Charles about the discrepancies in pictures and time served. Ray sat with his arms crossed. A time bomb was ticking and I worried it would go off. He uncrossed his arms and leaned in on the counter.

"Charles, thank you for letting us stay here. This has been a dream come true – like I won the bucket list lottery. You and your family must have spent many holidays here in Stowe. I can imagine tromping through the woods to find the perfect size tree."

"Ray, those trees are fake. Staff puts them up and takes them down the day after Little Christmas. My family has never been here."

I studied Charles. The feeling of *liking you just the way you are* was gone. I held my breath thinking Ray would capitalize on the reference to fake, but didn't.

"What a shame. I haven't had Christmas with my brother since moving to Daytona. He's in California, too far to travel … and flying this time of year can be a nightmare. Where does your brother live."

Charles's jaw dropped. He paused before answering.

"My brother is deceased and something I don't care to talk about."

We all were stunned by what he said. Carrie gave Charles a sympathetic look, and Roxanne studied Dad's reaction of dismay, while Dad glanced at his watch and nudged Charles in a light-hearted manner.

"It's four o'clock, old boy and we've been drinking your liquor without you. It's time to sit by the fire and enjoy a few. The little ladies can start dinner."

Roxanne rolled her eyes. "I have a pot roast cooking already, Frank."

After they left the room, Carrie and I said in unison, "That went well!"

"What went well?" Roxanne asked.

I looked to Ray to explain. He was reluctant to answer but finally said, "His Facebook picture doesn't match."

Roxanne appeared shocked. "You think he's an imposter?"

"We don't know what to think."

"Certainly, none of you think it's right to fraternize with a known criminal. I'll just go ask him," said Roxanne.

She called, "Charles!" in a loud voice as she left the room.

We followed.

"Charles, are you aware ... your identity has been stolen?"

"You must be talking about the Facebook photo. I wondered when it was going to come up. Since I'm growing fond of Carrie by the day, I might as well confess now. That's my evil twin."

I almost burst out laughing. Ray said he'd come up with something plausible, however, the evil twin story was simply a joke.

"I left home after high school, went to college, and started to make a better life. Calvin was not like me – we weren't close. That thing about being in the womb together isn't always true, and certainly not true for us. He got a construction job but kept showing up drunk, got fired, and once unemployed drank all day ... followed by drugs and money laundering. Once out of prison, he stole my identity. I just never figured out how to change the picture back. He's dead now and my parents blame me, except when they need money."

We all pretended to believe him, but of course, no one did.

"How do we know, you're not the evil twin and Calvin or Charles is dead?" Ray asked.

"I'm not sure, you're the detective, you tell me."

"Your brother was fingerprinted, we could have you fingerprinted and there's DNA testing."

"Sure, whatever you think, or I'll go upstairs and get my high school and college yearbooks."

Chapter 38

New Year's Day 2015

❦

"Mary Elizabeth, remember our Little Christmas celebrations?" Frank sat in the hot tub, New Year's Day morning. Roxanne was still sleeping. They had celebrated New Year's Eve at the Von Trapp Gala.

"You'd be having a hissy fit about a frost, and your brother would tease you about icicles hanging from your nose as a kid. For us, it was a religious holiday; the day the three kings came bearing gifts. But your family came from New York to be warm, not pray. They piled sleeping bags and cots in your sewing room."

Frank smiled as he reminisced.

"They stopped coming when Joy was about nine or ten. Your sister Patsy said, they were busy ... couldn't take time off. It was bullshit. I was running around with Diane. It's been my biggest regret."

He slipped underwater, came up for air, and took time to collect his thoughts.

"That's not everything that's on my mind, Mary Elizabeth. I'm starting to remember the good times. The party sound of people laughing and singing is back in my head. The shadow of sadness you left behind ... is gone. Roxanne's teaching me to enjoy life."

He looked to the sky.

"We're going to have our own Little Christmas once we're back in Florida ... No disrespect ... But ... I'm going to ask Roxanne to marry me. We've been going steady. You probably know all this, seeing you're in heaven, looking down."

Frank wiped the tears from his eyes.

"I want to get hitched. Not in church, of course, you'll always be my bride in the eyes of God. And mine, too! And I wanted to tell you personally, we'll be together again, when I die. Unless I'm sent to purgatory ... because ... I was a sinner."

Frank sat quietly and waited. A blurry vision of a woman seemed to appear in the distance. Maybe it was the steam from the hot tub playing with his eyes. But when he heard her voice, there was no doubt it was Mary Elizabeth!

> *"Roxanne's a good person. Her husband, Joe, talks about her all the time. I forgive you, Frank ... if you forgive me. I'll put in a good word for you with the Lord."*

And just like that, she faded away.

*****

Persuading Frank to wait, failed. "People, are partied out from the holidays," said Roxanne.

Frank disagreed. "Or, they just want to have fun." He sang Cindy Lauper's song, *Girls Just Want to Have Fun*, and twirled her around.

Little Christmas was held at Crane Lakes Clubhouse. Frank

hired a deejay and Roxanne told people to bring a dish to pass. Halfway through the party, the deejay announced there was a family feud to settle. Everyone stopped dancing and the room got quiet.

"Frank Webb and Roxanne Hart, you're the couple with a dispute. One of you wants to marry ... the other one doesn't."

Oohs and aahs exploded in the room.

"Come on down."

The guests applauded like a game show audience.

"Welcome to the Newlywed Game," declared the deejay.

"We are NOT newlyweds, and this isn't a game," said Roxanne.

"All the same, it's time to play!"

He explained the person with the most correct answers would decide if they should marry. Roxanne gave Frank the finger; Frank grinned from ear to ear, and the crowd went wild.

"Frank, what is Roxanne's favorite color?"

"Pink."

"Correct. One point for Frank."

"Roxanne, what is Frank's favorite color? The time was up before she could answer. "The correct answer is yellow. Two points for Frank."

It was decided quickly when the score was four to ten, that Frank was the winner.

He said, "Roxanne if I get down on my knee, I might not get up. So, I'll stand up ... Will you marry me?"

"I'll think about it," she said and walked away.

"She'll come around," Frank said to the crowd. And she did.

"Informal ceremony, no papers signed and I'll do it."

"Are you sure? There'll be one hundred witnesses to our 'I do.'"

"I'm not selling my house, either."

"I don't want your girlie touches in my man cave, anyhow."

Chapter 39

The Wedding Ceremony

Valentine's Day 2015

ॐ

"What is love?" Artie asked. The former priest stood facing a group of one hundred people, his back to the river. Dad wore a short-sleeved dress shirt with a palm tree print. Roxanne's white lace dress swirled in the breeze. We carefully selected the garment after debating the wind factor and sun setting behind them at the ceremony.

"Who can forget the photo of Lady Di not wearing a slip?" Roxanne had said in the specialty dress store.

The store owner responded, "The dress is fully lined, looks fabulous on you, and has a heart shaped neckline."

Roxanne had decided on a heart-themed wedding.

"After all, it is Valentine's Day."

There were hearts and kisses on the napkins, paper plates, and the cake was ... heart-shaped, of course!

Dad smiled at Roxanne and reached for her hands. All six of her boys, and their families had come for the happy occasion.

"Is it a feeling?" continued Artie with his hands in prayer. Red heart-shaped helium balloons bounced in the wind behind him.

"We think love comes from the heart, and that's truly the

start. Emotions and passion bind us. Ultimately though, love thrives in our mind."

Carrie and Charles smiled at each other. Dad was impatient.

"Love needs to be nurtured, kept alive by kindness and unselfishness."

"What is love?"

The question was repeated throughout the service and I realized my definition of love was different from thirty years ago.

Was it love to hurry down the college dorm steps, and drive away with the Dolans, to spare my mother the heartbreak of my pregnancy? Was it love to spare Ray from a marriage, I thought he didn't want? Was it love to secure a better life for my unborn son through adoption?

That young Joy was a scared immature girl ... but ... today, I still did not have answers.

A year ago, I'd returned with little expectation of happiness and unaware of my dormant feelings for Ray.

My father was happier than ever, the conflict and drama between us gone. How could I have been so wrong about the people I love?

I hated myself for what I put people through. And yet, they have forgiven me, even Jason. If I could just forgive myself.

Artie cleared his throat.

"The couple will now say their vows. And folks, I have no idea what they will say. But I do know, God is watching."

"Roxanne, I was a sorry sap worn out bum when we met. You changed all that. Now I feel like dancing every day. I promise to love you and take care of you. I'll even do the dishes. Will you be my ... partner ... significant other or whatever I'm supposed to call you, from this day forward?"

There was nervous snickering.

"I will ... And Frank, you can call me wife ... if ... you promise to scrub toilets."

People reeled with laughter. Roxanne continued with her hands on her hips.

"I'm only marrying you so you'll stop bugging me. The truth is ..."

Now the guests held their breath.

"I don't know why I love you ... but I do."

Frank and Roxanne sang the song, to the amazement of their guests.

Artie yelled, "I now pronounce you husband and wife!"

Cocktails and hors d'oeuvres followed the ceremony. The family planned to have dinner at Billy's Tap Room later.

Roxanne and Dad mingled, showing off her heart-shaped diamond wedding band.

Ray whispered in my ear, "Joy will you marry me?"

"Do you promise to scrub toilets?" I said, laughing.

His whisper sent chills down my spine. The proposal was unexpected, and what I thought I wanted ... until now.

I was no longer afraid to be alone or fearful of other people's judgment and disapproval. I liked having my own place and space and was thinking of going to law school.

"I promise to nurture you with kindness and understanding," Ray said and put his arms around me. "What if we can be happy together? Grow old together? Have our son and grandchildren in our lives?"

I did not want to say yes or no. It was strange after all this time, not to know for sure.

"Can I think about it?"

"Get a room, you two," said Dad as he approached us. He was grinning from ear to ear.

"I asked Joy to marry me and she wants to think about it!"

Ray stretched his neck from side to side.

"She'll come around, Ray!"

And Dad cha-cha-cha'd away.

~*The End*~

Acknowledgments

Prior to retirement, book reports, term papers, and newsletters were the only writing I did. Consequently, I had a huge learning curve when I took up writing as a pastime in my late sixties.

There are many people to thank.

My husband, Bob, aka, Mr. Wonderful or Bobbie C, is my word miser and first proof-reader. We've been married 52 years.

Janine, my daughter, helped in ways she's unaware of; her love, kindness, and support make a difference in my life. Her twenty years' of experience as a pharmacal copywriter gave me insight and positive feedback.

Florida Writers Association was and continues to be a learning vehicle for me. It was where I found out I didn't have a clue about what I was doing ... and ... it was okay. *Writers helping writers* is their motto.

Through FWA, I met Christine Speno, who took me under her wing and helped me learn how to blog. We'd meet in Flagler Beach with our computers to have lunch and coffee.

I am fortunate to have family, friends, and WordPress followers whose encouragement helped diffuse my doubts.

Judy, Marti, Mel, Abbie, Victor, Drew, Matthew, Louise, Laura S., George, Betsy, Nancy P., Chris, Jenny, Ellen, Kathe, Dennis, Marshal, Claire, Mary G., Mary S., Liz, Ronnie, Becky, Pat S., Pat P., Meredith R., Paul, Christy, Barbara C., Barbara

R., Joanie, Johanna, Pattie, Yvonne, Nancy H., Dorothy, Jeff, David, Judith, Michael J.K., Annie, and Lynette.

Cindy Casey, owner of CCE Publishing, and I met by chance. She had my confidence from the start. Cindy is not only a good listener; she understands what is being said, and is generous with her time and numerous talents.

Cindy put me in touch with Kelsi Lee, the illustrator.

Kelsi, has never been to Daytona Beach and lives more than one thousand miles away, but nevertheless, transformed my words into the book cover. The cover for Morningside Drive is one example of her many artistic abilities.

Thank you to Steve Hartman and his children, Emmett and Meryl, for the constant reminder to stay kind. Random acts of kindness make a difference in our lives.

About the Author

Claudia Chianese and her husband retired to Florida in 2008 and she began writing behind closed doors. After reading a newspaper advertisement for Florida Writers Association, she was inspired to attend the City Island Library where she learned to write and started blogging.

Three of her short stories, *Acerbic*, *Wheels of Circumstance*, and *First Step Back* have been published in Florida Writers Association's anthology collections.

Claudia graduated with a bachelor's degree in education from the State University of New York at Oneonta in 1970 and has a master's degree in education from the City University of New York Herbert H. Lehman College.

She was born in the Bronx. Her mother (pregnant with her fourth child and living in a two-bedroom apartment) prayed to St. Jude for a house. They moved to Long Island with a $25 deposit and sister Judith was born. In 1961 the family moved to Hensonville, New York and expanded; there were now eight children. All are still alive.

Memories of crumb cake started with her grandmother's visits to Levittown and Hensonville. She always brought an Entenmanns cake.

After she married and lived in the Bronx, the smell of crumb cake from the factory alongside the Bronx River Parkway permeated the area.

Buying a house and moving to Newton, created another

crumb cake experience. The town bakery's Sunday treat was crumb cake, circle in apple, peach and blueberry filling. If you didn't go early, they were sold out.

She never baked a crumb cake, until her Florida neighbor, Barbara, delivered her home baked crumb cake. A game changer. The recipe is included in the back.

Claudia's work experience includes:

- Adjunct Professor at Sussex CCC in Newton New Jersey 2002-2006
- District Manager/Avon Products 1985-2000
- New York City Public School System 1975-1981

While raising her children, Claudia was an active quilter and attempted to play golf. Her "dinners for twelve" still make people talk. She is very social and enjoys a good laugh, a good rant, a decent nap, and a walk on the beach.

She recognizes this is a different time in her life and has embraced writing.

She blogs at claudiajustsaying.com. Morningside Drive is her first novel. But a second novel is dancing around her mind.

Author's Note

Crumb Cake Memories

My love of crumb cake is associated with my grandmother. She would arrive with an Entenmann's cake, a bunch of bananas and slip a quarter into our hands when she kissed us goodbye.

I cannot remember her saying she loved me, but I knew she did.

As a bride, the smell of the Entenmann's bakery, not far from our apartment, permeated my senses as we drove the Bronx River Parkway. I thought I was in heaven

Once we bought our home in New Jersey, we'd wait in line to purchase Newton Bakery's coffee cake ring after Sunday Mass. As you ate your way around, you would encounter a variety of fruits: cherry, apple, peach. It was another kind of heaven.

Crumb cake has been around for ages. Americans call it coffee cake because in the 19th century coffee was added to enhance the flavor. Hence the association with a good cup of coffee. I can't have one without the other.

When we moved to Florida, my next door neighbor, Barbara, presented me with my now favorite crumb cake with *gigunda* crumbs. Her recipe is below.

Crumb Topping:

- 2 sticks of butter or margarine
- 2 1/4 cups of all-purpose unbleached flour

• 1 cup of sugar and 2 tablespoonfuls of cinnamon

Melt the butter and mix all together till it is well blended. Shape into a ball, place in plastic bag and refrigerate for about an hour.

I use a boxed yellow cake, and I take it out of the oven about 5 minutes before the package directions and then break up the ball on top of the cake and put back in oven for an additional 15 minutes.

Crumble starting at edges because center will push down and move crumbs around towards center.

Sprinkle with powdered sugar once cooled.

Claudia, the trick is when to put the crumbs on. The first time I did it, the batter was way too soft and the crumbs migrated to the bottom. It was not edible because once the crumbs were on, it did not continue to cook. If it is set and still golden, it is fine. If it giggles in the middle, cook it a little longer.

Good luck! This is one of my favorite recipes because it is easy, can be done in advance and everyone LOVES it!

ENJOY! Barbara

I would love to hear your crumb cake stories. Send me an email at claudiajustsaying@gmail.com or let me know on Facebook. You can find me at facebook.com/claudia just saying.

I'd also love to know what you think of my first book!

Thanks for reading!

www.ingramcontent.com/pod-product-compliance
Lightning Source LLC
Chambersburg PA
CBHW071249300726
48975CB00002B/602